ST. MARTIN'S

MINOTAUR
MYSTERIES

GET A CLUE!

Be the first to hear the latest mystery book news...

With the St. Martin's Minotaur monthly newsletter, you'll learn about the hottest new Minotaur books, receive advance excerpts from newly published works, read exclusive original material from featured mystery writers, and be able to enter to win free books!

Sign up on the Minotaur Web site at:
www.minotaurbooks.com

"Karen Harper brings England alive."   —*Rendezvous*

The Thorne Maze

"Brisk, energetic writing and terrific historical color."

—*Kirkus Reviews*

The Queene's Cure

"Fascinating series."   —*Library Journal*

The Twylight Tower

"Her attention to the details of the Elizabethan court—dress, food, pomp and circumstance—works very well . . . Conspiracies and lies within lies take the story through twists and turns."   —*Booklist*

"Ms. Harper has done her research well and comes up with an interesting spin on the story. Fans of historicals as well as mysteries will enjoy this book."   —*Romantic Times*

"Karen Harper has written an exciting Elizabethan mystery that contains meticulous research and detail . . . The sleuthing is fun, but what makes *The Twylight Tower* comparable to the fine works of Allison Weir is the strong writing of the author, interweaving historical tidbits into a powerful story line."   —*Internet Book Watch*

The Tidal Poole

"Fans of Elizabethan historical mysteries will find ample sustenance here: a fiercely independent young queen, a loyal but feisty band of assistants, a plethora of historical characters, and an all-encompassing knowledge of the times. Excellent."   —*Library Journal*

Elizabeth I Mysteries
by Karen Harper

The Fyre Mirror

KAREN HARPER

St. Martin's Paperbacks

THE FYRE MIRROR

Copyright © 2005 by Karen Harper.
Excerpt from *The Fatal Fashione* © 2005 by Karen Harper.

Cover painting of Nonsuch Palace © Syndics of Fitzwilliam Museum, Cambridge.
Cover portrait of Queen Elizabeth I from *Atlas of the Countries of England and Wales.*

Library of Congress Catalog Card Number: 2004056654

ISBN: 0-312-99622-5
EAN: 9780312-99622-2

Printed in the United States of America

St. Martin's Press hardcover edition / February 2005
St. Martin's Paperbacks edition / February 2006

St. Martin's Paperbacks are published by St. Martin's Press, 175 Fifth Avenue, New York, NY 10010.

10 9 8 7 6 5 4 3 2 1

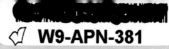

As ever to Don
And for the newest family member—
wishing you much love

Sean Patrick Armstrong

1533   Henry VIII marries Anne Boleyn, January 25. Elizabeth born at Greenwich Palace, September 7.

1536   Anne Boleyn executed in Tower of London. Elizabeth disinherited from crown. Henry marries Jane Seymour.

1537   Prince Edward born. Queen Jane dies of childbed fever.

1538   Henry VIII takes over village of Cuddington and begins to build Nonsuch Palace.

1544   Act of Succession and Henry VIII's will establish Mary and Elizabeth in line to throne.

1547   Henry VIII dies. Edward VI crowned.

1553   Queen Mary (Tudor) I crowned. Tries to force England back to Catholicism; gives Margaret Stewart, Tudor cousin, precedence over Elizabeth. Queen Mary weds Prince Philip of Spain by proxy.

1554   Protestant Wyatt Rebellion fails, but Elizabeth sent to Tower for two months, accompanied by Kat Ashley.

1558   Mary dies; Elizabeth succeeds to throne, November 17. Elizabeth appoints William Cecil secretary of state; Robert Dudley made master of the queen's horse.

1558   Elizabeth crowned in Westminster Abbey, January 15. Parliament urges queen to marry, but she resists. Mary, Queen of Scots, becomes queen of France at accession of her young husband, Francis II.

1560   Death of Francis II of France makes his young Catholic widow, Mary, Queen of Scots, a danger as Elizabeth's unwanted heir. Elizabeth names Earl of Sussex lord lieutenant of Ireland.

1561   Now widowed, Mary, Queen of Scots, returns to Scotland.

1563   William Cecil drafts a proclamation designed to control productions of Elizabeth's royal likenesses.

TUDOR FAMILY

House of Lancaster
Henry VII
r. 1485–1509
m.

House of York
Elizabeth of York

HOUSE OF TUDOR

Arthur
d. 1502

Henry VIII
r. 1509–1547
m.

Margaret Tudor
d. 1541
m.
James IV of Scotland
d. 1513
|
James V of Scotland
d. 1542
m.
Mary of Guise
|
Mary
Queen of Scots
m.
Francis II
of France
d. 1560

Margaret Dougla
m.
Matthew Stewar
Earl of Lennox
|
Henry Stewart
Lord Darnley

1509 Catherine of Aragon
ann. 1533
d. 1536
|
Mary
r. 1553–1558
m.
Philip of Spain

1533 Anne Boleyn
ex. 1536
|
Elizabeth I
r. 1558–1603

1536 Jane Seymour
d. 1537
|
Edward VI
r. 1547–1553

1540 Anne of Cleves
ann. 1540
d. 1557

Mary Tudor
d. 1533
m.

m.
Archibald Douglas
Earl of Angus

Louis XII of France
d. 1514

m.
Charles Brandon,
Duke of Suffolk
d. 1545

1540 Catherine Howard
ex. 1542

1542 Katherine Parr
d. 1548
m.
Thomas Seymour of Sudeley
Lord High Admiral

Mary Seymour

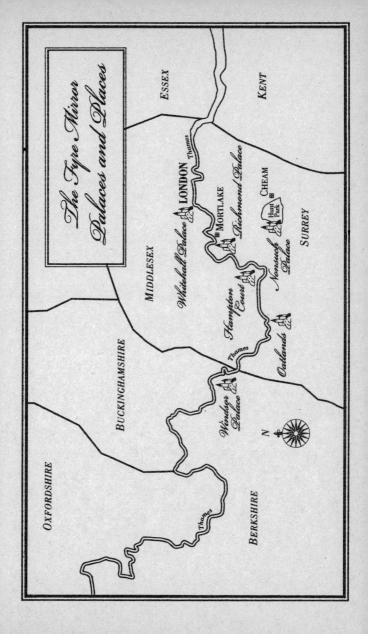

The Fyre Mirror

Prologue

I flatter both kings and shepherds.
I correct faults without knowing them.
I do not speak but I counsel.
Often when I am true, I am not believed.
And when I flatter, I am always believed.

What am I?

No crooked leg, no bleared eye,
No part deformed out of kind,
Nor yet so ugly half can be
As the inward, suspicious mind.

—ELIZABETH REGINA
1565

LONDON, APRIL 23, 1565

 "WANT TO GET YOURSELF KILLED?" SOMEONE SHOUTED.

Gilbert Sharpe threw himself out of the way of the lumbering cart and just missed being hit by another. He knew better than to dart across the street while looking back over his shoulder, but he'd been fearful that the man was following him again. Now he hoped it had been just his imagination.

Another voice yelled, "Stand aside, you clay-brained cur!" Curses chased Gil as he silently thanked God in both English and Italian for his escape. His broken leg had never healed quite right, so he couldn't run anymore. Gripping his hemp sack of sable brushes, rolled canvases, and clothes packed around his precious Venetian mirror, the seventeen-year-old pressed himself between the arches of the huge gateway and let the carts and horses supplying Whitehall Palace stream by on Kings Street.

As he scanned the passing flow of faces, Gil shook his head to clear it. Surely he was safe in the city, for he'd been certain he'd given his nameless, faceless pursuer the slip at Dover. If Maestro Scarletti had hired someone to silence him, would that man pursue him even into the depths of the queen's court?

He heaved a huge sigh and surveyed the area again. On one side of the gate lay the symbol of his old life, the Ring and Crown Inn. It was there that he and his mother, while trying to steal draperies years ago, had been caught by the queen. Partly because of his artistic talent, instead of sending them to prison, she'd taken them to the palace on the other side of the gate and into her care.

Now Gil noticed something he would never have seen when he left London three years ago: this gate which straddled the street was an awkward blend of English and Italian. Its style was like his own, he thought, and he could only pray that his beloved queen would like the pastiche. After all, what he'd become was partly Her Majesty's doing.

As he walked on, Gil felt utterly grateful to be back home. His travails in Italy—his initial lack of the language, his painful yearning for England, the difficult days cleaning others' brushes and filling in their backgrounds, even his precipitate flight— would all have been worthwhile if his enhanced skills at portraiture could please his royal patron.

Limping markedly, as he did when he was tired, Gil hurried down the street toward the towers and turrets of Whitehall Palace. He knew this massive beehive of buildings like the back of his hand holding brush to canvas, yet after studying art in the ducal court of Urbino and his visit to Venice, he saw it all with new eyes.

The rose-hued walls looked lacy with the cross-hatch pattern of the bricks. Above, opened to catch the sweet spring breeze, the thick-leaded windows of the queen's favorite London residence cast diamond designs on patches of waxy green ivy. Windows, however high, used to mean nothing to him, for he'd once scrambled through them from rooftops or trees as if they were ground-floor entries.

He raised his voice over the street ruckus to call to the nearest guard at the gate, "Please send word to Her Majesty that Gilbert Sharpe, queen's painter, is returned from Italy and requests an audience."

The man guffawed in his face, belching out garlic breath. "Sure, an' I'm her sec'tary of state, Sir William Cecil, just takin' a respite from my business runnin' the realm this fine spring day." He nudged Gil with the butt of his pike. "Be off wi' you, then," he added, squinting at the lad's disheveled state.

Years ago, Gil would have cursed the lout with hand signals, for he used to be mute, or dumb, as they called it. Then he would have scaled the back orchard wall and gotten on the grounds until Her Grace saw and summoned him. But what if these years away had changed everything? He should have gone to his mother's house to wash and change his attire, then sent word ahead to see if he was welcome here.

"Give access, give way, ho! Make way for the queen's master secretary!" Gil heard the shouts in the street. He saw that the small party on horseback did indeed include Sir William Cecil. In his mid-forties, he looked the same to Gil, maybe thinner and grayer but still reeking royal command. The crowd stopped and gaped, as it did at anyone important going in or out.

Gil summoned the last remnants of his strength. Though he was shoved back in the crush and his words were nearly drowned in the mingled huzzahs, he took the chance of calling out in Italian to catch Cecil's attention. Like the queen herself, Cecil was learned in languages. The great man had given Gil a purse of coins and a task when he left England, so Gil considered himself to be working for Cecil as well as for the queen.

"*Me é, la'artista della regina,* Gilberto Sharpino!" he shouted as loudly as he could. "*Sono ritornato!*"

Cecil craned his neck and reined in, frowning, scanning the sea of faces. Hoping to be recognized, Gil snatched off his hat.

"*Sono spora qui! Qui!*" Gil shouted, waving.

Cecil's face registered surprise—as much surprise as ever crossed that long, guarded countenance Gil had sketched more than once.

"Let that lad pass to me!" Cecil said, pointing.

Gil was handed through the crowd and hustled into the courtyard where the party of six men was dismounting. Secretary Cecil handed his satchel to another and motioned Gil forward, then clasped his shoulder in greeting.

"The queen's little painter scamp Gil Sharpe has grown up, has he not?" Cecil asked as Gil swept him a half bow.

"Grown up to be Gilberto Sharpino, trained in the Della Rovere painter's school in Terra del Duca, Urbino, under Maestro Giorgio Scarletti, my lord."

"A place full of artists, no doubt, but papists and pro-Spaniards, too, eh?"

"Oh, yes, my lord, and I have much to tell."

"Her Majesty and I want to hear it all. It's ironic you have come home now, for the Queen's Grace and I are determined to select an official portrait of her to be sanctioned, copied, and distributed in the realm. Walk with me, lad," he said, starting toward one of the guarded doors to sprawling Whitehall.

Gil's pulse pounded. He walked with the most influential man in the realm—unless Her Majesty was still smitten with Lord Robert Dudley, whom the queen always called Robin. While yet in Italy, Gil had heard that Dudley had been named Earl of Leicester, elevated, some said, so the queen could pass her former favorite off as a possible English and Protestant husband to the Catholic Queen of Scots.

They strode past groups of courtiers and deeper into the palace, toward the royal chambers. Surely, Gil thought, this was a sign that he was destined to do great things for the queen at court. Did Lord Cecil imply that he could paint the queen's official portrait?

"Two years ago," Cecil went on, not turning his head and talking out of the side of his mouth as if nothing were really being said, "the queen signed a proclamation designed to control productions of her royal likeness. Everyone was painting or drawing her, and she hated most of the results—you remember that."

"I do, my lord. Do you think that I might be allowed—"

"I know you came to speak later in life than most, lad, but

have you not learned yet to listen more than you talk? The act prohibits painters, printers, and engravers from creating her picture until Her Majesty chooses a portrait of which she fully approves, which may then be copied."

Gil nodded. The standard method of punching holes in the outline and smearing the pattern with charcoal to reproduce the likeness on a surface beneath, which would then be filled in and colored, was the old way the English still used. Gil had spent backbreaking hours studying his maestro's identical technique. But then he'd stumbled on the carefully guarded secret some Italian artists, including Scarletti, used to both charm and cheat their noble clients. One reason he'd clandestinely left for home was that he feared his master would discover he knew of that dark deceit.

"She's put the portrait business off of late," Cecil went on, "but has now begun to pose for selected persons."

"Oh," Gil managed as his hopes deflated. "Well-established, sanctioned artists, you mean?"

"The point is, not sanctioned yet." Cecil rounded on him, and they stopped walking. "My lad, I want a full report of Urbino politics rather than portraits later. Meanwhile, I will send you with one of my men to wash up a bit while I speak to the queen about your return. If she still favors you, perhaps you can serve her yet, though I'd say the selection of three artists for her portrait is firmly established and finally well under way." He gestured down the hall, and they began to walk again, with his entourage several paces behind.

As they passed the double doorway of the privy gallery, which Gil recalled the queen often used for a council chamber, the boy glimpsed a makeshift artists' studio set up inside. The long table had been shifted to the wall, and the queen sat on a dais in strong window light with the easels of three artists—two men and a woman—facing her with their backs to Gil.

Though Cecil didn't notice at first, Gil stopped walking. The boy lingered as the sun cast its rippled light through the mullioned windows like flickering flames on the red hair, golden crown, and crimson costume of the queen.

Elizabeth Tudor had spring fever, yet here she sat for the initial posing which would lead to a selection of her official portrait. Though a dozen or so of her closest courtiers stood nearby, whispering and gesturing, she remained stiff and still while her thoughts raced.

The spring rains had abated of late and she yearned to leave London for the countryside or to go out in her barge—if the Thames wasn't still so unruly. Sitting ramrod straight, holding the pose she herself had chosen, perspiring in the elaborate ruff and ermine-collared mantle draped with the heavy gold chains of state, she slanted her gaze around the room.

She detested this process of trusting others to convey her presence and person to the world. She fully intended to look in a mirror as she examined each painting to be certain the art told the truth—but for a few details she might change, of course, such as her long nose and sharp chin. But her eyes were good, she assured herself, her mother's dark Boleyn eyes, which offset well her father's ruddy Tudor coloring.

This was sheer agony, but she and Cecil had agreed that a standard must be set. A carefully crafted image must speak of her serene power and control to friend and foe alike, especially with her Catholic cousin, Mary, Queen of Scots, spinning her webs of subtle rebellion even on England's northern borders.

Elizabeth's eyes skimmed the massive painting on the far wall, the one her father's court painter, Hans Holbein, had done of King Henry VIII in all his glory. Though he dominated the piece, it also included his third queen, Jane Seymour, and their son, Prince Edward VI, Elizabeth's long-lost, dear half brother. How she missed the boy, who had died in his fifteenth year. How she wished she could see him again and comfort him from night frights and fear of their own father—

The queen started and stared. As if her longing had summoned her dead brother, in the doorway stood a tall, lanky boy peering in; with this light in her face, she could not clearly see his own.

To the obvious dismay of her artists, she rose and shaded her eyes. The lad was Edward's height but had more girth. He held some sort of sack. Oh, someone with Cecil, she thought as she saw her master secretary appear in the doorway and speak in earnest to the boy.

Her lady-in-waiting, Rosie Radcliffe, hurried to take the heavy gilt scepter and orb from her hands. "Your Grace desires a respite?"

"She desires to fly this hot cage," Elizabeth told her, stepping away from the throne and dragging her heavy train, which others of her ladies hastily lifted from the floor. "Yes," the queen mused aloud, "maybe I shall go elsewhere. Send for Lord Arundel and tell him I long to take the court to his fine Nonsuch while this place is swept free of winter woes."

Cecil had entered and heard her words. "Your Grace, isn't it a bit early for a progress with possible mired roads? Besides, the

Queen of Scots' envoy Maitland should be here soon with her decision on her marriage."

"*Do not* get me started on that today, my lord," she said, shrugging off her train into the arms of her women. "It's bad enough to have to sit here while my very being is copied for the likes of my enemies to possess."

"And your own people to see and cherish, Your Grace."

But she felt petulant and strolled behind the artists' easels, however much that rattled them. "Lavina," she told the woman who usually painted miniatures of court personages, "you always make me look whey-faced. It may not matter as much in a tiny, closed locket around someone's neck, but life-sized, I can't abide it."

"Hm" was all Elizabeth said as she glanced at the partial portraits that Will Kendale and Henry Heatherley had done. She looked skeletal in both, but she had lost weight this winter, and they were only sketching outlines so far.

And then when the boy at the door, who had reminded her so of her brother, stood his ground, she knew who he was. Gil Sharpe! Gil had grown up and was back from Italy. He'd been gone but three years when she had assumed he'd not be back for at least five.

"Gil?" she cried, and stepped around Kendale's easel so fast her skirts caught its legs and he had to lunge to save it. The boy flew through the door and knelt before her in such a blur she could hardly note how his face had matured, how he'd grown sturdier and handsomer.

"Gilberto Sharpino at your service, Your Majesty," came from a mouth muffled by the big hempen sack he toted.

"I hope you learned a thing or two on the Continent besides how to Italianize your name, Gilberto Sharpino," she replied with a little laugh. "It's hotter than the hinges of Hades in here, so the court will be moving to the sweet, cool countryside, but you may come along—with my other artists, of course—and I'll pose in the sun where there's a decent breeze."

Smiling as the boy rose, she began to signal messages with her quick hands, and he silently chattered back to her in turn, just the way they used to communicate before Gil began to talk. She ignored the mutterings and murmurs of her painters and her people, for the lad seemed to bask in her presence as if she were the sun.

Chapter the First

CHAOS COMMANDED THE COURT THE NEXT DAY AS THE royal household packed for Nonsuch Palace a day's journey away. When the queen's retinue went from place to place, it was like moving, not a mere visit. Linens, tapestries, tableware, favorite furnishings, and trusted servants made a long cavalcade of horses, litters, and nearly three hundred carts. Ordinarily, Elizabeth traveled with over a thousand, but not to the petite Palace of Nonsuch.

She heard running footsteps in the halls, the banging of goods, shouted orders. Lord Arundel, who had bought the former royal estate from the previous Tudor queen, had gone ahead to prepare for the arrival of two hundred guests. Most of them must reside in tents in the meadow because the apartments of the charmingly sized palace would be taken by the queen's closest courtiers and staff.

"What is that sweet-smelling stuff?" Elizabeth asked Meg Milligrew, her strewing-herb mistress of the privy chamber. On her knees, the girl had her red head bent over a chest of the queen's clothing she was scenting. Elizabeth halted as she entered the chamber from the inner sanctum of her bedroom.

"Fresh potpourri from the first apothecary roses, Your Grace. I was wearying of the dry dust of the wintry sachets. Gracious, this journey to Nonsuch will be like a breath of fresh air."

Meg Milligrew had always been that for the queen. They'd gone through some difficult times these last seven years Meg had served her. Because the young woman somewhat resembled Elizabeth Tudor and was one of her most trusted servants of the privy household, Meg sometimes became more than a mere herbalist, especially when some mystery or crime needed to be secretly solved.

"You'll soon be fetching in all sorts of green and growing things again," Elizabeth told her jauntily, though the queen's heart was heavy as she went out into the corridor. She headed two doors down to a small chamber where her dear old friend Lady Katherine Ashley was living out the winter of her life in a state the royal physicians deemed "second childhood."

As the queen had been only three when she lost her mother, Queen Anne Boleyn, Kat had been her nursemaid, her early governess, and later first lady of the bedchamber and mistress of the royal wardrobe. Above all, Kat had been the nearest thing she'd had to a mother these thirty-two years.

Elizabeth halted in the doorway. Kat, in a carved armchair by the window, was slumped in sleep with the sun on her robed knees. Floris Minton, the nursemaid who had been hired with highest commendations in January, looked up from her embroidery frame and jumped to her feet to curtsy.

The queen gestured for Floris to join her in the hall, and the sprightly woman obeyed instantly. Floris was a real find, a gem, as

Lady Rosie and Meg, who had previously helped tend the failing Kat, always said. Floris's face might be plain and pale, her nut-brown hair and eyes unremarkable, but she was clever and always radiated care and concern for Kat.

"How do you think Lady Ashley will abide the trip?" the queen whispered to Floris with a nod in Kat's direction.

"In the padded litter you propose, well, I think, Your Majesty. The sweet country breezes of Surrey will do her good."

"Tend her well on the journey and send word to me if aught is amiss. Of course, both of you will be lodged near the royal chambers. Mistess Minton, I trust your opinion in all this."

The short woman gave a pert nod. "I note well the love you bear her. You suffer to see her so much as buffeted or discomfitted."

"Has she addressed you as her daughter of late?" Elizabeth asked, for Kat sometimes had hallucinations that Floris was her own progeny she must tend to.

"Off and on, Your Majesty. She—"

"Who is that come calling?" Kat's tremulous voice cried out.

"It's me, Elizabeth," the queen said, stepping into the chamber and slowly going closer. "Remember me?"

"Of course I do. And I see you've borne your child, flat as a board you are again."

"I—Kat," Elizabeth said as her hands fluttered to her stiff satin stomacher, "I told you I am not wed nor have had a child."

"Pity," Kat clipped out, frowning. "My Floris needs friends."

As queen she could not tend Kat for hours, as she'd like, but it cut Elizabeth to the quick that it was Floris whom Kat held to now. "We all need friends," Elizabeth whispered, and merely touched Kat's shoulder, though she wanted to hurl herself against the old woman's breast and weep for her losses, as she had so many times in her childhood. But the queen blinked back tears and fled before she made a fool of herself, crying before Floris and further upsetting Kat. Each time Kat was with Elizabeth lately, she seemed not only agitated but angry.

As the queen stepped into the corridor, she saw William Cecil, with several others in his wake, bearing down on her, waving a parchment. Cecil always had queen's business on his person, sometimes literally up his sleeve. But this paper was crushed in his fist, and that meant a show of temper her brilliant chief secretary of state seldom demonstrated.

"Bad news, my lord?" she threw over her shoulder as she proceeded him into her privy chamber. Meg was still on the floor, doling out rose petals.

"Hell's teeth! Queen Mary of Scots' envoy Lord Maitland is in Berwick and will be here in a day or so," Cecil said so loudly that Elizabeth knew he meant his words for others. He took care not to close the door completely. "But, Your Grace," he raged on, "this paper from a well-placed informant says she's determined to wed Lord Darnley, no matter how much you promote the Earl of Leicester! Ah, Mistress Milligrew, I didn't see you," he went on in a more subdued tone. "Could you step out?"

"Oh, of course, my lord." Meg darted out and closed the door behind herself.

"Did I look vexed enough?" Cecil asked the minute they were alone.

The queen smiled grimly. Cecil had said he might put on a show for any Scottish informants who had infiltrated the court. This winter they'd had a bellyful of them lurking about and reporting every word and move to Mary, Queen of Scots.

" 'S blood, it was a fine performance, Cecil, one I warrant even my clever master of revels Ned Topside and his former Queen's Country Players would cheer. I've been feeling low, but this perks me up indeed. Of course, we must still publicly 'promote' the Earl of Leicester with the Scots queen so that the defiant, headstrong schemer will be sure to wed that sot Darnley and be weakened from within, so to speak."

"But from without, we must yet fear her Scots lords and what they and our own northern Catholics could do. Those damned English papists near the Scottish border have been hoarding arms and conducting masses in secret for years."

"And in secret they champion my cousin Mary, who covets my country and my crown. At any cost, I cannot allow her that victory."

"Your plan to refuse her Darnley to make her want him all the more is brilliant, my queen. And now, your removal to the country will mean Ambassador Maitland must come to seek you there, only to be told you still will not sanction her wedding the man. The only risk in all this, of course, is that we may soon have not only Mary to fear as a magnet for Catholic rebellion, but a legal child of her body."

"Yes," Elizabeth said, and turned away to the window to gaze out over the privy gardens. She pressed her flat belly hard into the jutting windowsill. "But pray do not preach to me about my own need to wed and bear a child, my lord. England," she whispered to herself, "shall ever be both my husband and my child."

"What's that about a child, Your Grace?" Cecil asked, stepping closer.

"I said," she added as she spun back to face him, "Gil Sharpe is no longer a child, and I'm including him with the three other artists going to Nonsuch. I cannot wait to hear his report of all things Italian."

"Which reminds me, the artists have asked to see you, though I put them off."

She heaved a sigh. "I am in need of a walk outside, so send to them that they may join me in the privy garden forthwith."

As Cecil bowed and left her, Elizabeth gazed out again at the greening grass and tiny buds popping on the bare limbs of trees. This winter had been a bitter one, but now that spring was here—and Gil had come home early—better times were surely soon to come.

"Is there some concern about accompanying me to Nonsuch, or painting there al fresco?" the queen asked her three artists as they joined her in the privy gardens. "The background of the portraits must, of course, be a rich interior with my throne, but I trust you have the skills to manage that while painting out of doors."

"Oh, indeed, and we are deeply honored to be included in the royal retinue," blonde, big-boned Lavina Teerlinc said, gripping her hands together. Though tall, the queen's only female artist had to stretch her strides to keep up with the queen's quick pace on the geometrically laid out garden paths.

"Ah, yes, back to Nonsuch," Will Kendale, fat as a woolsack and already puffing, put in from her other side. "You may recall, Your Gracious Majesty, that I myself was one of the artists your royal father chose to bestow the fantastical beauty that is Nonsuch. I lived there nearly six months, painting several scenes on interior walls when the building was going up. It will be, in a way, a home going for me, though my great successes were also achieved here in London after I studied with great painters who—"

"Master Kendale," Henry Heatherley said as his highly polished boots spit gravel, "we do not need a recital of your well-known list of good fortune. You are hardly being attentive to Her Majesty's expressly voiced concerns. I have studied my craft under Master Hans Holbein himself, but I'll not flaunt that here. Yes, Your Majesty, a slight concern exists about the conditions under which we go to Nonsuch in your retinue."

"But not," Lavina added, "about the conditions of painting outside or living there in a tent. I am sure dat vill be quite pleasant."

Lavina had been reared in the Netherlands with Dutch as her first language; *dat*s and *vill*s crept back into her speech when she was excited or upset, which, Elizabeth noted well, she must be now.

"Are we correct to assume, Your Majesty," Heatherley said, "that the work of at least one of us three will be the final, officially approved portrait? Odds then are one-third for each of us that it will be a marvelous opportunity—that is unless . . ."

"'S blood, unless what?" Elizabeth finally got a word in as she halted and faced them near the marble fountain.

"Unless dat lad vill be included," Lavina blurted, but so quietly that the queen almost had to read her lips.

"Gil Sharpe?"

"Ah, yes," Kendale said with a sharp sniff, "or Gilberto Sharpino as he styles himself now."

"It was my suggestion and my support," the queen explained, "that sent Gilbert Sharpe to the ducal court of Urbino to study portraiture. And yes, I intend to see what he can do, though God knows, he is so greatly gifted—as I'm sure all of you were in your youth before someone taught and gave you opportunities—that he almost didn't need the help. Why, Lavina, you were reared in a painter's household, so how could you begrudge the boy some teachers? And Masters Kendale and Heatherley, both of you have just emphasized to me that you studied in the schools of masters."

She stared down the disgruntled Lavina, who was trying hard to hide how annoyed she'd been the other day at the queen's critique of her style. At last, looking abashed, Lavina dropped her sharp blue gaze and unfolded her arms from across her broad breasts to clasp her hands together as if in petition.

"Of course, Your Majesty," Heatherley put in, "I'd be willing to help the lad in any way I can." Elizabeth turned her gaze on him. He was as compact and dark-haired as Kendale was fat and silver-haired. Heatherley's olive complexion made him look Mediterranean, quite swarthy in a land of fairer folk.

"That is kind of you, Master Heatherley."

Though she'd heard the man drank too much expensive Bordeaux, his hand was still steady with a brush, and his work was as polished as his deportment. Yet, today, for the first time, Elizabeth sensed burning ambition beneath that suave exterior, the like of which she'd seen only in her own dear Robin, Earl of Leicester.

In this day of unsigned portraiture, Henry Heatherley liked to sign his paintings with a grandly flourished *HH*. It was not only his initials, she thought, but his way of reminding everyone he had studied with Hans Holbein, her father's genius of mirrorlike portraits. Heatherley's movements—mouth, gestures, steps, everything about the man—were quicksilver fast, like a fine Barbary horse straining at the bit.

Finally, the queen regarded Will Kendale, still apparently seething. She supposed that despite his impressive credentials, she should have listened to Lord Arundel when he called the man "a flap-mouthed magpie as full of bombast as he was of any sweets he could get his hands on."

"Then," Kendale said, "is the boy to be included among those of us you will consider, Your Majesty?"

Elizabeth's temper nearly broke at his baiting tone. "I haven't yet decided," she informed them, "but this audience has been most enlightening, and I look forward to viewing more completed portraits at Nonsuch—four of them."

She smiled stiffly. Lavina, having been at court off and on for years, evidently recognized the tone and look of her royal mistress, for she dropped a quick curtsy and, linking her arm through Heatherley's, who looked as if he'd like to dig his heels in, urged her fellow artists away.

In the late afternoon of the next day, as she approached Nonsuch Palace, set like a jewel in the rolling green hills of Surrey, Elizabeth summoned Gil Sharpe to her open coach from his place far back in the royal retinue. Again, as he approached, he reminded her of her half brother, though the boy rode awkwardly, while Edward had been a fine horseman. But then Gil had been reared poor in the city. What was important was his gift from God to paint. She recalled the first sketch the boy had done of her, scribbled on crumpled paper, but so skilled that she thought at first her master of revels, the wily Ned Topside, had done it.

"Such a beautiful sight, Your Majesty," Gil called to her as, at her cue, the entourage halted behind, overlooking the palace and its hunt park. Elizabeth alighted from the carriage in which her people had cheered her on her way, and waited for her mount.

"I am going to ride ahorse the rest of the way," she explained to Gil, "and I want you to approach Nonsuch without everyone else in your way for the first time. Though faces may be your forte, mark my words, someday you will paint this vista, and I shall keep it with me all winter long."

When the queen was mounted sidesaddle and had led her entourage into the gentle slope of rolling meadow before the walls, she rode slowly to savor the moment and allow Gil to keep up.

"However did your royal sire find such a perfect site?" the boy marveled. "I heard he built this place in his old age for a hunt lodge, but ended up making it his most wonderful building project."

"This site is the single sad thing about fabulous Nonsuch," she told him. "A village stood here with a Catholic church and manor house—Cuddington, it was called. But when Great Henry wanted his palace here, the townsfolk were moved, the entire village was razed, and this was built—plain on the outside, but wait until you see within! It is the ultimate blend of the English with the Italian."

"If your father loved it and you do too, Your Grace, then why is it Lord Arundel's possession now?"

"It was too fancy for my sister, Queen Mary, and she hated the place. She sold it to Lord Arundel for a pittance," she said, her voice not betraying her anger at her sister for that and so much more.

"But I heard Lord Arundel favors you and if you but asked for it back . . ."

"Gil, you must learn not to blurt your thoughts, though to me in private you may say all. Yes, Lord Arundel, Catholic that he is, has hopes of being my suitor to save my Protestant soul and bring his own great name into the ruling family. As for keeping this palace myself, isn't it better to have a wealthy, devoted host to care for it?"

"Of course, Your Grace, like dining at someone else's table. And my lord Cecil has lectured me more than once to keep my ears open and my mouth closed. I swear I was quiet as a mouse in Italy, though that was partly because the place overwhelmed me and it took a while to learn that singsong language."

They laughed together as they rode onto the wide gravel avenue that headed straight as a die for the great north gate. "Gil," she said, raising her voice over the noise of hooves and the rumble of the retinue behind them, "I hope to hear what you observed in Italy. But I warrant my master secretary does too, and even helped support you as I did."

Gil almost managed to cover his surprise. "He said to tell no one, but I'm sure he didn't mean you—if you asked."

"Exactly. You see, my lord Cecil often has English visitors abroad do more than visit. They become his eyes and ears on my behalf. Ah, I see Lord Arundel standing inside the gate to welcome us. Best drop back with the other artists, then."

"Yes, Your Grace, but I wasn't riding with them. I was back farther with your servants Meg Milligrew, Stephen Jenks, and Ned Topside, remembering old times and getting caught up on the new."

"One more thing," she told him, even as she lifted her gloved hand in distant greeting to Lord Arundel. "As I was saying, the secrets and wonders of Nonsuch are not visible until one reaches the innermost court, as in coming to know a person. Gil, tread carefully with the other artists until you know them better and . . ."

The clatter of hooves on gravel and excited voices drowned out her words as the boy was swallowed by the closest riders. To remain at the head of the onslaught, the queen spurred her mount through the tall, turreted brick gate.

Elizabeth rose, late for her, at midmorn. It had been a short night since her wealthy host had given a welcoming feast followed by a masque. But this was her favorite time of day at Nonsuch, and the morning was stunning with a clear blue sky, brisk wind, and strong sun already casting off its heat. She scented faint smoke and wondered if someone was burning dead leaves nearby.

She favored strolls in this inner courtyard when the sun climbed above the eastern walls and shone upon the western ones. Then, sharply defined in their life-sized relief, the classical gods and goddesses of gleaming white marble seemed to leap to life.

She walked among them and recalled their stories and how her father had loved these gilt-framed granite panels flaunting the labors of Hercules in powerful bursts of energy, balanced by the more gentle figures of the Graces. As she touched them and marveled at their contrasting strengths, she realized that she must radiate these varied virtues to her people.

Her eyes, as everyone's here must do, then came to rest on the massive statue of King Henry VIII enthroned in splendor, presiding over the array of deities which he had commanded built here. Unlike her father, she would not hide her kingdom's grandeur within the walls of privacy and privilege. She, Elizabeth, meant to use portraits of herself, carved or painted, to reach her people and to help her rule.

"Your Grace! Your Grace!" a man's voice called, much agitated.

As the Earl of Arundel ran toward her, Elizabeth came back to the present with a jolt. The four ladies-in-waiting she'd brought along came closer as if to shield her, but she stepped out from them.

Henry Fitzalan, Lord Arundel, was forty-four, a wealthy widower with two grown daughters, who fancied himself a suitor for her royal hand. But above all, Arundel was a bred-in-the-bone Catholic. And so, though he seemed to serve her well, and she had granted freedom to worship privily as one willed in her kingdom, she could not completely trust him.

"My lord, what is it?" she asked. The usually elegantly attired man looked rakish and hastily clothed.

"A fire among the tents! I've sent men out with water buckets to help fight it—fire, like a flaming torch!"

"Then let us go out and be sure no one is hurt," she cried, and lifted her skirts to break into a fast walk. "Pray God it doesn't spread, as those tents are cheek by jowl."

"I hear not, but they say the cries were dreadful."

"What cries?" she asked as she rushed from the inner courtyard to the outer, with Arundel and her ladies behind.

"They say one of your artists was trapped in a tent," he told her, gasping for breath.

Elizabeth of England left him and the women in her wake as she hiked her skirts higher and broke into a dead run.

Chapter the Second

 OUTSIDE THE PALACE GATE, ELIZABETH TURNED RIGHT and ran toward the haphazardly pitched white canvas tents. From the far fringe of the encampment, she could see and smell smoke.

The immediate area seemed deserted. Trailed by Arundel and her women, she tore down a zigzag grass path, avoiding tables set outside the open-flapped tents. Ribbons fluttered in the breeze on tent poles; here and there were remnants of last night's revels, a dropped tankard, spilled food, an overturned bench or stool, a cold cook fire.

She saw everyone had gone where she surmised. Courtiers and servants stood in a circle, gaping at a collapsed, blackened tent. It was the only one, as far as she could tell, which had been engulfed in flames, though others near it looked soot-stained. The grass in an oval around the ruin lay burned and black. The tent had been pitched on the outer edge of the encampment in the meadow about fifty paces before the thick trees of the hunt park began.

Though several men heaved useless buckets of wash water on

the charred, sodden mass of canvas, it still smoked. One man tried to lift the edge of the tent with a lance, as if someone inside could yet escape the collapsed weight of devastation. Women shrieked or cried. Someone began a dreadful wail as if she were a professional mourner in a funeral procession.

"Let me pass!" Elizabeth commanded, though her voice was tremulous and she was panting.

People gasped to see her and parted as if she were Moses at the Red Sea. The first face that emerged from the blur of horrified countenances was that of her longtime guard and groom, Stephen Jenks. Though Jenks's wit was mostly for horses, he was ever loyal, and she trusted the brawny man with her life. She realized it was Jenks who had pried two of the tent poles from the ground and tried to lift the canvas with a lance in an obviously doomed effort to allow those inside an escape route.

"Jenks! Who?" she demanded.

Still squatting, then going to one knee before her, he said, "It was the artist with the boy—"

"Not Gil!" she shrieked.

"No, your painter Will Kendale and his lad Niles who mixes his paints and all," Jenks got out before Robin Dudley, Earl of Leicester, stepped between them.

Where had Robin suddenly appeared from? She always picked him out, even in a crowd. Now she noted other individuals, some with soot- or tear-streaked faces. But for the two distraught artists, Lavina and Heatherley, who stood in her line of sight, surely not many of these people had known Master Kendale. Since he had recently come to court, her people must be reacting to the sheer horror of this. Her own stomach roiled as she fought to keep control.

Robin's voice was much quieter and calmer than Jenks's had been. "Yes, Your Grace, it's Kendale's tent. His servant Niles was also evidently trapped inside, his artist's aide, cook, and, ah— body servant," he added, and lifted a sleek eyebrow at those last two words as if to insinuate something she didn't even want to contemplate.

"According to Lord Arundel, there were screams," she said. "If they were awake and aware, why did they not escape?"

"Yes, my man told me dreadful screams," Arundel repeated, for he'd now caught up with her and had pushed his way through the crowd. He was sucking in great breaths and holding his side as if he had a stitch in it. "But then, evidently," he went on, "either the fire or the choking smoke silenced them. The tent must have gone up quickly." Arundel began hacking into his hand.

Despite his coughing fit, others now stood silent, staring at the tomb of two lives snuffed out within. Again the queen fought to keep from vomiting. The odor of charred flesh emerged from the mass as surely as some strange, acrid scent she could not place.

Her knees went weak with relief when she glimpsed Gil's frightened face in the crowd. Thank God he was safe. Like the child he had once been, he waved to her, then signaled with quick hand gestures, *I was in that tent last night. No one but one man, one boy there last night.*

At least Gil had not stayed with Kendale and Niles, but had probably been with Jenks or Ned Topside. She must question the boy about it all later. She shuddered and took Robin's arm to steady her weak knees, but it was her trustworthy Jenks who thought to fetch a stool for her.

"Your Grace must surely want to go back in now," another voice behind her said as she sank onto the seat. Cecil had appeared from the palace. "Arundel, Leicester, and I," he went on, "can see to the removal of the bodies, the clearing up of all this."

"Yes," she said, and her voice rose, "the clearing up of this, indeed. My lords, send everyone back to their tents and tell them to guard their cook fires. We will hold a memorial service in the chapel later today. I will go inside the palace soon but not quite yet."

The three men hovering over her exchanged swift glances. Robin, the love of her life, though she prayed he did not know it, had never gotten on with the other two older, more conservative men. Nor was her indispensable Cecil liked or appreciated by Arundel, for the aristocratic earl felt Cecil was a pushy "new dealer" whom she heeded far too much. Still, at least when any sort of upheaval threatened, her triumvirate of close advisers managed to work together for queen and country.

"Yes, Your Grace, anything to help," Robin said, and began to urge the curious onlookers away. She heard him even mention the cook-fire explanation she had put forth, though she wasn't sure that was the cause of the conflagration. After all, artists carted about with them all sorts of oils, resins, and strangely concocted paints and powders. It might have been an accident.

She was not surprised to see Cecil still at her side. "Your Grace," he said, his voice low as he bent down, "Dr. John Dee arrived just after dawn with his new wife. He's come from Mortlake with news for you. I had planned to meet with him in my chambers just now. If you wish, I shall remain here while you see him, as it's best you not sit out in the open here—like this. With this smell and the bodies in there, it isn't seemly."

"Seemly?" she cracked out, glaring up at him, though she had to look directly into the sun. "I will be the one in this realm to say what is *seemly*, my lord. If you had your way, it would not be *seemly* that I rule without a husband or heir. What is seemly is to look into this, just to be certain it was an accident."

"If you mean to inquire into this tragedy, can you not do so from within the palace?" he argued quietly, not budging.

"Cecil," she said, her tone more tempered as she stared back at the fatal tent, "I shall go inside only if you and Jenks remain here as witnesses and report forthwith to me every detail, however dreadful. And place all the evidence of these dire events under lock and key inside the palace—the tent, its contents, however charred, except the corpses, after they are examined. I shall go inside and ask Dr. Dee to view the bodies. He may not be a medical doctor, but he is a learned, brilliant man, and I value his advice." She lowered her voice even more. "And if I must, I shall convene my covert Privy Plot Council just to rule out any sort of foul play."

"Forgive me, Your Grace," Jenks put in, stepping between her and the ruins and doffing his cap in his blackened hands, "but I'd wager foul play for certain. See," he rushed on, gesturing, "I only tried to lift the bottom of the tent canvas to let them out *after* I saw the entry flaps were tied tight shut."

"You mean secured from the inside of the tent for the night?"

"Oh, no, Your Grace, 'cause I couldn't have seen the ties then. If the ropes for the flaps aren't all burned up under this mess, I think we'll find them tied—even knotted—from the outside, not within."

From the outside, not within. Elizabeth kept hearing Jenks's words as she went inside the palace and headed toward her second-floor apartments. "From the outside, not within," she whispered.

Had someone deliberately pulled the tent lacings—by which the flaps could be secured from the inside—to the outside and knotted them, as Jenks claimed he'd seen? She had ordered him and Cecil to be certain that that observation was correct before the bodies were removed and the interior of the tent was examined, and if it was so, to preserve whatever was left of the ties.

"Clifford, fetch Dr. Dee to me from Secretary Cecil's chambers," she told her guard at the door to her apartments. She sent her ladies away and went in through her privy chamber to her bedroom by herself. Only Meg was in the room.

"I heard what happened, so I'm mixing the strongest-scented elixirs and powders I have, Your Grace," she told her, fussing with a wooden box of herbs and a pitcher on the table. "Though I couldn't bear to go out to see the tragedy myself, I know you have a delicate sense of smell and—"

"But more than that has been thoroughly ravaged today," Elizabeth finished for her. "Two of my people are dead, under mysterious circumstances, and I'll not abide it. This is dreadful, as if it were an attack on my painters, and on myself for finally deciding to have my approved likeness completed and made public. Here, let me have some of that stuff and throw the windows open wider, as I smell like smoke myself."

"Shall I send for your ladies to help you change your garments?"

"I just sent them away and have summoned Dr. Dee."

"I heard he's arrived with his new wife, Katherine Constable. She's a London grocer's widow, not one with a good dowry, though he's always needing money, so I hear, but she's a fetching, younger woman. Didn't think he was the type to be swayed by all that, he's so brilliant and all, so deep into examining so many things."

"But he is a man," Elizabeth muttered as Meg dusted her sleeves and bodice with the sweet-smelling powder. The queen exploded in a huge sneeze. It was just as well; she was afraid she'd never get the stench of death out of her nostrils and her head. She took the scented, damp cloth Meg held out to her and rubbed her face and hands with it.

"If you're sending for Dr. Dee, is there something, well—that needs study and examining, Your Grace?"

"As you said, John Dee is skilled in all pursuits," Elizabeth muttered, giving her the cloth back, then pacing to the window. Already the bearded, black-garbed Dr. Dee was striding across the courtyard, his skullcap perched on his head, his robe billowing out behind him. Yes, his bride, a young blonde who trailed along, was beautiful, willowy and graceful, hurrying to keep up and chattering away at him.

"Opposites attract," Elizabeth said as Meg peeked past her shoulder. "I wonder if Dr. Dee ever proved that in his laboratories at Mortlake amidst his experiments with magnets, optical glasses, maps, and cryptic writing."

"Mayhap the brilliant doctor won't be traveling so much anymore then," Meg said.

"He will if Cecil sends him at my command."

The two figures disappeared below, and the queen sank into a chair behind the table. "Meg, where is that soothing throat elixir? I feel I could spit smoke, but I'm going to probe this tragedy, beginning right now."

Despite his forty-two years, John Dee always felt a childlike thrill to be summoned by his queen.

"But I don't see why I can't go with you to meet her now," his wife of three months, Katherine, coaxed. She pouted prettily and laced her arm through his when they were admitted through the guarded door into the wing with the privy apartments.

"Because, my dearest, she has summoned me. It's something, I surmise, about that dreadful, fatal fire this morning."

She gasped and tugged back. "But what could you possibly know about that?"

"Do not fret, my little love. As the Bible says, 'Do not fret because it only causes harm.'"

"I haven't caused any harm! I can't help worrying that you need to make your way with the queen and keep in her good graces."

He noted she managed to match him step for step up the stone staircase, however much shorter her shapely legs. She looked especially young this morning, all flushed with health and life, all passionate for building their future together on the petticoats of the brilliant, powerful queen. And, of course, he had no right to scold his Katherine for wanting to meet Elizabeth Tudor. He himself stood ever in awe of her quick mind, her tenacity to know things, her wide-reaching education, those very things which animated his being.

"And what would I know about the fire?" he repeated her question. "I'm Her Majesty's official court philosopher, a man in quest of universal knowledge, so she summons me for advice on many things, my dear, you'll see."

Katherine was always vexed that philosophers at royal courts were paid well on the Continent, but Elizabeth always paid him in books and favors. He never intended to tell his Katherine that books were what he wanted, what he loved almost more than life itself—and now her, of course.

"Do you think she'll visit us at Mortlake as she has you before?" she went on. "I mean, I know we wouldn't be worthy to entertain her there, but you promised I would meet her and—"

"Katherine, Katherine," he chided at the top of the staircase. Just ahead—he could tell by the two yeomen guards at the door—lay access to Her Majesty's privy chambers. "I promise you that you shall meet her soon, and I will indeed invite her to Mortlake."

Katherine sighed yet still stomped a foot, which rustled her best gown. She'd insisted on wearing it, though they were coming in by horseback from their Thames-side home at Mortlake, a good six miles distant. They had left shortly after daybreak, and he fully intended to head back to his work after he delivered his message to the queen. And now Her Majesty had suddenly summoned him for reasons of her own. Perhaps the queen's news wouldn't wait, but his was burning in his brain too.

"You'll wait here, then, my dear?" he asked, patting her hand in the crook of his arm, then bending down to kiss the Cupid's bow of her lips.

"If I must. But you must mention to her that she should meet me."

"Ah, perhaps the best time to meet her might be later, when she is not so busy and you have had time to change your gown. That one looks a bit dirty. Perhaps you brushed against something in the little walk you took around the palace grounds while I was waiting for Secretary Cecil."

"Really? Oh, no! Where?" she cried, pulling at her skirts and turning her head to peer at the back of them. All the while, the two stoic guards at the door didn't budge, as if they were statues like those in the courtyard below. "Well," she said, whispering now, "at least you must tell me everything she does and says, and I mean, every word!"

Sometimes, though John Dee usually had all the answers, he couldn't help but wonder if his wife hadn't married him merely to meet the queen.

Elizabeth's keen ears picked up voices in the hall. She shifted in her chair and downed the rest of the sweet spearmint elixir Meg had left her. Voices or footsteps, even rustling garments or the creak of boot leather outside her door—she'd never be used to them, never escape the memory of how they used to frighten her. Before she was queen, such sounds had meant spies, trouble, danger. The only noise that used to scare her more was the jingle of keys or their grating in a lock from her terrible time in the Tower.

She had been certain then that her life could be forfeit because her sister, Mary Tudor, then queen, hated her and could not afford to let her Protestant sister inherit her throne. And now, the great cosmic wheel had turned, and Elizabeth feared the same of the Catholic Queen Mary of Scots.

And Elizabeth recalled, sitting up straighter, that the crackle of flames was the other sound that sometimes tormented her dreams. She had pushed a certain memory to the back of her brain, locked it tightly away, but it came back now and again in flashes of fear. Twice, she herself had been trapped in a burning building, once just last year with Cecil and Jenks, during the Yuletide holidays, when the royal boathouse somehow caught fire. Even when she'd discovered who was trying to harm her, the villain had never admitted he'd lit that nearly fatal fire. She supposed it could have been an accident, set by a vagabond trying to keep warm in the wintry weather, one who'd seen what he'd done and had scuttled off into the dark night.

But it was an earlier blaze that had haunted her since she was thirteen. Not only had she nearly burned alive, but her sister Mary and brother Edward too, the entire hope of the Tudor dynasty. How terribly it had marred such a happy period in their lives, one of the few when they actually felt like a family. But that time, she knew who was at fault, though it was not the one who took the blame, for—

A knock on a distant door shattered her agonizing. She rose and went from her bedroom into her council chamber and sat again behind the long table there. "Open to me!" she called.

Her favorite yeoman guard, Clifford, stepped in. "Your Majesty, Dr. John Dee awaits."

"He may enter."

The tall, bearded man came in and bowed. He looked exactly as he had over a year ago, before he had left on one of his trips to the Continent. The learned man seemed ageless, unchanging. No wonder that during her sister's reign, some superstitious folk had imprisoned him for being a wizard. After all, Dr. Dee had done everything from appearing to make men fly during theatrical performances to claiming to aspire to universal knowledge, which was surely the realm of only God himself.

"I was surprised but pleased to hear you had come unbidden to Nonsuch," she told him, indicating he could sit in the chair across the table from her. "Your letters from abroad have been informative and welcome, Doctor, and Cecil's getting good at decoding them."

"I know Your Majesty could easily do so yourself if you but had the time."

"It is your cryptic signature that both baffles and amuses me," she confided. John Dee signed each communication to her with only what looked to be a three-digit number, two zeros and then a seven, the top of which extended over two small circles to its left. Since Dee, like others in her or Cecil's employ, was not only a traveler but an informant—"intelligencers," Cecil termed them— she took the symbol of what Cecil always called "007" to be a furrowed brow over two wide eyes.

Dr. Dee smiled tightly, then went deadly serious again. "Anything I can do to serve you is never enough for me—ah, and my new wife, of course."

"I am delighted you've found domestic happiness, and shall look forward to meeting her."

"Oh, that will please her mightily, Your Majesty. Meanwhile, I keep my eyes open in your behalf—hence the 007 signature."

"But to business. I can use your advice even now. You heard of the fatal fire this morning?" When he nodded solemnly, she went on. "One of my court artists, William Kendale—a man, by the way, who painted the frescoes in the lower hallway when my father built this fantastical place—was killed with his serving boy."

"Was killed or died, Your Majesty?"

"That may be the question, you see. My man Jenks insists the tent flaps were—are yet—tied from the outside. Even without that possible damning piece of evidence, inquiries must be made."

"Indeed, detailed observations and deductions aligned."

"And so I'd count it a great favor if you would examine the burned ruins with Secretary Cecil, especially the bodies, though I know you're not a medical man. I have a court physician here, a Dr. Forrest, whom I brought to tend Lady Ashley, but he's been ailing since we arrived. I regret it, but I've had to move him to a tent outside lest he make his own patient ill."

"I'd be pleased to help, Your Majesty. Is the inquiry proceeding now? I can hie myself down there. We rode in early this morn and saw no smoke then. But since they say where there is smoke there is fire, I must give you the news I've come bearing."

She sat up straighter. "These dreadful deaths have so distracted me—of course, you came for some purpose, since you weren't sent for."

"I know you and my lord Cecil feel that, despite the dangers to England which could come from the Continent, perils lie much closer to these isles, especially with Queen Mary of Scots to the north."

Her stomach cartwheeled. "Say on, Dr. Dee."

"I have something portentous to share, Your Majesty, something which may be rumor, but, ah, I think not."

"Tell me straight and now."

The usually calm Dee cleared his throat nervously. He gripped his long-fingered hands on the arms of his chair. "She—the Queen of Scots—had been lately looking in mirrors, making a big ado of it."

"Mirrors? They say she's pretty." Elizabeth shrugged. "The few portraits of her suggest that might be so, including one the Earl of Leicester has, the blackguard. But she is looking in mirrors for some other purpose, you mean?" She stood and leaned toward Dr. Dee with her palms flat on the table. "That she is fairer than I?"

"That would be a bald-faced lie, but it is far worse, Your

Majesty. Each time, looking in a mirror, she laughs as if she has not a care in the world and says the same thing, which is being reported far and wide, especially on your northern boundaries, which could flare up. But even if this challenge is exaggerated, I have it on sound authority that last week at Holyrood Palace, Queen Mary playfully pushed Lord Darnley, whom she swears she will wed, out of the way when he peered in the looking glass too."

"Yes, he would, the self-besotted popinjay. But each time, she says what?"

"Ah, with each glance in a mirror, I regret to inform you, Queen Mary publicly declares for all to hear, 'Look, I see the true Queen of England there.'"

Chapter the Third

"ARE YOU CERTAIN NO ONE SAW YOU BRING ALL OF THIS into the palace?" Elizabeth asked Jenks and her yeoman guard Clifford as the two men huffed their way up the servants' staircase of the privy apartments. The queen and Cecil had ordered them to take the burned tent, swathed in burlap, up onto the flat roof of the palace, so it could all be better examined without everyone staring. The canvas was so heavy that, however tall and strong the queen's men, they half carried and half dragged it up the tight, twisting staircase toward the roof.

The queen led their way with a lantern. In her other hand, though she'd had no time to study it yet, she carried a sketch Cecil had asked Gil to make, a diagram of the placement of the items in the tent as he recalled them from the previous night, before the fire. Soon she would question her young artist on all that had occurred during his visit to the victims that night. Dr. Dee was with the bodies, which had been removed to a cool cellar until their burial in the graveyard in the little village of Cheam, a few miles away.

The queen had decided the roof would be the best site to

examine the evidence for several reasons, besides removing the ghastly remains from prying eyes in the meadow. It was a sprawling space partly protected from wind by the teethlike crenellations around the outer edge, yet enough breeze came through to blow some of the heavy smell of death away. She wanted the good lighting of today's strong sun. And though she had shared her last thought with no one, she hoped the open air would dispel her own desperate memories of another conflagration.

For, unlike from the boathouse fire this winter, the queen kept suffering strange flashes in her mind's eye of that fire at Oakham, which had nearly trapped her and her half siblings years ago. They had been in a tent then too, so that was no doubt the connection which provoked these swift, sharp images and made her dread sleep tonight. Either this fire had set her off or Kat's being so strange . . . so angry with her. . . .

Elizabeth shook her head to clear it as she opened the door to the roof. By the time the men had the tent laid out and then went back to fetch and spread out its burned contents, Cecil had joined them.

"A fine place for this," he said, puffing from the steep climb. "I was thinking of arranging it in the back corner of the privy gardens, but then some could have seen it from their windows."

"And there is another good reason I hadn't even thought of to do this up here," Elizabeth said as she stepped away to peer through a lower section of wall at the tents below. "From this bird's-eye view, we can discern the relative positions of the tents and paths between them. Perhaps the arsonist darted into his—or her—tent nearby after igniting Kendale's."

Cecil only nodded, but Jenks said, "I could tell you who had tents nearby Master Kendale's, Your Grace, and Ned Topside could too. It was your other artists, mostly. We were talking with Gil late last night and saw all your painters. Ned kept asking Gil all kinds of questions about whether he had seen any theatricals in Italy, but I was just trying to calm the lad after Kendale insulted him."

Elizabeth's wide gaze snagged Cecil's. "Kendale insulted Gil about what?" she asked, trying to keep her tone of voice level when her heart was nearly beating out of her bodice. Surely, however abusive Kendale might have been to Gil, the lad would not have retaliated in some way that got out of hand.

"He said Gil was a climber far above his station," Jenks went on, "and that Kendale bet he couldn't paint worth a fig to rival himself or even the other two painters. That—"

"I plan to question Gil myself about all that soon," Elizabeth interrupted, hoping Cecil wasn't already suspecting poor Gil. "But first, let's lay the groundwork for all else we must do to establish foul play and then to discovery by whom."

With the blackened canvas tent positioned in the same direction it had been in the western meadow below, the queen saw indeed that the rope lacings at the flaps were tied tightly shut from the outside. Really, they were more than tied; rather, they were neatly laced.

"When we finish with all this, Jenks, cut out that section of the tent and save it," she ordered. "Who knows but that pattern of laces and knots isn't—pardon the pun—tied to some particular person through a hobby or avocation."

"Like sailors' knots?" Jenks asked, frowning. "It's not what we use in the stables, and I've not seen their like."

"Your Grace," Cecil whispered, sidling closer to her, "I do not desire to speak ill of the dead, but rumors have been bandied about that Kendale's interest in the boy Niles was not only to mix his paints, if you take my meaning."

"In short, Kendale and Mary of Scots' pretty and beloved Lord Darnley are of the same sexual persuasion," she whispered back.

Cecil nodded. "So, you see, the tent flaps could have indeed been tied closed—for extra privacy—but—"

"Not from the inside," she finished for him. "Yet these laced ropes could mean two things. First, since many people react violently toward those who practice sodomy—especially with boys—someone may have wanted to kill Kendale for that, and the fire snagged young Niles, too."

"At any rate, we have murder, I warrant," Cecil said as Jenks and Clifford finished arranging the tent's charred items next to the remains of the tent itself.

"A double murder," she corrected. "And lest we have a random murder by an arsonist among us while many of my people are housed in tents, we must move with great haste. I am immediately calling a meeting of my Privy Plot Council members who have helped me solve attacks and full-fledged plots before. Jenks, fetch both Mistress Milligrew and Ned Topside. Clifford, go out to the back cellars and see if Dr. Dee can join us with whatever he may have deduced by now. I hate even to contemplate it, but I may have to take a look at the bodies myself."

"So, we are gathered yet again for the desperate task of unmasking a murderer," the queen began when her group of covert detectors stood around the layout of the tent and the separate spread of items it had held but the day before. Meg, between Jenks and Ned, the queen's handsome, mercurial master of revels, nodded solemnly. Cecil looked grim, as he did when anything hinting of violence came near his queen; John Dee, who had joined them for the first time in an investigation, stared at the evidence. Elizabeth could tell Dee's mind was working at lightning speed, but so was hers.

"Ned and Jenks," she went on, "I am going to have you lie down over here, assuming the position of the bodies, amid this arrangements of items as we believe they were in the tent when it collapsed. Dr. Dee? Doctor?" she repeated when he didn't respond at first.

"Ah, yes, Your Majesty, I can testify to the corpses' positions and placements. No one had disturbed the heavy, smoking canvas before we uncovered the—ah, remains. With your permission, I'll show your men exactly . . ."

"Yes, go ahead."

"The big body, Master Kendale," Dee said, moving Jenks near where the tent flaps would have been, "was here, facedown, with both arms out toward the tent's tightly closed opening—so."

Watching Jenks get into that position, Cecil observed, "He might have been reaching for the tent flap."

"My thought exactly, my lord Cecil," Dee said. "Perhaps he had been clawing at the flaps, even desperately reaching through to untie them. The boy was not with him, nor helping him with that task," Dee went on, positioning Ned on the opposite side of the tent, lying curled up, facing the very outer edge of the tent. Ned, who was used to taking the lead parts of dukes and kings, had played more than one corpse before, the queen thought.

"The boy could have been trying to get out under the canvas," Cecil said, pointing. "See, they aren't near their beds."

"Not beds—bed," Elizabeth said, handing him the sketch Gil had made. "I'd wager Kendale slept on this wide cot and the boy had a blanket or pallet—which Gil has not sketched in here."

"Or he slept with Kendale," Cecil whispered.

"Be that as it may," she went on, "the most damning thing—along with the tent being laced from the outside—is that Gil sketched no place for food preparation, and no remnants of a cook fire are in the tent."

"Then the fire came from without indeed," Meg put in.

"I'd best go with Dr. Dee to view the bodies myself," Elizabeth said while the others walked among the items laid out on the roof as if they stood in the death tent itself.

"I'd advise against it, Your Majesty," Dee said. "To put it crudely, both corpses look like roasted game. And for another, ah, both are unclothed with no signs they wore garments when they died, which I'd deduce was from suffocation by smoke, and *then* they were burned. I surmise that from the fact that neither seemed to be in positions of agony that being burned—alive—would engender."

"I hope it's so, that they didn't suffer, beyond the panic of knowing they were going to be burned or die," Elizabeth said solemnly. "Hence those dreadful screams . . ." She shuddered involuntarily, not at the imagined screams but at the memory of her sister's and brother's shrieks from the lockbox of memory. . . .

"Maybe they even hesitated to rush directly out at first," Dee went on. "Perhaps they were fumbling for clothes. The man may have been clutching his, including a large, charred leather vest.

Here," he said, pointing to an article that, unlike much else, was discernible as a tooled Spanish vest as big as a knight's saddle. "As far as I can tell from examining the bodies, Your Majesty, there were no signs of man or boy being struck or cut, no noticeable blows to the head, if that is what you planned to look for."

"Yes, it was in part."

"Since it is proven that smoke, even in an enclosed area, rises," Dee continued, gesturing with his long hands, "we can surmise that either they were on the ground because they dropped there to get better air, or the weight of the collapsing tent took them down. Before the time of the fire, I take it from my own observations when my wife and I rode in, many in the encampment were risen, but who is to say some could not still have been abed when it began? The victims may have been dazed—disoriented—when the smoke began. Although I warrant we'd need to actually, ah, cut into their lungs to see if they are blackened by inhaled smoke, I surmise that suffocation was the actual *causa mortis.*"

"Since the evidence testifies to suffocation," the queen pronounced, "I have no intentions of having anyone cut into those bodies which have already suffered so grievously. And, thanks to Dr. Dee, I shall forgo looking at them myself."

She heard Cecil heave a sigh of relief she herself could feel, yet her tensions only twisted tighter. "But if many were up and about when the fire began," she reasoned, "how could someone sneak unseen to the tent to start the conflagration? I don't care if it was on the edge of the encampment. Ned, I'll ask you to inquire if those nearby saw anything strange. And I shall ask Lord Arundel, since his apartments overlook the scene."

They all stood silent for a moment. It was as if, Elizabeth

thought, fire had struck from the very heavens. "Jenks," she said, turning toward him, "are tent poles always pounded in the ground so strongly that they can't easily be pulled out?"

Still holding his position on the floor as Kendale's corpse, Jenks answered, "I know you haven't pitched too many tents, Your Grace, but they got to be tight in, specially if a wind comes up. The weather turned good a week ago here, I heard, so's the ground would have hardened up from the earlier spring rains."

"Yet I shall ask you to see if other tent stakes are in the ground so hard that they can be pulled out only with difficulty." She still stood by the blackened canvas, staring at the top, then the bottom of the tent. "Dr. Dee," she said, bending to touch a corner of it, "is this the same sort of material used to make sails on ships?"

"It is indeed, Your Majesty. And, ironically, artists' canvases, though those are washed over and over again, bleached and stretched over a frame in the sun, and then treated with several coats of solid paint as a base, though some artists use varnished boards, of course, and . . ."

His voice trailed off, evidently when he saw them all gaping at him. Few knew, the queen thought, as she did, what a compendium of universal knowledge was her Dr. Dee.

"Bleach and varnishes," Elizabeth said. "That reminds me, could Kendale's own artist's concoctions in the tent have started the fire? There was a strange, acrid odor."

"Remnants of paints were within, as well as burned brushes of all sizes and an easel, too," Cecil put in, glancing from Gil's sketch to the clutter of items laid out on the roof. "I suppose something like that could have started it."

"And where are the remains of my portrait Kendale had

begun?" the queen asked, glancing over at the contents of the tent. "I see remnants of an easel, paint jars, and brushes."

"No portraits were within, Your Grace," Jenks said, sitting up as if he'd decided it was time to resurrect himself. "There's charred rolled canvas—see there? But none stretched on any frame or any board."

"Then I must remember to ask the other artists if they know where he might have kept it. And yet," she said, folding her arms, "I think Master Kendale's artist's supplies were not the cause of the fire. Not unless they flared up very high."

"Ah, yes," Dee said, following her gaze as she fixed it again on the ruined tent canvas. "A most unusual burn pattern."

"What do you mean?" Cecil asked as Ned jumped up from playing a corpse. Meg came closer, peering down at the blackened canvas where the queen now pointed.

"You see," Elizabeth said as Dr. Dee nodded his approval of what he must have guessed she would say, "the tent is burned more heavily toward the top than the bottom, hence, from the top toward the bottom."

"But the fire did flare high," Cecil said. "Everyone said they saw that."

"But no arsonist would or could start a fire on the roof of a tent," she argued. "Even if it was laced shut from without, a fire set high would give those inside more time to escape and would be more quickly visible to others, who could put out the flames earlier. It would be highly unusual to start a fire on the roof instead of on the ground, where it would move upward to engulf the entire thing."

"You're thinking someone heaved a torch atop the roof?" Cecil asked. "They would hardly climb a ladder to set a fire where they could be spotted. But, Your Grace, the other artists' tents were near this one. You *have* rather fostered a competition among them, but I can't imagine ..."

"I don't like the sound of that, Cecil!" she exploded before she realized she would sound so angry. Pictures of that other fire so long ago streaked through her brain. "In this realm, contests and competition are healthy, not harmful," she said, her voice controlled again.

"I didn't mean you could be to blame, Your Grace," Cecil said.

Frowning, Elizabeth walked away and leaned on her elbows against a shoulder-high section of the wall around the roof. Standing on her tiptoes, she squinted into the bright sun at the blackened oval below among the scattered white circles of tent roofs. Soon the others came to look down from other notches in the wall, with only Cecil sharing her spot.

"I want to speak with Gil Sharpe first and then with my other two artists and Lord Arundel," Elizabeth told him as he looked over the edge with her. "The rest of you, be ready for further tasks, for I'll not have someone loose who likes to set fires on tents or elsewhere in my court or kingdom. Dr. Dee, we shall see that you are allotted a tent for the next few days, so that we might further use your service in the examination of the fire and the other matter you brought to my attention. We can provide an escort back to Mortlake for your wife if you like."

"I shall be honored to remain to be of assistance, Your Majesty, but I am certain my wife would like to stay."

"Granted."

"Your Grace," Cecil said, "since no storm clouds threaten today—not the skyward kind, anyway—shall we leave these things laid out on the roof for a while longer?"

"Yes," she said, and leaned farther out, trying to fix every detail in her mind. Like the area around the pretty pavilion she and her half siblings had been playing in so long ago, the death site was not far from the fringe of the forest. Though the foliage was not full, she could look a ways into the deer park where she had often led the hunt.

But now she had on her hands another chase, one in which she could see only partway. It was a hunt in which she must corner and capture a villain before he—or she—killed more prey.

A quarter hour later, trying to calm herself, Elizabeth gazed out a window into the privy garden while she waited for Gil to be brought to her. To her surprise, Kat and Floris were just slipping out toward the forest through the garden's postern gate, which the queen knew was kept locked from the inside. Any palace her father had built or renovated had privy entrances. Perhaps Kat needed a breath of fresh air. Elizabeth dared to hope that her old friend had recalled that the key was kept in the crotch of the corner pear tree.

Let Gil wait for her, the queen thought, for she needed to see how Kat was doing. She told her yeomen guards at the door that the boy should wait in the hall until she returned, then, on second thought, took Clifford with her. With the big man keeping a bit back as she had ordered, she hurried down the privy staircase and ran across the garden beneath the first blossoms of the pear and plum trees. The postern gate was closed but unlocked. Glancing in both directions and seeing no one but the two women, the queen stepped outside.

Elizabeth followed them along the strip of grass between the fringe of the hunt park and the palace walls. They strolled toward the wildflower meadow near the south gate, at the opposite side of the palace from the encampment. Before she could catch up, they had crested a knoll and settled themselves in the tall blowing grass, which bobbed with spring flowers. On the hillock stood a few bricks atop some sort of cornerstone, perhaps some rustic remnant of the village or manor of Cuddington.

The sunstruck sight made such a lovely pastoral scene that Elizabeth stopped and stared. Kat looked so content, Floris so perfectly at ease, that she felt closed out, as if she were staring at a painting of them she could not enter. She did not want to risk upsetting Kat, yet she needed to be with her for a moment, to talk to her, and not only to see if she was well. She needed Kat to help her dispel the terrible waking dreams she was having of that childhood fire, because Kat had been there too.

Glancing behind herself once to be certain Clifford was waiting, the queen strode toward the grassy knoll. Obviously startled, Floris saw her first and dropped whatever she was doing in her lap.

"Look, Kat, the queen has come to visit," Elizabeth heard her say, for the wind carried perfectly in her direction.

"I suppose we have to stand and curtsy, then," Kat said, shading her eyes, "but I don't think my old bones will abide it."

"No—do not rise," Elizabeth called to them, hoping her voice sounded brighter than her mood. But whenever she saw Kat hardly heed her but look to Floris, it swamped her spirits. She climbed their hill and plopped down in the grass on Kat's other side. Both women had been lacing flower stems to make necklaces.

"I heard about the . . . the sad event," Floris said.

"Yes, but I am heartened to see you two enjoying the lovely day. How are you feeling, my Kat?"

"Very well. I always did like it here at Hampton Court. Floris has been telling me all about it, you know, where she used to live."

On Kat's other side, the queen saw Floris dramatically shake her head, then point to it, as if Elizabeth needed to be reminded that Kat had lost her faculty of logic.

"Oh, yes," Elizabeth said, and patted Kat's hand. "Hampton Court always was your favorite place."

"Floris's, too," Kat confided, squeezing Elizabeth's hand. And in that fleet, passing moment, she smiled at Elizabeth. The sun lit that dear face, now webbed with wrinkles, and the sky blue gaze, now cloudy. But it was as if she had her Kat back again, and they were younger and would protect each other at any cost.

The queen almost burst into tears. She rose quickly. "Floris, I appreciate your friendship with Lady Ashley. I must inform you that the incident from this morning you mentioned may not have been an accident. So when you leave the walls of the palace, always take that guard there"—she pointed to Clifford waiting patiently at the edge of the hunt park—"as an escort."

"Oh, I didn't know. You mean, I—we must be wary out here? But there's another woman even farther out from the palace, that way," she added, pointing toward the meadow. "See, by the old apple copse. It's your lady artist, I think, painting."

Elizabeth looked over her shoulder. From this gently sloping height, she could see Lavina Teerlinc sitting with her back to them and a blank canvas before her. Elizabeth wanted to get back to Gil, waiting for her inside, but she didn't like Lavina wandering off by herself. Hadn't Cecil told her artists to keep close until they could be summoned for questioning?

Kat was humming an old dance tune while she went back to lacing flower stems. Elizabeth summoned Clifford with a flick of her hand and walked down the far side of the rise toward Lavina.

The shadows of the hunt park seemed to reach for her artist as she sat motionless but for the breeze slightly shifting her skirts and cloak. Strangely, as sturdy as she was, Lavina looked frail and fragile out here. She sat motionless, hands in her lap, staring either at the blank canvas or beyond. She wore a big-brimmed straw garden hat which sat askew but shadowed her shoulders. As the queen came closer, she could see Lavina had no paint or brushes with her, unless they were hidden in her lap or in the tall grass.

Again, Elizabeth turned back to Clifford and motioned for him to keep his distance. On the hill behind him, she could see Floris watching and Kat bent to her task.

"Lavina?" Elizabeth called before she came too close, so as not to startle the woman.

The hatted head turned. She jumped up, hitting the small camp stool with her skirts so that it collapsed against the easel and toppled it. Lavina curtsied hastily, shakily.

"Your Majesty, whatever is it brings you out here?"

To the woman's obvious dismay, Elizabeth retrieved the canvas for her and placed it on the easel Lavina righted.

"I hadn't started even to sketch yet," Lavina said, stating the obvious.

"Because you forgot your charcoals and paints?"

"I—yes. I was so distraught about Will's death that I just

wanted to get away—into fresh air. I planned to do his portrait—in remembrance, though he never married, and I have no idea whom to give it to. Would you like to sit on the stool, Your Majesty?"

"I'll stand. Lavina, where were you when you learned Master Kendale's tent was afire?"

"In my tent, shared with several of your women's lady's maids. You can ask them, of course."

"Why would I not believe you?"

"I did step out earlier to . . . to relieve myself at the forest's edge. There's a sort of women's place there, well hidden from the camp. When so many of us are living together without jakes and clothes stools . . ."

"I understand."

"They say—I saw it too—that Will's tent was laced shut from the outside. It's dreadful. I—I don't know if I can get his face out of my mind to paint yours again, Your Majesty."

"Perhaps going on with normal things after the memorial service for him and the boy will be the best help for us all. Lavina, it may indeed have not been an accident, and everything is being looked into."

"By Dr. Dee and Cecil, I take it? We all saw them hanging about."

"More or less, yes. Lavina, were all the artists getting on? I realize you were discomfited by my bringing Gilbert Sharpe into the competition, but was there rivalry among the group of you beyond that?"

The artist flinched. "You're not implying—that Henry Heatherley or I—"

"I'm implying nothing, but asking a flat question."

"No, then. We were all getting on, colleagues in the same endeavor, though each wanted his or her portrait chosen, of course."

"Then can you tell me where Master Kendale was storing the portrait of me he had begun, as it seems not to have been in his tent? Had the three of you placed them somewhere for safety?"

"What they've done with theirs I know not. I have mine in my care and am extremely pleased with the way it is begun. The whey-colored face you alluded to can be altered, Your Majesty," she said, her voice rising, and her usually stiff gestures becoming more expansive. "A bit of rose hue and your complexion will appear to be country cream gilded by the sun."

Elizabeth regretted questioning Lavina, for she was obviously distraught over Kendale's death; yet, was that not the best time to press for the truth? But that subtle insult of her complexion *appearing* to be country cream gilded by the sun—that would be curdled cream indeed. Had that criticism the queen made to Lavina in London made her so resentful she'd turned reckless and tried to eliminate a competitor?

"Have you summoned Master Heatherley to question him, too?" Lavina asked, pointing. Not only Floris, Kat, and Clifford were in view but Henry Heatherley, striding toward them from the south gate of the palace. In his hands, he too had a canvas, a draped one, as if he and Lavina had made some pact to meet out here to paint.

"Your Majesty," he said, bowing but ten feet from them, "I had no notion you would be out here too. I came to ask Lavina about this before I showed it to you."

"And what is that?" Elizabeth asked, though suddenly she thought she knew.

"The portrait of you Will Kendale had begun," Heatherley

said. "One of the lady's maids in Lavina's tent just brought it to me and said it was hidden there among her own can—"

"No! That's not true!" Lavina cried, striding toward him with her arms straight down at her sides and her fists tightly balled. "I never put it there. Let me see it!"

"Yes, let me see it too," Elizabeth said. Lavina halted and stepped aside, as if shocked she'd turned her back on the queen.

"But there is another surprise to come," Heatherley warned, "one I swear I had naught to do with. Brace yourself, Your Majesty."

He removed the cover from the canvas almost reluctantly. It was indeed Kendale's sketched portrait he had planned to embellish later. But now, only the edges of the portrait were intact, for the queen's face and form had been slashed to pieces.

Chapter the Fourth

THE QUEEN'S STOMACH KNOTTED AT THE SIGHT OF THE ruined portrait, and not only because it was an attack on her. Such a furious slashing was exactly what she had been tempted to do to a painting of her cousin Mary, Queen of Scots, when she discovered that Robin kept a likeness of the queen behind a curtain in his privy chambers, as if he could hide it.

"Lavina," she cracked out, "what do you know of this?"

"Not a thing, truly, Your Majesty. I can't help that it was put with my canvases—if indeed it was."

"Do you imply I'm lying?" Heatherley demanded, glaring back at Lavina. "That I would do such a low thing as secreting this and then accusing you? Your Majesty, you may ask your lady's maid who found it and brought it to me."

"Lady's maids or maid?" Lavina demanded. "Your story seems to change. One maid or two? All three? How interesting that they would run to you. Give us their names so th—"

"Your Majesty," Heatherley interrupted her, "God as my witness, I have naught to do wi—"

"All right, none of you know anything!" Elizabeth cried, holding up both arms stiffly as if to keep bullies from cuffing each other. She saw her guard had come closer as the voices rose. "Clifford," she called to him, "take this ruined portrait into custody and escort my two artists back to the encampment straightaway, for I would see the very place this was discovered."

Elizabeth was relieved to see that Floris and Kat were going back inside the palace as she and the others headed toward the cluster of tents. Her poor Gil would have to wait for his interview a little longer.

"Which tent?" she inquired of Lavina as they approached them. The queen noted thankfully that few courtiers were still in the area, for they must be about their various duties and pursuits. Most were probably within the palace, thinking she was there.

"This one next to where Master Kendale's was—and Master Heatherley's yet is," Lavina said as Heatherley shot her another hot glare.

The three artists' tents, which the queen had heard all but Kendale had shared with servants other than their own, had stood in a nearly perfect triangle. Since the three lady's maids who also resided within Lavina's tent were gone, it was deserted. The maids would be easy to question, the queen thought, for she had daily access to them. She stepped inside; her eyes skimmed the small, dim interior of the tent.

"My sleeping pallet is there," Lavina told her, entering and pointing a trembling finger, her voice deadly calm now. "And the few canvases I brought are there, against the inside of the tent."

Elizabeth went closer. Three stretched canvases leaned on their sides, shrouded in separate hemp sacks. She bent to pull each forward in turn and unwrapped a corner of each to peer at the canvas. The partial portrait of herself was the second one in and, thank the Lord, undisturbed.

"Was this," she asked Master Heatherley, "where the maids—or maid—say they found the slashed portrait?"

"Yes, Your Majesty. They admitted they wanted a peek at the one Mistress Teerlinc had begun of you—and found the ruined one."

"'S teeth, Henry," Lavina cracked out, "if I'd harmed Vill, I'd hardly have secreted his painting vit mine!"

The queen let them rail at each other this time. If they were guilty, they might let something slip. Indeed, Lavina's accent was doing just that. "And vat a coincidence the maids ran right to you!" the woman repeated, pointing straight-armed at Heatherley.

"Because I happened to be here, not out in the middle of some field as if you were skulking away or feeling guilty!"

"Guilty! I vas mourning the poor man in my own vay, though you seem not to give a fig vat happened to him!"

As Elizabeth put Lavina's canvases back against the edge of the tent, she noted how loose it was. Hadn't Jenks said the tent stakes were pounded in tight?

She moved the canvases out again and pressed the toe of her shoe against the side of the tent. It poked out so far that she almost went off balance, though she was certain her broad skirts hid from others here how loose the tent wall was.

She placed the canvases on Lavina's pallet and asked them all to wait there a moment. Alone, though Clifford stood in the entry to the tent, keeping a nervous eye on them and her, she circled the exterior to its loose section. The stake which should have secured it was pulled completely out of the ground, as was the one next to it.

Aha! Elizabeth thought, feeling she was getting somewhere—but where, she did not know. This meant, at least, that Lavina could have crawled out of the tent without being seen by the sleeping maids. Or it could be just the opposite: someone had reached in, pulled out the portrait, slashed and then replaced it. But it was far too early for accusations: the background sketch of this double murder was barely filled in, and many details were yet needed.

Again, the stench of smoke crept into her nostrils and lumped in the pit of her belly, for it seemed to have permeated the nearby tents. Despite the fact that she must now suspect her two remaining artists—not counting Gil, of course, who had been in a more distant tent with Jenks and Ned—with good conscience she could not ask those living closest to the site to remain here. After all, she had invited these people to accompany her. She owed them kindness and hospitality, at least until she could prove someone's guilt.

"I'm going to order these closest tents to be pitched on the other side of the encampment," she announced to Lavina and Heatherley as she returned to the entry of the tent. "It won't do anyone any good to try to sleep near this site. I suggest you go inside the palace to get something to eat, then attend the memorial service. Afterward, you will find your tents on the far side of the encampment with everything moved for you."

Both of them looked immensely relieved, as if they had just been exonerated from any wrongdoing. They had no notion that she, Cecil, and Dr. Dee were going to give their tents a thorough tossing before they saw them again.

———

As if he weren't on edge enough, Gil fumed, the queen kept him waiting outside her apartments a good hour after she sent for him. He paced the grand, ornate staircase up and down. Each time on the ground floor, Gil studied the frescoes of cavorting gods and goddesses that Master Kendale had boasted he'd painted in the six months he'd lived here while the palace was being built. Gil could almost hear the man's voice now, for his bragging last night had been as bloated as his flesh. But now that the blowhard was dead, Gil had regrets.

"Great King Henry visited many times to see the progress we builders and artists were making, and he complimented me especially," Kendale had boasted just the night before, after he'd invited Gil into his tent and, stupidly, Gil had gone. The man had been drinking overmuch; he reeked of wine and slurred his words. "Complimented me especially" had come out more like "come peaceably." He'd looked unsteady on his feet too, though the cause of that might have been balancing his excessive girth on those spindly ankles.

Gil had replied, "Her Majesty fondly recalls how proud her royal sire was of Nonsuch." As he pictured Master Kendale's annoyed expression again, suddenly the entire encounter came rolling back in a vividly colored scene in his mind.

"Oh, flaunting that you're more'r less her foundling again, eh?" Kendale had goaded. Gil could tell that Niles, the young artist's assistant, was vexed with his master for baiting another young man, or at least that's the way Gil read things.

"I'm just recalling something she said yesterday," Gil replied, and sidled toward the open tent flap.

"As if she'd share personal mem'ries of her royal family with a vagabond like you," Kendale said with a hiccup. "A pox on you wi' your inflated sense of worth, you rough-edged whelp. So what if you had three years'n Urbino or wherever—"

"And a four-month visit to Venice," Gil said, his bile rising at Kendale's insulting tone and glare as well as the pointed words. This man annoyed but didn't frighten him. What scared him to death was the possibility that he'd been followed here from Urbino. Master Scarletti had said the guild of artists would kill to keep its secret. Could it have hired the man who might have been following him in Dover and again in London?

"Venice, eh? 'S 'at so?" Kendale needled, but Gil could tell he was impressed despite himself.

"Aye, Venice, where I met the artist I admire most in all the world, Tiziano Vecellio, called Titian."

"Who? Well," Kendale said, moving his bulk to deliberately block Gil in the tent, "Her Majesty'll be sad to hear you ven'rate a foreigner over a pure English painter, like at least two of us she selected to do her official portrait."

"One thing I've learned on the Continent, Master Kendale," Gil countered, "is that the talent of true artists knows no boundaries. Henry Heatherley and you are pure English, as you say, so perhaps your work will remain provincial. However, Titian sells paintings to King Philip in Spain, as well as—"

"You young whelp, half schooled, thinkin' you've all the answers! You're outta your el'ment!"

"My element, Master Kendale, is to serve Her Majesty with my hands and head and heart."

"Heard you were born deaf and dumb, but you've got a quick

lip now, however dumb you still act to be so flippant with your betters!"

"I was not born either deaf or dumb, but was scared into silence as a lad by an explosion. Aye, the queen good as plucked me off the streets to help make me what I am today. And whatever I am, that which you are so disdainful of, best you'd complain to her then!"

"If you open that quick mouth to tell'r one thing about what I said—"

"Good night then, Niles. And Master Kendale, *buone notte ed arrivederci, lei il maiale grasso!*"

He prayed Kendale had no idea he'd just been bidden good night as a "fat pig." Gil turned sideways and managed to get past the man. He hoped Kendale wouldn't take his temper out on his boy.

"Boy! Gil Sharpe!" a tall queen's yeoman guard called over the banister to where Gil glowered and even gestured at Kendale's frescoes. "Her Majesty will see you now."

Taking two steps at a time, Gil hurried upstairs and into the first chamber past the guards. The queen sat at a table, eating figs and drinking wine. After Gil bowed, she pointed to the chair across the table and pushed the dish of figs toward him. Compared to her high mood yesterday, her spirits seemed low. She looked both weary and wary, but surely not of him.

"I have so much to ask and you so much to tell, yes, my Gilberto Sharpino?" she said with her mouth half full.

"Oh, yes, Your Grace, of artists, and Italy, and anything else you would know."

"In due time. My lord Cecil and I want to discuss your impressions of politics and papists as well as paintings. But for now, tell me about your contretemps with Master Kendale last night."

Gil sat up straighter, his heart pounding, though he knew by now not to be surprised that the queen seemed to know everything. "Yes, Your Grace."

"Then I want you to go up on the roof with Jenks to view the way we've laid out the things from the burned tent and see if you can add or change anything. And sketch it for us again, lest we need to store the things away."

As he explained to her his encounter with Master Kendale, he tried not to sugarcoat what had passed between them on the last night of the man's life. But he intentionally muted his own anger.

"So he was drunk," she said. "Perhaps his besotted state is why—besides his weight and girth—he might have been slow to move when his tent began to smoke and flame. Beyond the fact, of course, that someone had laced the fat man in his tent as tightly as a fat woman is laced into a corset."

"What is it, Your Grace?" he asked as she jumped up and began to pace. "Murder for certain, you mean?"

"We've already established that. But I hadn't thought of something before, that those ties were laced the way a woman would close a corset with a single, flat bow at the bottom."

"A woman did it?"

"I don't know! Never mind for now. Gil, I must ask you something else. Although Master Kendale insulted you last night, you did nothing to retaliate, did you? I know you will ever answer me truthfully."

Her dark eyes burned into his. He silently thanked God she had not asked another question, for it was nearly impossible to lie to her. "I tried to insult him back—circumspectly, Your Grace— and did manage to get him doubly vexed. And one more thing."

"Which is?" she asked, still looking worried. He realized again how blessed he was that, for some reason he would never grasp, Elizabeth of England cared deeply for his well-being. It was his amazing, grand good fortune of all time, even more precious to him than his gift to draw and paint people.

"I do admit at least, Your Grace, I reviled him all the way back to my tent with every foul, cesspool Italian curse word I ever knew."

She smiled stiffly. "Then, if that was your only retribution, I may need your services, not only to paint a portrait or sketch a tent, but to help Cecil and me with the investigation into Kendale's and the boy's deaths. But best you go now. Find Jenks before you go up on the roof, for I must attend the memorial service I have ordered in the chapel. As he bowed and headed for the door, she called after him, "Gil, one thing more."

He turned back to face her. His heart began to pound again.

"Why did you return from Italy two years earlier than expected? I suggested five years of study, and you agreed to that."

He almost blurted out the truth—all of it, painful and terrible. But instead what came out was, "Because I yearned for England and to serve you."

The corners of her mouth tilted into a hint of a smile. "And I am glad you are back." She stared at him strangely, with misty eyes. "In a few days," she said, "I shall pose for you and the two others, and then we shall see what you have learned."

He bowed again, turned, and went out, but his hair prickled along the nape of his neck as if he'd been out in a field when lightning struck. She had stared at him so eerily, as if she'd seen a ghost. In his mind's eye, he could almost see one himself, which haunted him. It was Kendale, screaming and burning as if he were trapped in hell itself, and Gil regretted that.

After the memorial in the chapel, in which the queen had the minister give a little speech for calm among her courtiers, she was escorted out by both the Earl of Arundel and the Earl of Leicester. During the short service she'd been agonizing about who the arsonist-murderer could be. But it was only when Arundel began to comment about the large size of Kendale's coffin that she recalled something else: Arundel had once called Master Kendale a "flap-mouthed magpie full of bombast" and urged her not to include him among her official painters at court. And so their host himself, who surely knew each stride of the Nonsuch park and grounds, must have held some sort of grudge against Kendale.

"My lord Arundel," she said as they walked across the half-shadowed courtyard toward her apartments, "though none of us like to speak ill of the dead, pray tell why you advised against my employing Master Kendale for my official portrait."

"The man turned out to be trouble, did he not? Rumors are flying about his relationship to the dead boy, he argued with your other artists, was full of braggadocio, I hear, and then did something to get himself killed."

Frowning at that cruel assessment, she merely inclined her head, biting back the urge to rebuke him. Had he just revealed more about himself than about Kendale?

"The reason I advised against Kendale, Your Grace," Arundel

went on, "was that, quite simply, the man was a baseborn braggart, just trading on his talent."

Elizabeth bit her lower lip and let him talk, however much she wanted to tell him that she fully intended to encourage such men who traded on their talent to serve queen and kingdom, no matter what their social rank. But if what Arundel was saying of Kendale's birth was true, it flew in the face of Kendale's rejection of Gil for being baseborn and trading on his talent. Evidently, Kendale not only had hidden his own humble beginnings but dared to lord it over those who reminded him of his past.

"You see," Arundel continued with a sharp sniff, "Kendale did a portrait of me about ten years ago that was passable but not inspired. He made me look dour, actually, stuffy and old-fashioned."

"Imagine that," Robin said, his face stoic despite its rising color.

Elizabeth bit her lip harder. Robin was getting red in the face, and she feared he'd burst out with one of his guffaws. Arundel not only did not have a sense of humor, but usually failed to recognize it in others.

"The wretch charged me a pretty penny for it too," Arundel plunged on, "and told everyone I adored his work, which I'd never said. That was as good—as bad, I mean—as lying, if you ask me. Not to mention the man paid too much heed to my page boy, of all people, while he was around, and the lad was too young to know better. This was before Kendale turned as corpulent as your fath—" He stopped talking midword.

"As corpulent as my father," she finished for him. "I do see the picture you paint, my lord."

Robin stifled a snicker, which, fortunately, Arundel did not hear. "Of course, you have every right *not* to heed what I advise," Arundel said, tugging his ruffled satin cuffs down over his beringed hands. "God knows, your royal sire did not. When he saw the site for Nonsuch—I was with him, you know, on a boar hunt—I suggested he build the palace at the far end of the meadow and use the little village of Cuddington as a place where courtiers and servants could live. But no, he would have it exactly here on the rise of ground and said leaving Cuddington would ruin the view, so out the village folk and the family of the manor went and down came the buildings."

But Elizabeth was only half listening now. She could see through the ornate gate into the outer courtyard, where three riders were dismounting from lathered horses, and she was suddenly certain who had arrived.

"Well, my lords," she said, looking back over her shoulder to catch Cecil's eye, "it seems Queen Mary's Lord Maitland has arrived from Scotland—via London, if he went there first. I'll see him forthwith. Despite who his royal mistress is, I have found him a forthright man with only his country's best interest at heart, and who can ask more of a man than that? Cecil, with me, if you will."

Just as the chimes rang four of the afternoon, the queen and her secretary of state walked together to greet Maitland under the tall clock-tower gate. He had been the Scottish secretary of state for years, appointed before Mary was queen. Though Mary had not officially demoted him, she'd used him lately more as an envoy or liaison to the English court, partly because he was a staunch Protestant and frowned on her increasingly reckless behavior. But Mary could not argue with the man's wily ways or the fact that he and Cecil had lately managed to keep peace between the two countries.

"My lord Maitland," Elizabeth called in greeting, and the man swept off his hat and shaded his eyes before a low bow. "You are welcome here at Nonsuch."

"I take it the court's movement was a sudden decision, Your Most Gracious Majesty," he replied, "for when I crossed the border, I heard you were still in London."

Sir William Maitland of Lethington was tall and sturdily built, a jouster in appearance but, like Cecil, a lawyer at heart. Bearded, approaching age forty, he seemed bluffly honest and had the brains *not* to favor Lord Darnley as his mistress did, so Elizabeth liked the man despite her aversion to his Catholic queen.

"Who can resist this country air after such a winter, my lord," she said. "Come inside, and I'll see you and your men are well cared for. And what is the message from my cousin, dear Queen Mary?" she added as they walked toward the royal apartments.

Maitland's clear blue gaze met hers, then Cecil's. "I regret to inform both of you," Maitland said, his voice so low and rough that it sounded as if he were grinding out his words, "she is yet besotted with Lord Darnley and, I fear, will have him."

Elizabeth tried to convey both surprise and concern. "I feared so too, and in defiance of my counsel."

"And mine. God's truth, Your Majesty, this is something upon which you and I agree. I know young Darnley's your second cousin, but he's a preening milksop and he galls me sore. She's beyond listening to either me or the Earl of Murray on it."

The shadows of the arched entryway leaped over them as they entered the building, and for a moment, the three of them blinked like owls to see better. A lad appeared with three goblets of wine on a silver tray, and Maitland took his readily.

"I wish we could drink to better news," the queen told the men solemnly, though she could hardly contain her excitement. Mary had not only bit on the bait, but was going to be quite caught in the net. Darnley would surely drag her down. Maitland might call the pompous lad a milksop, but indeed he was a sodomist, who must be playing Mary for all she was worth. The man's passion must surely be only for her power, not for her person, so there might not even be an heir from their marriage that Cecil so feared.

They emptied their goblets silently. Let the pretty Queen of Scotland gaze in mirrors and jest about taking England from its rightful queen, Elizabeth thought grimly. Just let her try.

While Maitland and his men refreshed themselves and rested, and two tents were pitched for them, Elizabeth, pretending she was merely going for a stroll, went out with Cecil and Dr. Dee to look through Lavina Teerlinc's and Henry Heatherley's tents. The servants who lived here were being kept busy in the palace, so although others walked or rode the grounds, no one was nearby now.

"Even if we disturb the order of their things," Elizabeth assured her companions, "they'll think it just happened when their domiciles were moved."

Dee and Cecil took Heatherley's tent while Elizabeth looked through Lavina's more carefully than she had before. She peered into and sniffed at pots of paints, bottles of what smelled like linseed oil, and something more acrid in which a single, short brush sat, so perhaps it was some sort of cleansing liquid. Lavina had bouquets of brushes, from squat and short to lean and long, all made with various animal hairs, soft sable to stiff boar. There were, of course, lanterns in the tent, three of them with fat, half-burned candles. Could a candle have begun the blaze by being thrown up on the roof?

"Dr. Dee," she said, going to stand in the opening of Heatherley's tent as the two men searched his things, "could a candle heaved on one of the slanted tent roofs catch and start a fire?"

"Canvas doesn't catch easily, Your Grace," John Dee told her, straightening from his own perusal of paint supplies. "Granted, tallow could have melted and the wick burned in the blaze, so we'd find no evidence. But I'd say a candle is as likely to gut itself out as catch an entire tent afire. Now a torch might be a different thing."

The queen suddenly broke out into a sweat. It had been flames larger than a candle which had caught afire that gay, brightly hued pavilion when she was thirteen. That had not been sturdy canvas, but mere material in pretty colors with fluttering flags and pennants. . . .

To get away from the warmth of the late-afternoon sun, she went to stand in the shade on the eastern side of Lavina's tent. As she gazed up at it from this angle, her eyes widened. What appeared to be a scorch mark, walnut brown, perfectly round, was on the sloped roof just below where the tent pole emerged.

Elizabeth circled the tent. She saw only that one strange spot. As she circled Heatherley's, peering up at his roof but seeing nothing amiss, Cecil and Dee came out to inquire what she was doing.

"Look!" she told them, motioning them to her earlier vantage point. "That mark up there. What is it? Could a candle or flame have been thrown on this tent roof, too, but failed to ignite? Strange that it seems so perfectly round."

"But for your keen eye, it would have been a perfect crime, Your Majesty," Dee said, so quietly that it was if he spoke to himself. "With the bright morning sun and the angles of refraction, I should have thought of it myself."

"Thought of what?" Cecil said. "You don't mean something like a—a spot of sunlight started that fire?"

"Have you ever heard the story of how Archimedes burned the Roman ships that were going to attack Syracuse?" Dee asked, folding his hands across his chest and tapping an index finger over his mouth. "Your Majesty, if you will come to visit me at Mortlake, I can demonstrate for you how that mark—and perhaps the deadly conflagration of the nearby tent—could have happened."

"Wait," she commanded, pressing her hands to her temples. "As I recall, Archimedes used a huge concave mirror to catch the sun's rays and burn the canvas sails and ignite the ships. But here?"

"Even a small mirror would do," Dee said, nodding as he bent his knees slightly and lifted his hands to peer through them at the circular stain. "A small mirror, that is, in the hands of a very daring and determined killer."

Chapter the Fifth

"MY DEAREST! KATH-ER-INE!" JOHN DEE SANG OUT AS HE hurried into their hastily pitched tent on the other side of the encampment from the scene of the fire. He saw she'd been scrubbing at the dirt spot on her skirt, for her ministrations had turned a circle of the dark green damask black. Besides her wash bucket, around her lay scattered items from their four saddle packs, so she must have been unpacking.

"What is it?" she cried, looking up. "I'm hungry. We are to be allotted some fine fare while we're here, aren't we, I mean, considering your status? Why, you seem at her beck and call every bit as much as her secretary Cecil."

"Good news!" he told her, chortling. "Your wish has come true, my dearest."

"To meet her? Now—with my best gown all blotched up?"

"Ah, better than that. The queen and a small retinue are coming to visit us at Mortlake on the morrow."

"Tomorrow?" she cried, and leaped up from the single stool in the tent. "But—but—I'm here, and Sarah won't know to clean and to prepare food and to—I can't leave here without meeting her, why, coming all this way and not so much as laying eyes on her. Surely we'll go ahead of her to Mortlake, so she won't be walking in with us when I haven't been there, didn't know. . . ."

Dee sighed and sank into the stool she had just vacated. He was aching from the ride to Nonsuch, then from running hither and yon to examine corpses, tents, and scorch marks. But he was honored to be in the thick of things with Elizabeth Tudor and William Cecil, the two brightest and most powerful people in the kingdom. Though, God as his judge, he couldn't see why Katherine had to fuss at him when she was being given the desire of her heart. All he'd heard was queen, queen, queen, and now . . .

"Let me explain it to you clearly, my dear," he said, tugging Katherine down on his knees. "It's actually an important trip for Her Majesty as well as for us. She wishes to see some things in my laboratory which tie into the investigation here of that fatal fire."

"In other words, she is coming to work with you," she said, sitting stiffly, almost warily, in his lap. "Whatever is she thinking caused that fire?"

"Never mind all that, my love. We must send for our horses and set out so we can be home before sunset tonight. You see, that will give you all evening and part of the morrow to prepare things for the royal arrival."

"But just one night? Well, I shall do what I must, of course."

"There, you see, and you can talk mirrors with Her Majesty, as you favor them, and she is very interested in them now, especially my concave looking glass. Ah, I think we shall set up the demonstration in our garden in full sun. Now what?" he asked, seeing her stricken expression. "Don't be vexed, for everything will go well."

"Mirrors?" Katherine demanded, seizing his sleeve as he headed out to send for their mounts. "What about mirrors? I mean, you've many mirrors, so why that special one?"

"Ah, it is your favorite, is it not? She may wish to take it with her for a while," he said ruefully, for it was his favorite too. The mirror was fearfully expensive. He'd bought it in Venice, where glassmaking guilds on the islands of Murano guarded the secrets of their craft, he'd heard, on pain of death. The Italians were that way, apparently effusive but actually as defensive as their city-states.

As for his precious mirror, he'd spent hours studying its angles, its ground surface, its silver backing, its pinpoint focusing power, and especially its distortions. He cherished it because it had taken him a long time to discern its mysteries. But not, he feared, as long as it was going to take him to understand his wife.

"What's keeping that boy?" Elizabeth muttered as she and Cecil awaited Gil in her audience chamber.

"Perhaps Clifford couldn't find him," Cecil said, stacking the bills and grants she had just signed.

"Which reminds me, how did you find Lord Maitland in your meeting this morning?" She rose and went to stand in the splash of sun through the window, resting one arm on the deep ledge and soaking in the warmth. "You know, my lord, he's the only Scot I trust in this subtle struggle with Queen Mary. I truly believes he fears her wildfire actions as much as we do."

"Agreed. He says Darnley's already throwing his weight around, acting arrogant and insulting her longtime counselors right and left. With that sort of help from her betrothed, the queen may soon alienate all who have been loyal to her, the Protestant lords of Congregation like Maitland and Murray anyway."

"She's been content to let them advise and nearly rule, but will Darnley allow that, especially as her husband?" She hit her fist on the windowsill. "This covert policy of ours to plant him in her life has been a gamble, my lord. Yet I still believe their marriage will weaken both of them, just the opposite of what they are expecting. Dr. Dee's report on her mania for mirrors shows she is rash enough to make public that she covets my throne. 'S blood, we don't need *my* northern Catholic subjects joining *hers* in a rebellion to topple me."

"Your Grace?" a voice called from behind them.

She started when she saw the boy simply standing in the door, for she hadn't heard it open. "Oh, Gil! Enter, then. I did say they should send you straight in. Ignore what we were saying if you overheard, or I shall have to have you put under lock and key."

When the lad's eyes widened, she smiled to assure him she was jesting. "My lord Cecil is going to take a few notes," she said as Gil dipped a bow to her. "We are most anxious to hear everything Italian you have to share." She sat at the table again. "Will you sit or stand, Gilberto Sharpino?"

"May I walk a bit, the way you do when you're thinking, Your Grace? It will help me remember. I dared write nothing down."

"Of course. My lord Cecil, do you have a particular thing you would ask Gil first?"

"How tight is the court of Urbino to Rome and to Spain?" he asked as he poised pen over a fresh sheet of paper.

"Very close ties, my lord, to Rome especially. And correspondence is exchanged—ambassadors are too—with King Philip of Spain. He buys artwork and, I don't doubt, information too from Italy. They think our queen's father and she herself are heretics of the worst order, of course."

"Of course," the queen clipped out, "and I've no doubt I'll be excommunicated by the so-called His Holiness someday. But my people will rally behind me—that is, the ones who don't take that as their battle cry to rebel or try to kill me."

Cecil and Gil both gaped at her. "'S blood," she cried, "I am not some innocent ninny lost in the woods!"

"Hardly that, Your Grace," Cecil said. "To carry on your conceit, I just want to be certain we always see the forest for the trees, that is all."

"Meaning not to let our enemies like Mary of Scots, King Philip of Spain, and the pope himself cause us to react instinctively instead of calmly, without viewing the broader picture? I can't help it, Cecil. After all, politics and history hang greatly on the personalities of the participants."

"I cannot argue with that, Your Grace, for you are England."

"But I meant not to digress. Gil, tell us about the art school there, about people—you see, there we are again—people making policy. Who is the most interesting person you met?"

She and Cecil listened raptly while Gil painted word pictures for them of the Italian painter Titian's genius, especially of Gil's favorite masterpiece, the *Venus of Urbino*.

"Naked?" the queen said when he described it. "He painted his Venus quite naked, but she looks to be a real woman, not the goddess?"

"Oh, she's real, all right," Gil vowed. "And I've met a woman,

Dorothea, who looks a great deal like Titian's model. Dorothea's a model too. I'll sketch her for you sometime, Dorothea that is, as I've drawn her before—with clothes on."

"This Dorothea is Titian's model?" Cecil asked, frowning as he looked up from taking notes.

"No, my lord, she poses for my maestro, Giorgio Scarletti."

"But were we not speaking of Titian? Forget this Dorothea unless she is of import here."

The queen noted that Gil looked crestfallen. Because of Cecil's scolding tone or because this woman evoked sadness in the boy? His face had lit like a Yuletide candle but a moment ago. But she'd broach that subject later.

"Anything else of import about Titian?" Cecil asked.

"He's painted for King Philip of Spain," Gil said, his voice quiet now. "Religious paintings, mostly of saints."

"And who knows what else Titian sends him."

"I doubt that, my lord," Gil said, seeming to perk up again. "He's obsessed with his art. He doesn't even sell his own works, because a patron manages it all for him, keeping him in the eye of the nobles who would commission him. And so his fine reputation is spread far and wide on the Continent."

"Who is this patron promoter?" the queen asked.

"One Pietro Aretino, a big bully of a man, but he keeps Titian's name and reputation and work disseminated everywhere."

"Hm," Cecil mused, "a genius of another sort, to make and sway public opinion."

"As I mean to do through my portraits and appearances over the years. Tell us more of Italy, Gil."

He described Terra del Duca, the town of Urbino with its massive fort and ancient palace on the tops of two hills. "In truth," Gil confided, glancing out the sunstruck window as he passed it in his pacing, "the landscape of Urbino reminds me of this area with its gentle hills and mix of meadows and forests. Both places have scattered remnants of stones or bricks, a few foundations hidden in the grass from buildings which came before, places where other people lived and died."

"You've become a poet as well as a painter, Gil," the queen pronounced, and then they fell silent for a moment. She watched Gil's eyes glaze over as if he saw Italy even now, built upon the ruins of its past. She'd never given much thought to the demise of little Cuddington on this site, but she'd seen the few surviving stones. In a way, it was sad that her father had built his fantastical Nonsuch on someone else's beloved manor and town.

"And, Your Grace," Gil's eager voice interrupted her thoughts, "women are important in the Italian city-states, for the men are oft gone to war, sometimes as mercenaries, sometimes for their own or the pope's cause. Dukes' wives rule when they're away and even make laws, receive ambassadors, and oversee the education of their daughters as well as their sons."

"We educate women with their brothers here," Cecil proclaimed a bit too loudly, as if he'd had enough of Gil's extolling another country. He tossed his pen on the paper, flecking ink spots across the page.

"Those Italian women are not comparable to me," the queen said. "I don't rule in the place of a duke or king—a man—and never shall. Though I do recall when my father went to war in France late in his life, he named my stepmother Katherine Parr as regent in his stead. And she took all of us— his three children—to await his triumphant return home at Oakham Manor in Rutland."

"Times," Cecil said, "were different then."

"I meant not to reminisce," Elizabeth whispered, turning away from both of them as she, like Gil, gazed outside into the blaze of sunlight. Curse it, she fumed, but the tent fire here kept resurrecting her terrible memories of that fire at Oakham. It was there, the very day she so proudly presented her stepmother with her gift, that she got in trouble, not only for her choice of a gift but for the nearly fatal fire itself.

Cecil cleared his throat and shifted in his chair. "Gil," he said in the stretch of silence, "pray tell who else you saw in Italy of import to us."

"Well, Dr. Dee, of course, when he passed through. He told me some of the latest news of home and made me yearn to be back all the more."

"Cecil, did you know John Dee passed through Urbino? Why did he not tell us?"

"Hm, perhaps he did and I forgot to say."

"Too many things churning in that brain of yours," she agreed.

"Dr. Dee didn't stay long, then went to Venice," Gil put in, "though not when I was there observing techniques in Titian's studio to compare them with those of my own maestro Scarletti's."

"What techniques have you learned, Gil?" she asked, though her mind was still on Dee. He should have reported, written at least, about how the boy was doing in Italy. "Gil, what techniques?" she demanded when Gil, after being so talkative, said nothing.

"Just brushstrokes, that's all, the vibrant use of color, perspective and the depth of shadowing—things like that."

But the boy had stumbled through that answer; she could sense he wanted to say more. He looked as if he'd been caught at something, just the way her brother used to, like that time he brought a pregnant dog into his bed and could hardly hide the mess—or six new puppies in the morning.

"After my lord Cecil and I return from Mortlake late this afternoon," Elizabeth told Gil, "perhaps we shall use the warm glow of the sinking sun for our first portrait session here—outside. And then we shall see what techniques you learned in Italy, Master Gilberto Sharpino. You just be certain, my young man, you paint your queen fully clothed."

The lovely early-afternoon ride toward the tiny Thames-side enclave of Mortlake calmed the queen. The river glittered in the sun as they rode the rutted path which followed its south bank-side contours. She usually took her royal barge up and down this, the greatest waterway of her realm, but today it felt good to ride. It reminded her that she had hoped to go hunting at Nonsuch—though for deer, not for a double murderer.

Her entourage consisted of Robin, who had been tutored years ago by John Dee and who had originally introduced Elizabeth to the learned man; Cecil, who hardly had the time or the inclination for a ride, but wanted to see Dee's latest experiments; one of her ladies, Rosie Radcliffe; and four guards, including Jenks and Clifford. She had been to visit Dr. Dee's home and laboratories only once five years ago, for her 007 usually came to court or was abroad in her secret service. When he was home in Mortlake, Dee still lived with his elderly mother, who doted on him and his genius, but now he had to contend with a young wife the queen had only briefly glimpsed from afar.

As the royal retinue approached Mortlake, it was apparent that someone had spread the word she was coming. Men with children on their shoulders lined the river path; women waved tablecloths from front yards or upstairs windows. Two lads had climbed one of the cottages and sat waving from its thatched roof. On the fine old Riverside Inn, which the queen had often noted from her barge, bunting made from skirts and cloaks was draped from sills, while makeshift flags flapped in the breeze.

"I can't believe Dr. Dee told people," Elizabeth said to Robin as she smiled, nodded, and waved amid the cheers. "He's usually so secretive."

"I'd wager an entire week's primero winnings," Robin said, "it wasn't him but his new little bride."

Dee, looking as surprised at the noise and fuss as the queen felt, came out with his stooped mother, walking with a cane, and Katherine to greet them. The pretty blonde wore a forest green damask gown and curtsied so low and grandly that she almost sat down on the grass. After pleasantries, introductions, and a few more waves to the lingering crowd of several score, the queen's party went inside.

"I regret the swarm outside, Your Majesty," Dee whispered to her. "It seems Katherine only told one person, and then—"

"I understand. It is ever my joy to greet my people, but it will make your mirror demonstration difficult, will it not?"

"Though we have an enclosed garden, I set it up in the larger courtyard away from prying eyes," he told her as Katherine came in with plates of food and a serving girl with a ewer of wash water. Dame Dee, whose age must have been near Kat's, retired to a chair by the hearth, so Mistress Dee was obviously overseeing things here. She looked quite nervous, Elizabeth thought, and her heart went out to her. To calm her, the queen remarked, "You are a fortunate woman, Katherine, to have wed a man with so many mirrors, are you not?"

To everyone's dismay, the young woman started and spilled the meat pastries at the queen's feet.

Gil sat alone in the still dimness of the small tent he shared with Jenks, Ned Topside, and two grooms. He kept hearing the queen ask him, *What techniques have you learned, Gil?* He'd so wanted to tell her, to seek her help and make her understand his fears and why he had acted as he had.

He'd been sitting right here, alone too, when he'd heard the queen outside with Cecil and Dr. Dee decide that someone might have lit Kendale's tent with a mirror reflecting the sun. He knew mirrors could do amazing things, things that could get people killed if they knew about them—and told. He raked his fingers through his hair, as if he could pull it out by its very roots in his frenzy.

He moved aside the easel he had brought from London and his canvases from Urbino. Beneath lay his pack, quite flat now since he'd taken most things out of it. But within lay his two work shirts and paint rags, all wrapped around the mirror.

He uncovered it and stared down into its fine surface. He stroked the inscription etched into its steel back and whispered its words aloud, first in the Italian in which it was written and then in English: " '*Lamentare non a me, O la donna, per gli ritorno soltanto che lei me ha dato*'—'Complain not to me, O woman, for I return to you only what you gave me.' "

A beautiful woman had, more or less, given this mirror to him. How he wished her fabulous face were still reflected in it, peering yet over his shoulder and laughing and telling him that his painting had made her look so beautiful. He cherished the mirror for its memories as well as for its beauty. Dorothea had been a model of Maestro Scarletti's, and Gil had borrowed her. And then she'd borrowed his heart and as good as pierced it when she told him to stay away and he'd realized she was bedding with Scarletti. Anyhow, he'd kept the mirror she'd accidentally left behind, in exchange, he figured, for the portrait Gil had done of her—one the maestro had locked up. He'd painted another one of her since. But now Gil wanted to experiment with the mirror again.

Pushing it up under his shirt, he peeked outside. No one was watching. The three tents of the artists were gone from this spot, and the entrances to the nearby tents all turned away from the western edge of the forest, where he was going.

He sauntered a ways into the trees, then looked around again. He prayed that even if he had been followed from Italy to France and then to London, no one would risk tracking him here. Surely what he had discovered in Urbino watching Maestro Scarletti was not something he could be killed for.

He situated himself in a patch of afternoon sun that pierced the leaves of the new-fledged trees. He played the sharp beam of reflected light up, down, around. Then, wishing his once-broken and still weak leg were as hale as it had once been when he'd climbed trees and even buildings at will, he approached a tree with a girth about as fat as Kendale's. Taking great care not to drop the mirror, he hoisted himself into the crotch of the tree. How good it felt to climb again. It didn't hurt his leg at all. From here, he shot the beam of light toward Lavina Teerlinc's tent roof.

Yes, it was possible. Entirely possible.

The queen quickly surveyed Dee's workshops. The two rooms at the back of his house, which in this fine weather opened onto an enclosed courtyard, were cluttered with glassware, measuring devices, prisms, alchemy jars, and burners. Books on shelves lined the walls between the windows, an amazing collection in an age when large libraries might contain twenty titles. Elizabeth noted several volumes she herself had given him. Only she and Cecil stood with Dee in his realm of rapacious knowledge now, though his wife kept flitting in and out.

"Ah, I quite forgot I have a book here on the lore and power of mirrors, Your Majesty," he told her, reaching for a leather-bound volume. Turning away, he blew the dust off it, and opened it to skim its index. "Oh, yes, I remember this now. It seems the ancients were quite superstitious about them. The Chinese used to mount polished brass concave mirrors on doors so that marauding spirits would frighten themselves away."

"That's a good one," Cecil said, chuckling. "I may have some of those put on my work-chamber doors."

"And the Japanese," Dee went on as if Cecil had not spoken, "held them before the faces of prisoners being questioned to detect guilt."

"Yes, I can see that," Elizabeth said. Cecil reacted to her pun by lifting his eyebrows, but Dee read on.

"The Roman god of fire, Vulcan, supposedly had a mirror which could reveal the present, past, and future. And Merlin, King Arthur's magician, presented someone named King Ryence with a mirror capable of exposing secret plots, treasons, and projected invasions."

"And that," Elizabeth declared, "figuratively speaking, is what I'm hoping your mirror demonstration helps us to expose today. At least, Doctor, in this new age of knowledge, we are a far cry from those days when the Catholic Church forbade people from having them because they led to pride and lust. Let's see your experiment, then, if you please."

"Here, outside, as the sun should be exactly right for it just now," Dee said. Reluctantly he put the book down and motioned them into the sunny courtyard. He had set up a primitive tent—some old canvas stretched over two tall poles—and a small platform with two small boxes on it.

"Herein, Your Majesty and Secretary Cecil," Dee said, seeming suddenly more formal, "are two from my collection of mirrors, which some still call 'looking glasses.' I will demonstrate that any of these could have not only left that round scorch mark on your lady artist's tent but turned Kendale's into a fiery death trap."

Elizabeth and Cecil stepped up onto the plank platform with him.

"Why this elevated height?" she asked. "Because the scorch mark was on the tent roof and the fire evidently began high and moved low?"

"Exactly, Your Majesty. And because of the nearby hunt park. If we could have staged this outside, as I had originally hoped before all the gawkers descended on us, I would have climbed a tree for this. Experimentation and proofs demand authenticity. There is a slight rise of elevation just inside the hunt park, but I'm betting the arsonist scaled a tree."

"If so," Cecil said, "it's a man—someone who could climb."

"Don't you think that if I wanted to, I could not climb a tree?" Elizabeth demanded, and Cecil merely nodded. "Which means," she went on, "when we return, we shall examine trees in the line of—of fire—to see if we can discern a possible perch or perhaps even find a snag of clothing or hair."

"Ah, that reminds me," Dee said, "though I'm no artist, I walked the edge of the hunt park and made a sketch of what I theorize happened." He pulled from inside his robe and carefully opened a folded piece of parchment. On it he had crudely drawn the edge of the hunt park near Kendale's tent and noted the slight rise of ground within. He had drawn only four trees, and had put a star next to the two that had—according to his drawing— elevated limbs on which one could perch, and in which sat stick figures holding up mirrors to catch the sun's rays. He'd also sketched dotted lines from the sun in the sky to the mirrors, and two more dotted lines to both the roof of Lavina's tent—so labeled—and then to Kendale's. He'd added flames and smoke engulfing the latter.

"So, if this is valid," Cecil said, "the arsonist evidently tried to light Mistress Teerlinc's tent after igniting Kendale's—or before—and it didn't catch. But when the first fire drew attention, he decided to run or hide."

"Or merely return to his—or her—nearby tent," Elizabeth added.

"There are, of course, other options," Dee said, handing the paper to the queen. "Mayhap he had the wrong tent at first and realized it. Or he was just randomly targeting tents. Fire is fascinating, is it not? I fear some have a sort of cerebral sickness which makes them revel in the fear and awe flames cause."

Elizabeth studied the strange look on Dee's face as she folded the sketch and put it up her sleeve. "Let us go back to your experiment, Doctor," she urged.

They watched intently as Dee unpacked his smallest mirror, tilted it toward the sun, and placed a perfect scorch mark on the roof of the mock tent. Then he held the mirror steady while the canvas at that spot began to smoke, then flame.

Both Elizabeth and Cecil nearly jumped off the platform when Dee shouted, "Ready, my dear!" and Katherine rushed out from the kitchen and beat the fire out with a flat, long-handled wooden paddle before it could spread.

"What she uses to get bread out of the oven," Dee explained somewhat sheepishly.

"I hope you won't mind if I borrow one of these mirrors, whichever you think may be most like the one the murderer used," Elizabeth whispered to Dee as Katherine hung about with her paddle, watching them. "And who knows," she added, "but I won't have to hold it before the face of someone I suspect while I question him or her. Perhaps, like Merlin's mirror, it will lead me to discover a secret plot or treason."

"You may borrow whatever you wish," John Dee told her, and made a shooing motion to his wife to go back inside. With a stomp and flounce of her green skirt, she obeyed. "This flat mirror could be the culprit, but a concave one is more likely." He repeated the demonstration with the second, larger flat mirror, then called out "Kath-er-ine!" again. She rushed in and smacked the fire out.

This was, the queen thought, stifling a smile despite the serious purpose of this endeavor, rather like a raucous comedy Ned Topside had performed for the court once. Each time the old, cuckolded husband in Ned's play had called for his wife to wait upon his table, she had rushed in and hit him with a meat pie. And since Elizabeth still had the remnants of such on her feet from Katherine Dee's dropping meat pastries, this effort did smack a bit of a domestic farce. The only thing was, well she knew that comic relief often came before the worst part of tragedies.

When Katherine went back in again, Dee said, his voice still soft, "Your Majesty, after the grievous news I brought you about Queen Mary's gazing in mirrors and suggesting treason, you don't mean to imply you think the tent fire could suggest an attack on you? Or some secret plot or treason against you as well as your artist?"

"I didn't tell you, Doctor, but the portrait of me that Kendale had begun was evidently stolen from his tent, slashed to bits, and then taken and perhaps placed in Lavina Teerlinc's tent. Yes, I fear there may be more afoot than a single fire meant to kill one of my artists. The fire and the events surrounding it may be symbolic at best, and a deadly threat to me at worst. Besides, when anyone attacks my staff and my citizens, it is an attack on me."

"Then best I show you the mirror that I believe is very probably like the fine concave one that was used for the fire, Your Grace."

"But these two mirrors made the tent burn," Cecil cut in.

"Granted, my lord, but the other would have done it more swiftly and surely; and I believe," Dee said as if he were pronouncing a life-or-death verdict, "the fire caught quickly—hence, a fine-grade concave mirror like the one I bought in Venice. It may distort some images, though it magnifies wonderfully. I will fetch it straightaway."

Elizabeth and Cecil waited, unspeaking, while Dee darted into his laboratory and out again. "And now," he told them, placing the black tooled-leather box on the edge of the platform, "though Katherine will be loathe to part with this, here it is, the most precious gem of all I've seen so—"

He opened the box with a flourish. It was empty but for the crushed black velvet form where a round mirror with a thick handle had lain.

"Ah—forgive me, Your Grace. She must have taken it out to preen—or polish it, more like. Katherine!"

Still holding her wooden oven paddle, Mistress Dee came out instantly as if she had been lurking just inside the door. "Where is my Venetian mirror, my dear?"

Her eyes widened and her Cupid's bow lower lip dropped. "But you said—I thought I suggested," she stammered, "you could demonstrate with the others."

"I need this one of necessity, wife. Please fetch it."

"I cannot."

"What?" Dee demanded, his voice rising.

Katherine burst into tears, dropped the oven paddle, and ran back inside.

"If she broke that mirror," he said, his voice quavering, "my mirror . . ." He could not finish the thought.

"I see we must have that mirror or proofs of its fate," Elizabeth said, and patted his arm. "You men stay here, and I will speak with her on it."

"But Your Maj—," Dee protested as the queen descended the platform and went out of the bright sun into the dim house. Even from here, Katherine's wails sounded entirely wretched, even panicked, as if she couldn't catch her breath. And Elizabeth meant to find out why.

Chapter the Sixth

THE QUEEN THOUGHT AT FIRST THAT KATHERINE DEE might have run sobbing to her mother-in-law, but she soon saw that was not true. Still in her chair by the kitchen hearth, Dame Dee sat alone, shaking her head as Elizabeth walked into the cluttered kitchen. She motioned for the old woman not to rise. When she evidently realized her queen sought Katherine, she gestured toward the door that opened onto the kitchen garden. Stepping out into a sunny patchwork of herbal beds, Elizabeth saw Katherine had collapsed on a wooden bench in the only shadowed corner of the walled garden. Now she sobbed silently; her shoulders shook.

The wretched woman seemed to sense the queen's presence, for she turned her tearful face and jumped to her feet to offer a tipsy curtsy.

"Sit," Elizabeth said, striding toward her. "Sit and I shall too."

"Please forgive me, Your Majesty," Katherine said, swiping tears from her cheeks with both hands as, looking awestruck, she made room for the queen on the bench. "You see, I so hate to disappoint him—John—when he knows so much—*is* so much to so many—especially to you—and here I am, trying to please him, but stumbling along. . . ."

"Buck up, girl. The man loves and dotes on you."

Katherine sniffed hard, and Elizabeth offered her an embroidered handkerchief from up her sleeve. Hesitantly, she took it.

"Dotes on me, maybe," she said. "Loves me in that way men love when bodily smitten, though their minds are oft elsewhere." She wiped under her eyes. "But I want to be needed for his work—admired by him, Your Majesty. You see, my father and then my first husband owned a grocer's shop in London near Cheapside. They relied on me. I kept the tallies too. But here, with all these experiments and theories and long, difficult books . . ." As if overwhelmed, she stopped talking and blew her nose.

"But surely," Elizabeth said, "Dr. Dee did not expect or desire a helpmeet who could assist him with his unusual and abstract work."

"But it's what he thinks about day and night. And now I've ruined everything."

"Hardly everything. The mirror, you mean? What became of it?"

"I should never have had it out of its case, of course, at least not when he wasn't here. You see, it distorts terribly but it magnifies wonderfully. It's good for plucking wayward eyebrows and finding freckles to wash with milk."

"You are speaking of it as if it still exists. Do you know where it is?"

Katherine shook her head so hard her eardrops rattled. "Gone," she whispered, not meeting the queen's gaze.

"Gone where?" Elizabeth could not help it, but her voice took on an edge. 'S blood, she had come not to comfort this woman or hear her beauty secrets, but to get her hands on that mirror, which Dee claimed was the very type that had ignited Kendale's tent.

"I—I had intended to say I broke it, but that would be a lie. And yet I fear it's gone for good." Her eyes, gray as wet brook pebbles, widened as she stared into the distance. "I had it outside, here, in the sun only last week to see a blemish on my chin. I went back inside, perhaps for a quarter of an hour, remembered it was still out here, returned, and—it was gone."

"Stolen?"

Katherine nodded wildly. "Of course I asked Mother Dee and Sarah. Indirectly I inquired of my husband. But no one knew anything."

"On this very bench?" the queen said, rising and scowling behind it as if the mirror would emerge from the new-sprouted tansy, dill, and horehound.

"I guess someone could have climbed the wall," Katherine said, jumping to her feet when the queen rose. "Several trees closely abut it outside, and then there is that pear tree over there for an escape."

Elizabeth pictured the drawing Dee had done of the fringe of the hunt park near the burned tent. Someone who was adept at climbing trees had become her prime suspect. Yet what possible connection could there be between Dee's mirror gone missing from this bench in Mortlake and one evidently used in the hunt park?

"Well, I must confess to him," Katherine said. "What I can't figure is how someone knew to come over a wall he couldn't spy over, for a mirror I'd left behind for only a few minutes."

"You are certain your girl Sarah did not take it?" the queen inquired, eyeing the six-foot-high brick wall. The only exit from this small area was the door into the kitchen.

"She said not, and I've found her ever trustworthy——she came from London with me."

Elizabeth again sat on the bench, and bent over a bit to the height Katherine would have held the mirror, then craned her neck to look above the walls. After all, Dr. Dee had convinced her of the import of angles, slants, and slopes. She could see trees from here but mostly the very heights of them. The only man-made thing in sight was the top floor of the Riverside Inn. Could someone have watched a comely woman from there, then seen her leave the mirror behind? The queen bent farther to the level where the mirror could have lain on the bench. Yes, the inn's top windows were still barely visible. The mirror could have shone in the sun that day to draw attention to itself.

"Did Dr. Dee have someone about the house or laboratory helping him the day the mirror disappeared?" she asked Katherine.

"He was not at home that day. He'd gone out to prepare for his annual May Day celebration, where a bonfire is built on a distant hill. He amuses everyone with his big mirror by sending signals from it, flashes of lights in some sort of code. I've never seen that event, but everyone far and wide in these parts looks forward to it. It's an old Celtic custom——forgive me, Your Majesty, but quite pagan in origins."

"Now that is something I would like to see."

"I know he planned to invite you today, Your Majesty——and your courtiers at Nonsuch. Since Richmond Palace lies close by Mortlake, perhaps you could move there for the celebration."

Elizabeth studied the young woman in the sun. She seemed so sincere, yet there was something too planned out about all this.

"Though this is your first year here at Mortlake, Katherine, do you know how large a signal glass he uses for his May Day revels?"

"It's under a shroud in his workshop. As big as this," she said and, childlike, rounded her arms over her head so her fingers almost touched.

"I'd almost forgotten," Elizabeth mused aloud. "He's spoken to me before of wanting to experiment with large mirrors from fortress to fortress or from ship to ship in some sort of code." Though she did not let on, she also recalled that Dr. Dee himself had mentioned how Archimedes had burned ships' sails from afar with his huge concave mirror. But all this meant nothing. The profound Dr. Dee and his flighty new wife were not under suspicion for anything yet, though, indeed, they had ridden into Nonsuch shortly before the tent caught fire. And Dee had let slip that his wife took a walk in the woods just after they arrived.

As if her thoughts had summoned him, the queen saw John Dee in the kitchen door, an anxious look on his face. "When you did not return, Your Majesty," he called out, "I thought it best I look in on both of you. Besides, the Earl of Leicester believes it is time for you to head back to Nonsuch."

"And so it is. Katherine, you will speak with your husband on the missing mirror. Dr. Dee," she said as she passed him, "I bid you good day and tell you I have accepted Katherine's invitation to join you this year for your May Day celebrations. I shall bring a party of forty or so and will leave a man here tonight to find us accommodations. Richmond Palace is being cleaned, and I'd rather not move everyone there for just one night."

"But of course, you may stay with us, Your Majesty," Katherine put in, hurrying behind. "As for forty, though . . ."

"I would not impose. As I said, I will leave my man Jenks with you this night and will see you again in but a week. Until then, Dr. Dee, I shall send for you if there is more you can do in the matter of the fire murders."

She swept through the kitchen and into the small solar, where her retinue amused themselves over a chessboard. Clifford and Jenks jumped to their feet while Robin and Rosie stood more slowly with a bow and a curtsy. Cecil must still have been outside.

"Jenks, to me," Elizabeth said, and stepped into the narrow hall with him. "I am leaving you here one night to do two things. Arrange for myself and a party of forty or so for May Day in the Riverside Inn just across the way."

"That big old place? But Richmond is so close—"

"Do as I say. I want to be near events, not walled off in a palace which is being cleaned. Except for that one night, I am determined to stay at Nonsuch until we find our arsonist."

"Yes, Your Grace."

"Also, keep your eyes and ears open for whatever passes between the Dees about a lost mirror. And while you're about all that," she whispered, "see if you can butter up that serving girl Sarah to find out if she saw what happened to the mirror Mistress Dee says she left on the garden bench before it simply disappeared."

"Like magic?" Jenks lowered his voice even more. "Some say John Dee knows all the sorcerer's arts, you know."

It was later than Elizabeth had intended when the royal retinue returned to Nonsuch, so she did not summon her artists to paint her. Instead, to help foster the feeling of normalcy, she hosted a dinner set up on plank tables in the outer courtyard, followed by a recitation of rural love sonnets by her master of revels and principal player, Ned Topside. The festivities, the queen had announced, were in honor of Lord Maitland's visit. He was leaving for Scotland the next morning, so she and Cecil spoke with him in private after everyone else was dismissed to return to their tents.

"I charge you to continue to counsel my dear cousin Queen Mary not to wed Lord Darnley," Elizabeth told Maitland as the three of them sat in her outer chamber over wine. Though she had set this marital trap for Mary, she wanted to clear her conscience somewhat. "Tell her the man's character is not well proven."

Maitland shook his big head. "Unlike you, Your Majesty, Queen Mary has little wit for knowing whom to trust truly, especially when it comes to dashing men."

"Or she would trust you more, would she not, my lord?" Cecil needled him. Elizabeth was ever amazed by how well the two of them, considering their opposing loyalties, got on.

"I wish it were a laughing matter," Maitland replied. "Indeed, not only her passion for Lord Darnley, but her leaning so hard on the Italian upstart, David Rizzio, shows how misguided she has become. The man began as one of her musicians and has become her closest adviser!"

"Is he handsome, then?" Elizabeth asked, and sipped her wine.

"Strangely not, Your Majesty. Dark and swarthy, but he favors her match with Darnley. Rizzio's getting as arrogant and greedy for power as Darnley himself," Maitland groused, twisting his big signet ring on the middle finger of his right hand. "I tell you, I do not look forward to going home. But is there any other message you would send to Her Grace?"

"Yes," the queen said, rising and setting her goblet down so hard that wine sloshed from it as both men also stood. "Tell her this, my lord, word for word. If she must gaze in mirrors to admire herself, best she not be so dangerously confused she does not realize she sees only the Queen of Scotland there and no other."

"And," Cecil added, "tell her if she does anything to incite our northern shires to rebellion, she might as well break every mirror in her kingdom and add up seven years of bad luck for each. The Queen of England will not allow her people or her places to be inflamed against her."

The next morning, the queen posed for Lavina, Henry Heatherley, and her Gilberto Sharpino in the meadow between the hunt park and the palace. Cecil had counseled against it, but she wanted to demonstrate she was not afraid to sit near the spot where the tent had burned. Despite the tragic loss of Will Kendale and his servant boy, life must go on.

Besides, she'd argued, if her posing drew out the arsonist with the mirror, so much the better. Next time, they would catch him. Ned Topside had reported that no one he'd interviewed had seen anything unusual the morning of the fire, so she was getting desperate to flush someone out.

Her people seemed to be defiant too, for both courtiers and commoners from the palace and the encampment sat or strolled nearby, enjoying both the weather and the sight of their queen, sitting still as a statue for once. Floris had brought Kat out, and both women sat at their apparently favorite pastime when outside, stringing flower necklaces for everyone. But it warmed the queen like the sun to have her Kat content.

"I must admit, Your Majesty," Henry Heatherley pronounced, grandly flourishing a crimson-tipped brush, "this is the best light an artist can have. It will help me keep the colors true, and it brings out your fine features."

"It casts wonderful, stark shadows," the queen heard Gil murmur under his breath, though no one reacted to that.

Lavina said, "Oh, yes, I like it too, Master Heatherley. Your Majesty, being in the sun of late has put the pink back in your cheeks."

Elizabeth was tempted to say, *So I no longer look so whey-faced?* but she kept silent. Posing here was much better than sitting within the confines of a palace in London or even inside Nonsuch. The air was fresh and cool, and she did not feel trapped. And no foe, threatening fear at the most and fire at the worst, was going to steal all this from her.

"Gil, how is this alfresco studio for you?" she asked as she rose to take her first stretch of the morning. Hoping to lighten his mood, she was anxious to see how the lad was doing after all that talk of Italy, Titian, and live models. She handed her scepter and orb to Rosie and loosed the heavy ermine mantle from her shoulders to let it fall back on the large chair which the artists would transpose to a throne.

"I am barely begun," Gil said as she strolled toward him, "but I much favor these conditions and this style."

"Oh," she said, peering at the vibrant multicolored sketch he had made of her on stretched canvas. "Despite how I've posed, you don't have me looking straight ahead. But a foursquare gaze traditionally evokes an aura of royal power and vigilance."

In her peripheral vision, she could see the smug look on Heatherley's face, and Lavina elbowing him as if to say, *The upstart boy has gone too far already.* Floris and Kat had come closer with some others to gaze at Gil's work too.

"I realize, Your Grace," Gil said, still finishing the sketch, "that other English artists tend to turn the head a bit but not the eyes. Yet you sent me abroad to learn what I could. As I said, I admire Titian, and he often paints his royal and noble subjects not only turned to the side but looking to the side."

"But our queen," Heatherley put in, "cannot be compared to others. Turning the head with the eyes makes her seem uninterested, even reticent."

"Never our queen!" Gil flared. "This position says she is so great and powerful that she need not watch us directly, and yet is in command of all things. Why, even now, she glanced aside to see her artists smile when she questioned me. What, exactly, is she thinking? people will wonder. How at ease in her power she is, how in control, and hardly stiff and still but living and so genuine and real!"

The queen could not help but smile. She and Cecil in their quest to promote her power through a portrait could not have said it better. Gil's style was fresh and free, but solid, too. Yet she regretted that Heatherley looked livid, and she was sure Lavina would soon start spouting her *vills* and *dats*.

"I believe I like it," the queen pronounced. "One of my mottoes is *Tutto vedo and molto mancha*—I see everything and much is lacking. I rather think it conveys that idea."

"Vell," Lavina put in, "his colors are goot. Brought pigments back from Italy, I guess."

"Just this yellow and red to mix for Her Majesty's unique and glorious hue of hair," Gil answered, pointing to the outline he'd done of her coiffure under the crown. "Titian paints Venetian women with rich hues, especially red-gold hair, though theirs is bleached, then tinted with henna. Our queen has no such need of artifice. And these lines suggest movement, not a static figure needing to be copied by mere tracery as we do here in Eng—" Gil stopped in midword and looked around as if he'd just emerged from a dream—and perhaps stepped into a nightmare. "I don't mean to sound as if I boast," he said haltingly, almost as if another person spoke.

"So," Heatherley said, stepping even closer and squinting at Gil's canvas, "is there some other way the Italian artists reproduce a portrait? If yours cannot be copied with punching and tracing the outline, what good is your work, for our queen will order her official portrait reproduced time and again."

"I didn't mean it could not be copied," Gil clipped out, looking suddenly stricken. "Your Majesty, may I take a moment away, if you please?"

"Of course," she assured him, but she was greatly vexed that something was wrong. Each time her young artist spoke of Italian artists' techniques, it seemed something frightened him, something he could not say. Gil had never been one to keep secrets, even when he and his mother made their living from climbing trees or crawling in upstairs windows to spy out what goods could later be stolen with their long-armed angling hooks.

"I wouldn't doubt," the queen overheard Henry Heatherley say as Gil walked rapidly toward his tent, "he simply copies paintings he's seen in Italy. He told me the first day we met that he's been working on reproducing his favorite Titian, called *Woman at the Mirror.* I glimpsed that canvas. And this one"—he gestured at Gil's portrait of the queen—"may be just another version of that."

Elizabeth's insides cartwheeled, and not at Heatherley's snide insult. She turned to him and Lavina. "Gil told me his favorite work by Maestro Titian was the *Venus of Urbino* and never mentioned painting someone with a mirror."

"The mirror portrait is the one the boy's been painting on the sly," Heatherley replied, placing undue emphasis on those last three words.

Fretting over Gil's behavior and realizing she must interrogate him about it, the queen sat to pose again. As if he'd been watching, Gil returned quickly and began to work. Most courtiers had gone back to their own pursuits, but Floris and Kat stood watching Gil, and Elizabeth let them stay. When the queen finally stood to stretch again, Floris came up to her with Kat close behind.

"Your Majesty," Floris said, keeping her voice low and ignoring Kat, who insisted on putting a laced crown of daisies on her head, "I've been thinking about that fire, especially after Ned Topside asked everyone if they had seen anything suspicious that morning."

"Yes, Floris?" Elizabeth said, holding up a hand to keep her ladies back a moment.

"The boy," Floris said. "What about the boy being the cause?"

Elizabeth held her breath, for it seemed Floris had guessed her own fear, her need to question Gil further. "You mean my young artist?" she whispered.

"Oh, no, of course not. I can see how you favor him. I just mean that everyone assumes it was your artist Kendale the fire demon meant to harm. But what if everyone is barking up the wrong tree because the target was that poor dead boy Niles?"

"They say Gil Sharpe's taken a walk in the woods, Your Grace," Ned Topside reported to the queen when he returned to her privy chambers without the young man. She had just come inside; the three partially completed portraits were still sitting outside on their easels drying while her courtiers amused themselves.

" 'S blood!" she muttered. "Best he be careful out there. Then I shall keep my eyes open for him, because I intend to walk into the hunt park too, to see how Dr. Dee's sketch matches the trees there. Ned, since Jenks has not returned from Mortlake yet, come along with me, and fetch Clifford too, unless he's out somewhere guarding Kat and Floris Minton."

"Yes, Your Grace," he said, starting for the door. She appreciated his immediate acquiescence to her wishes for once. Though Ned Topside was trusted and appreciated, the same bright talents which made his onstage dukes and kings leap to life sometimes made him more cocky than circumspect with her.

She began to pace but kept talking so that Ned turned back at the door. "I shall tell everyone that I mean to take a short constitutional walk without my ladies, that's it," she said. "And when I return, I've a good mind to ask Floris Minton to join our Privy Plot Council. How could I—all of us," she added, hitting her forehead with an open palm, "have ignored that the boy Niles could indeed have been the target? It's not as likely as that Kendale was, but I pride myself on following each lead to its possible end. Kat used to be a part of our council, but now she could be replaced by Floris. She'd be able to join us only when Kat was sleeping, of course, but we often meet at night."

"Yes, Your Grace," Ned said, and hurried out, even as Meg came in.

"Are you feeling well, Your Grace?" Meg asked.

"Just vexed with myself," the queen admitted, still pacing. Her heart had dropped when Floris had first said "the boy" could be the cause. Though she hated to admit it, even to herself, Niles aside, she must acknowledge that her dear Gil must now come under some suspicion.

The queen stood on a knoll as high as a man within the edge of the hunt park, with the encampment in view, including the charred grass where Kendale's tent had been. Yes, the sketch of trees Dr. Dee had done clearly matched ones she could see here. And two of them, as he had noted, had big limbs or crotches where someone could have elevated himself slightly to catch the sun in a mirror. If she were in boy's breeches, she'd climb the trees herself.

She peered up each of the two trees, then had Ned scale them to look for snags of cloth or hair. She had Clifford with her too, for Floris had taken Kat into the palace and didn't need him just now, but Clifford was too big and bulky to climb well. Ned, just as agile as he had been when she'd taken him away from his life as a roving actor with the Queen's Country Players six years ago, went smoothly up and peered down at her.

"Shall I recite something lovelorn as from a balcony or parapet, Your Grace? And Clifford can, of course, play the disapproving father."

"Stow the ad-libbing for now, man," she clipped out. "Do you see any signs someone has climbed that tree? Broken branches? Anything?"

"Nothing here, but I do see a brown deer yonder, standing as still as this investigation of ours is going."

"Enough! Come down then."

As she stepped back from the tree and nearly stumbled down

the slope, it struck her that this treed knoll was similar to the grassy one on which Kat and Floris had sat stringing flowers the day of the fire. Did this area simply sprout random yet similar hillocks, or were these matching, man-made rises? Strangely, both of them had some remnants of weathered stones, perhaps the foundations of some sort of very small buildings, such as watch-towers. Perhaps that was what these hillocks had once held. The elevations had no use now, but had perhaps served some purpose, even before the long-lost village of Cuddington was built.

"Your Grace," Ned interrupted her thoughts as he leaped lithely down, "I don't think it was a deer after all, but Gil Sharpe I saw through the screen of trees. You said you wanted to speak with him."

He pointed north; she didn't see where he meant at first, then noted the flash of brown, which could well have been a deer. It *was* Gil, she realized as she squinted in the direction Ned indicated. He wasn't walking but was staring at something.

"Shall I call or fetch him for you?" Clifford asked.

"Let's go to him quietly, lest he bolt like a deer," she said.

As they went closer, Gil saw them. He'd been leaning against a tree. Now he bent, evidently to brush leaves off his knees and shins, then hurried toward them.

"Is everything all right, Your Grace?"

"I might ask the same of you, Gilberto Sharpino. I want to continue our discussion of things you learned in Italy and how much you gleaned about Kendale's boy Niles in your brief time you knew him."

Gil's ruddy complexion paled. "I observed him, of course, but didn't really know him. Master Heatherley has tried to slander me again, has he not? It was he, I've learned, who was plying Master

Kendale with wine the night before he died, Heatherley with his favorite Bordeaux who got Kendale so drunk he insulted me and mayhap Niles, too, for all I know."

"I will look into your claim about Heatherley, as I must all accusations which might lead to—"

A woman's shriek shredded the quiet of the forest. The buzz of voices from the encampment rose to a roar. Lifting her voluminous skirts, the queen rushed with her men toward the tumult.

They broke from the hunt park beyond the clusters of tents, near where some courtiers still lingered around the three easels with their drying canvases. And one—the partially completed royal portrait by Lavina Teerlinc—was in flames.

Chapter the Seventh

 AS ELIZABETH RAN FROM THE HUNT PARK WITH CLIF-
ford, Ned, and Gil, she saw that a crowd had gathered around the easels. Amid the hubbub of voices
and people, she picked out separate voices.

"Smother the flames!"

"It's too far gone!"

"How in the deuce did that get started?"

"But I was nearby. No one even approached it just now and
certainly didn't light it, so——"

Elizabeth saw no reason to douse the fire. It had quite consumed the portrait, and had burned most of the wooden easel on
which the canvas rested. Lavina had appeared, panting and wringing her hands. She did not cry or speak, but gaped at the charred
ruin. Henry Heatherley shoved past Gil, not to see Lavina's work
but to check his own, and cried out, "Hell's gates, would you look
at this!"

The queen rushed to Heatherley's portrait. Two neat oval

scorch marks marred her face, which he had begun to flesh out today.

When Cecil suddenly appeared in the crowd, Elizabeth pointed at the marks and asked, "My lord, do you recognize these shapes?"

"Recognize them from where?" Heatherley demanded. "Who ruined my work? I suppose it could be somewhat painted over, but who dared throw circles of filth on this work of Her Majesty's fine face? And so now," he cried, rounding on Gil, who stood at her side, "only your portrait of the queen remains untouched!"

"Enough!" Elizabeth cried, and held up her hands for silence. "Clifford," she said in a clarion voice, "take other guards, hasten back into the forest, and question anyone you find therein. Ned, fetch more of my guards to join the search. Listen! Listen, everyone, to me."

As the two men ran to their tasks, the crowd gathered around her even closer. "It is now obvious we are facing a threat of fire from some unhinged person who wishes my artists or their work harm. We believe these fires are being set from a distance, possibly by a fire mirror tilted to concentrate the rays of the sun to ignite canvas. I tell you this to make you aware and wary."

Lavina looked puzzled and Heatherley shocked. Murmurs and mutterings followed from the crowd. Several craned their necks to look toward the hunt park or even the palace walls and roof.

"And so," she went on, "I am ordering all of your tents to be pitched within the palace walls in the privy garden, where reflected rays from the forest will not find canvas for further fuel. I assure you we will not remain long at Nonsuch if my men cannot find the villain who would wish my portraits, my people, or possibly my person harm. But I will not flee, and want to remain until we can catch the fire demon. If not, soon after May Day, we will be heading back to London. I expect your compliance and assistance."

"And if such a demented soul should follow us there," Heatherley said, "what of the city with its wooden-framed houses cheek by jowl and its thatched roofs? Why, all of London could go up in flame."

Elizabeth swung about to face him. That had sounded to her more like a threat than a question. Heatherley had a devouring ambition; she knew that. And if he had indeed gotten Kendale drunk the night before his death, and since he obviously resented her favoritism toward Gil . . .

But he was right: only Gil's portrait had not been harmed.

As courtiers and their servants hastened to their tents, Elizabeth stepped around Gil's easel to search his work for any signs of scorch marks. Nothing. Nothing but the fiery-hued sketch of her reddish hair and crimson cloak and the golden aura which seemed to come from her painted being. Dear Lord, she prayed, let it not be the boy behind this. Let it be someone else, let it be—

She nearly jumped out of her skin as a trumpet sounded down the lane before the castle. Turning, she peeked between Robin and Cecil, who had come to stand beside her like sentinels. Those five or six approaching had a banner flying, four horses and two carts. Not some official envoy then with bad news. Someone was waving, and that bold trumpet call sounded again.

"Who in the world?" Robin whispered.

Then the queen realized who it was. "It's Ned Topside's old troupe of actors, the Queen's Country Players. What timing. But we can use some distraction this evening within the crowded castle walls."

"Indeed," Cecil murmured. "Anything to lighten this siege mentality the fire-mirror murderer has forced upon us."

But even as the queen awaited their approach, she remembered her own silent prayer but a moment ago and wondered if the Lord High God had answered it so quickly. For well she remembered that Giles Chatam, now the leader of the troupe, had been under suspicion for murders in London last winter. He had been proved innocent, but she'd heard it was believed he'd begun a fire in his boyhood home which had trapped and killed both his parents. And actors always had mirrors about them. Last winter, Giles had sought attention from the queen, but, partly to protect Ned Topside, Chatam's rival, she'd sent the troupe away after Yule. But was this timing propitious—and suspicious?

As if he'd recognized his old fellows merely by their trumpet call, Ned came running from his tent to join them. He looked more vexed than she'd seen him in months, standing by her, solemn and silent for once.

"Shall I go tell them you'll hire them for one night?" Robin asked.

"Let them come on," she said, squaring her shoulders. "I would talk with their leader myself, not Ned's old uncle but their master player, the clever chameleon Chatam."

"But, Your Grace," Ned finally spoke up, "you know he was nothing but trouble last winter."

"As you were too, and only fortune's star—and my goodwill—kept you from being tossed out to ply your trade on the country roads with these men. Go inside, where you can speak with your former fellows later, for I would greet them without your sour looks and sharp words."

As Ned frowned, bowed stiffly, and retreated, she regretted

being so harsh, but she could not stomach Ned's constant, jealous bickering with Chatam again. After all, she merely wanted one night's good performance from the players. And, of course, to be certain Giles Chatam, who may or may not have burned his parents to death, hadn't been hiding in the hunt park flashing a cosmetic or costume mirror to get everyone stirred up here, so she would take them on.

But one way or the other, she did intend to take them on, take on anyone who might be guilty of murder by mirror.

"So you'll be heading back to Nonsuch now, Master Jenks?" John Dee called to the queen's man as he sat ahorse, just watching Dee and his old friend Simon Garver preparing to oversee the erection of the tall Maypole on Mortlake's green.

Dee wondered if Jenks was sweet on their maid Sarah, since he'd spent so much time in the kitchens, but he'd leave all that up to Katherine. Though she was still sulking over his explosion when he learned his Venetian mirror was stolen, she'd know about such things as someone being taken with another's charms. That was her realm, while knowledge beyond bed and board was his.

"Yes," Jenks said, "heading back, and grateful for your kindnesses, Dr. Dee. How tall is that pole, anyway?"

"One hundred and fifty feet, though nearly five of that goes in the ground each year to stabilize the top of it."

"Aye," the elderly Garver added, "can't have it wobbling when the dancing ribbons are attached to it and men and maids start cavorting around it and tugging on them, specially with a precious mirror tied to its top."

A longtime local friend of Dee's, Simon Garver had been a

woodcarver by trade, one who had specialized in felling, then chiseling, fine local oak so it resembled pleated fabric—linenfold paneling, it was called. Garver the Carver, some still called him. The Riverside Inn, which Simon and his wife owned, though they lived in a thatched house next to it, was full of his beautiful work, as was Nonsuch Palace, where he'd plied his trade years ago for King Henry VIII. The hoary-headed and hoary-bearded man was nearly three score and ten but still robust.

This sturdy Maypole had been donated by Simon years ago. But to Dee, this apparently frivolous extravagance was not only homage to his Celtic Welsh ancestry, but another experiment with signal mirrors and light. He had calculated the angles perfectly so that the celebratory bonfire set on Greenwich Hill several miles away could be picked up by his mirror mounted at the top of this pole and reflected here and there. The dancers might weave their ribbons, but Dee alone held the rope which turned the big mirror atop the pole to flash light signals back to Greenwich, a feat he would put to more practical purpose someday soon, especially now that he could convince the queen of its importance.

"How do you raise the pole then?" Jenks interrupted Dee's thoughts again. "Do you not need many men? I could delay my return a bit to help."

"All ropes, winches, and pulleys, my man," Dee said.

"I should have known it would be sleight of hand with you, Doctor. I'll be on my way then. And Master Garver, as I said, the queen's entourage will be at your inn come the morning of May Day."

"My goodwife and I are deeply honored," Simon said with a nod, "and I'll see the entire place is readied. Tell Her Majesty I worked for her father when I carved at Nonsuch."

"Good day to you then," Jenks said, doffing his cap, as he turned his horse away.

"Is your goodwife as thrilled as mine that the queen's coming with her courtiers?" Dee asked as he unwrapped the big mirror and began to mount it atop the pole before it would be winched into place.

"Oh, aye, but sad she was to have to evict that players troupe with that handsome Chatam fellow, even though they'd just taken the garret they hardly paid a farthing for." Dee's friend gave a hearty laugh and shook his head.

"The garret of your inn, you say? I haven't seen them about during the day."

"They're usually out and about, plying their trade. My old dame likes to hear them spouting their lines at night, and says they plan to be here to make a pretty penny at the May Day gathering. Wait till they hear they'll be performing for the queen!"

They shared a laugh together as they bolted the mirror to its revolving arm atop the lofty pole.

"It seems you have tracked me down," Elizabeth told the Queen's Country Players as they bowed before her at the entrance to Nonsuch Palace. Besides her guards, a cluster of her courtiers stood with her. Gil was sticking tight too.

"Indeed," Giles Chatam, their spokesman, declared as he dismounted and swept her a graceful, low bow. "At first we did not know you were here, Your Majesty, or we would have come sooner. We pray that the difficult events of last winter have vanished with the chill air of spring and that the desire to have a play for your people springs anew."

"Prettily said, as ever. Yes, I believe we could use a performance, especially if you would let me choose the play."

"But your wish is ever our command," Wat Thompson, Ned's uncle, put in. He had commanded the troupe when Ned was with them years ago. Randall Greene, once handsome but now fading, had also been a dominant player but had since been eclipsed by the clever, blond and blue-eyed Chatam. The players always had two boys with them to take the women's parts, and the queen saw Clinton, one lad she recognized, and a new one she had not seen.

"And my nephew Ned?" Wat asked, scanning the group behind her. "Is he not among your people here?"

"He is and will greet you later. I am thinking of a particular play from your repertoire," she went on, "one I saw years ago when I was princess and first met Ned Topside, so I am hoping you might let him again play his part in it—narrator, it was."

"But of course," Chatam said before Wat could answer. "I trust it's one which is especially delightful and soothing—to cheer one and all, lest anything has gone amiss of late."

She wondered how much the handsome man knew of what had taken place, but she did not enlighten him. At least, Elizabeth reasoned, Ned's taking a central role in a play Chatam was once no part of would smooth things over. For it wasn't Ned she was hoping to unsettle with this drama, but her poor Gil, who stood just a few feet away, watching her nervously. She would add a few lines to rattle him, then question him stringently about whatever he was hiding.

"What play would that be then?" Chatam was asking with a blinding smile that might be enough in itself to set something afire.

"If I recall aright," Elizabeth said, "it was called *A Potion of Pleasure* and took place in sunny Italy."

Her eyes met Gil's; his widened before he looked away. She was relieved to see Jenks riding in from Mortlake, for she would have him stick tight to Gil until tonight. Cecil had been right to declare that she was going into a siege mentality, for she must flush out her faceless foe. And if it was someone she cared for, someone she trusted, even then, justice must be done.

"Yes, we were drinking together that night," Henry Heatherley admitted when the queen summoned him to her council room. "Will and I were toasting our blessed fortune to be in such a lovely place and charged to paint such a lovely subject."

"Flat answers will do, lest you be charged with flattery, Master Heatherley."

"You—did not summon me to dismiss or—charge me?" he stammered. He stood across the table from her, turning his plumed cap in hands so tense his knuckles had turned white.

"Of course not, but you should have told me Kendale was possibly still besotted the next day. It could partly explain why he was so slow to move when smoke and flames spread."

"I—did not wish to besmirch his memory. Forgive me, Your Grace, but it was your young Gilberto Sharpino who tried to implicate me in this way, was it not?"

"I am asking the questions here. But I also sent to ask you if your portrait can be repaired or if you must begin again."

"I—thank you for allowing that, Your Majesty—for I believe I can salvage it. Holbein often painted over errors or problems, one of the many lessons I took from him."

"And I shall give Lavina time to begin again, hoping she can do some of it from memory. Master Heatherley, you do not truly believe that Gil Sharpe—for he is sharp in wit and skill—would be so stupid as to slash Kendale's work, burn Lavina's, and try to ruin yours, do you? It would be all too obvious then that he wanted to be the winner, and he would not risk all that."

"Point well taken, of course," he said. "But perhaps someone else who knows how much you favor him wants to help him by ruining your other artists. Though there is a renaissance of interest in classical things in our land, Italian things, as it were, you have oft said you are pure English, so I am certain your official portrait will be too."

"You're quite a speechmaker, Master Heatherley. Perhaps there will be a part for you in the drama tonight."

Again, she wished she hadn't been so testy with him, as she'd been with Ned earlier. All this was getting to her, when she had thought this sojourn at Nonsuch would be the perfect escape from London and its winter woes.

That evening, as the court assembled in the torch-lit inner court-yard of Nonsuch, surrounded by the panels of Roman deities and looked down upon by the enthroned figure of her father, the queen saw that Ned was in his element. He had apologized to her for ever so much as gainsaying her wishes and was grateful that she had stipulated he must be a central part of this drama.

Indeed, Ned's elevation relegated Chatam to a very minor role. It was a shot probably wide of the mark, she thought; but since Chatam no doubt resented being so used, then perhaps, if he was the fire demon, he would act again. At any rate, Ned was not only playing the main part in this play tonight, but had accepted the role of keeping a covert eye on Giles Chatam.

But now the queen's own eyes filled with tears as she heard the words from this play she had watched so long ago in the difficult days before she became queen. Then she had despaired for her own life and safety. Yet now, six years crowned, was she any safer? Or was the mirror murderer hoping to attack more than her portraits and her artists?

"We hope to amuse and amaze," Ned pronounced from the makeshift stage of planks in the center of the crowd. "We shall sweep you away from this place to other sites in this world, though none so grand as our fair England."

Elizabeth shifted slightly in her chair. Only she and Kat were seated; Floris stood behind them. Yes, she could see Gil's face from here. He was with Jenks, positioned just as she'd wanted so she could see the lad; then Jenks would bring him forthwith to her apartments for further questioning. Perhaps this nostalgic view of Italy would shake something loose from the stubborn boy.

"And now," Ned went on, "we shall present a few speeches and scenes from the new and fashionable Italian comedy *A Potion of Pleasure*. Drink up and dream you are in sunny Italy and have found such a magic liquor there as to make anyone who drinks it fall in love with you ..."

Gil started visibly at that. Because of the mention of sun or liquor or falling in love? the queen wondered. It was a charming, lighthearted play, but the stricken Gil looked as if he hardly heard another word.

Feeling sick as he faced the queen in her council chamber after the evening's entertainment, Gil stood as mute as he used to when he was dumb.

"You'd best answer each question Lord Cecil and I put to you," Elizabeth ordered. "After all, I'm the one who sent you to Italy, I'm the one who paid your passage!"

Gil knew the queen had been watching him during the play. Now he was so scared his knees were knocking. He dared not tell her he had a mirror. Or that it had gotten him not only into romantic trouble but deadly trouble, too.

"You'd best talk, lad," Cecil put in. They were the only two with him; the room echoed slightly when they raised their voices. "What Her Grace didn't put up for your purse, I did."

"I—yes, there were things I didn't tell you," Gil stammered, staring at his feet. "Things of the heart."

"Do you mean you came to love someone, or that you shifted your allegiance elsewhere?" the queen demanded. Her words frightened him further. Surely she did not think he would ever be part of some sort of spying against her. Was that why she and Cecil had questioned him about Catholics and Spaniards in Urbino? Maybe Dr. Dee, after his brief visit there, had reported to them that Gil had been working *against* her when he had merely tried to find out things *for* her.

He decided to tell part of the truth, hoping it would be enough. "You see, I came to adore Maestro Giorgio Scarletti's mistress, though I didn't know she was at first. Just one of his models, I thought. He was married, of course, though that doesn't seem to stop Italians from—"

"Or men in general," the queen clipped out. "Say on, Gil."

"She let me paint her . . . let me fall in love with her—I didn't know about her and the maestro."

"And when he learned you adored her, he cast you out in disgrace? Is that why you came home two years early?" she pursued.

"I—not exactly."

"What exactly, then?"

"I am not certain I can say."

"Gil, we are not just playing at guessing games of secret trysts here," Elizabeth explained. "Because of the attacks on my artists and their works of me and because the Scottish queen has been making remarks to her mirrors which hint she intends soon to be the next English queen—"

"No!" Gil cried.

"There are numerous reasons," Cecil put in, "that you must come forward with all you know, and now."

"But I know nothing of that, of—women and mirrors," he got out before he lifted both hands to his head. "Except I did a painting—of Dorothea with a mirror. . . . Has Heatherley told you of it? Pure happenstance, Your Grace."

"Yes, I have heard about the painting—your favorite, he said, when you told me quite another thing. Jenks!" she cried over her shoulder. "Bring in the work in question!"

Gil gaped as Jenks appeared through the door to the queen's rooms, holding the painting of Dorothea which he'd had secreted in his tent. In the work, she looked to the side toward a young man—a vague, idealized rendition of himself. And that poor, demented lover was holding an exquisite framed mirror behind her.

Gil start to shake even harder, from within. "It's more or less a copy of a Titian," he said. "See, Your Grace? As I told you, she looks to the side and has blond-red hair. But I put in Dorothea's face and her mirror. We were allowed—encouraged—to copy favorite paintings, to use the same models the masters used to learn their techniques. If the works were good enough, they belonged to our master to sell."

"But you left hastily with this favorite work—and without your master's favorite Dorothea, I take it?" Cecil asked, his voice quiet now.

"Yes, my lord."

"Is this technique of copying what you alluded to before?" the queen asked, her voice also kind now. "You became distraught each time you mentioned the Italian master's techniques, especially of copying, because it reminded you of Dorothea?"

Gil nodded, not looking into her sharp gaze again, but at the filigreed pomander of sweet herbs she kept fingering at her waist. He held his breath, praying that his clever queen would not ferret out the lies from his half-truths.

" 'S blood, but first loves are hard," she muttered. "And to have to leave before you wanted to, fearing you'd disappoint me . . ."

He nodded again. Thank God, she had not asked him if he had the mirror. If her goodwill toward him got him off scot-free from what she might have caught him on, he vowed silently, fervently, he would never commit another sin in his entire life. Besides, he tried to convince himself, his silence might protect her as well as him.

Elizabeth slept fitfully that night. In her dreams, her face exploded in fierce flames, then the tent around her whooshed red-gold in the conflagration. They were trapped in it, trapped, all three of them.

It had been a cloudy, chill day at Oakham Manor, and they

had thought to make a little fire to warm themselves in the gay tent in the back gardens. Her father's sixth queen, Elizabeth's fourth stepmother, was regent while their royal father fought in France, and so was busy with her council, signing documents, writing letters. Elizabeth's loyal Kat Ashley was the only adult with them when she and Edward scampered away that day, and their older half sister Mary Tudor tagged along. They had thought a fire would feel good on their hands, so at Edward's bidding, Elizabeth had lit his gathered sticks with a lantern she'd snatched from the gardeners' shed.

She had been so grateful to be with her sister and brother again, though Mary did not care for her, and she seldom saw Edward. More than once under her father's different queens, "Young Bess" had been sent to the country for asking about her mother. Or worse, off and on, she'd been declared a bastard. This queen, the strictly Protestant Katherine Parr, was kind, but she had not approved of the surprise Elizabeth had given her for a gift.

It was a translation from the French—in her dreams, Elizabeth could see it yet—a book bound in blue cloth and adorned with silver thread, a twenty-five-page poem, *The Mirror of the Sinful Soul,* written by Marguerite of Navarre, sister of King Francis I of France. Queen Katherine had said it was unseemly reading matter for a young girl, for it talked of false lovers sharing beds and torment and pain.

A false lover, her poor Gil had suffered that, Elizabeth thought as she thrashed in her bed, half awake. She had wanted to protect him as she had once tried to protect her dear brother Edward that day of the pavilion fire. But the flames caught the light material and the tent went whoosh. . . .

They barely escaped, and it was not her fault, but she took the blame, when she so wanted to please the queen, but she had to protect Kat, the only real mother she'd ever known. . . .

Drenched with sweat, Elizabeth sat up in a cocoon of twisted covers. Across the way on a pallet, Rosie Radcliffe breathed regularly. Elizabeth was grateful she had not cried out in that dreadful dream.

She shoved her hair back into her nightcap and thought again of Gil's portrait of his Dorothea and of his vibrant painted outline of his queen. She could not bear to believe that Gil had anything to do with the fires or scorch marks, any more than she really believed that the boy Niles had been the target of the tent fire. But she was appalled that neither she nor the members of her Privy Plot Council had so much as thought of that—and Flora Minton had.

She slid to the edge of the high bed and dangled her feet until she found her woolen mules. Thrusting her feet into them, she wrapped herself in a coverlet over her night rail and went out into the hall, thoroughly startling her half-dozing yeoman night guard there. She wished it were Clifford, but the man had to sleep when she did.

"Nothing," she murmured and waved him back. She padded down the hall to Kat's door. Lifting the latch slowly, silently, she peeked in.

A single fat candle lit the room in what seemed brightness after the dim chamber and hall. Kat lay, breathing heavily, in the big bed, but Floris was not in her trundle one. She sat at the dressing table, combing her long, loose brown hair, apparently staring out the black window—which may have acted as her mirror—into the tent-packed privy garden. The wan candle flame threw the shadow of her moving silhouette upon the walls and ceiling.

"Floris." Elizabeth barely breathed her name.

The woman gasped to see the queen and came quickly toward the door. In her long white night trail, she looked pale as a ghost.

"Your Majesty, is all well?" she asked with a curtsy.

"I couldn't sleep, that's all. How is she?"

"Resting well, as you can see. The sweet Surrey air does us all good. It's—inspiring."

"Floris, a favor."

"I am yours to command. Anything, of course, for you or Kat."

"I valued your suggestion this morning about looking into the boy Niles, though he seems a bit of a cipher."

"Some servants seems such, but you never know."

Elizabeth pondered that a moment. Floris was deeper than she seemed, and the queen was certain she could use her services, not only to protect Kat, but to help them ferret out the fire demon— a term Floris herself had first used and Elizabeth had now adopted.

"With Lord Cecil and some close servants, hardly ciphers, as you say," the queen went on, "I am personally looking into the attack on my artists and their art. And hence on me."

Floris clasped her hands between her breasts. "You believe it is truly a threat to your own person? But I cannot think how."

"There is much to tell which I will discuss with you tomorrow, if you agree to help us."

"Of course, in any way, though I will not commit Lady Ashley's care to any other, a charge you gave me when you took me on, Your Majesty."

"And a charge I will hold you to."

"Who then is in this group? I would wager a guess on Mistress Milligrew, your Ned Topside and Jenks, perhaps your guard Clifford and your Lady Radcliffe, too."

"You are a godsend in more ways than one with your sharp wit and discerning eyes. Kat does not have nightmares, does she?"

"To tell true, she does, Your Majesty. Ironically, I have discovered it is something about a fire—and not the recent ones, for she's had them from the first day I came. Something in her, or your, past perhaps?"

"Yes, but I did not come to unburden myself to you of that. The night and lack of sound sleep do strange things. I shall see you on the morrow."

"Good night then. My own mother always used to say not the usual adage, 'Don't let the bedbugs bite you,' but 'Don't let your nightmares fright you.'"

"Did she? Is she still living then?"

"Dead. Long gone from here—from this life."

"But still living in your memories, no doubt."

"Oh, yes. Very, very much alive that way," Floris whispered, and closed the door quickly and quietly, even before the queen could.

Chapter the Eighth

"I HOPE YOU WILL ENJOY YOURSELF TODAY, BUT BE EVER vigilant for our covert purposes," the queen told her Privy Plot Council members as they met briefly in her large second-story room in the Riverside Inn at Mortlake.

Her trusted group did not include Gil or Dr. Dee this time. But Floris, who had brought Kat with her, was present for her second gathering, as the group had met the last four days to lay strategy. Blessedly, nothing else amiss had occurred at Nonsuch, but the queen hadn't posed outside or allowed anyone to camp outside the palace walls either.

"And," Cecil urged, "watch for anyone with a mirror, besides Dr. Dee, that is."

"But remember," the queen added, "Dr. Dee's wife is to be observed, since she supposedly lost that mirror I told you of."

May Day in Mortlake was as lovely as the other country weather. The queen had brought her closest courtiers and servants along and housed them in the inn, while most of the others of her entourage had tagged along on their own.

She had been tempted to order her three artists to remain at Nonsuch, but eager to see the celebration, they had made the six-mile journey. Lavina and Henry Heatherley had found housing in the village; Meg and Jenks were to discover exactly where and keep close to them. Gil was staying with the Dees. Kat and Floris were in the room next door to Elizabeth at the inn. Everyone was eager to see the torch-lit Maypole dancing and, as the queen had overheard it called, "Dr. Dee's fantastical reflections of fire."

When the other Privy Plot Council members had filed out, Cecil closed the door and lingered by it. Elizabeth motioned for him to join her at one of the diamond-paned windows set ajar to catch the breeze. The spacious chamber took most of the second story, with sweeping views in four directions: the river just outside to the north, the village green to the south, Dee's home to the west, and a charming thatched cottage, owned by the innkeepers next door, to the east.

Like everywhere the queen visited in her kingdom, her chamber, which in this instance had beds for herself, Rosie Radcliffe, and two other of her ladies, smelled of a hard scrubbing and fresh whitewash. The noontide sun on the Thames was so bright that reflections of the water danced in wavering patterns on the ceiling. The effect was mesmerizing but discomfiting, too: it reminded Elizabeth again of mirrors throwing light.

"Your Grace," Cecil said, "are you not going out to enjoy the early revelries? Those who didn't see you when we rode in are hoping for a glimpse of their queen."

"I can see that," she said, gazing out the window, beneath

which a country fair was blossoming. Standing beside the window, Cecil watched with her.

People were pouring into the village, and small groups waited below; occasionally, someone stooped to a child or pointed at the inn to a friend, all the while talking and nodding. Their happy voices carried easily to her ears. Arrayed in finer garb than the villagers, her retinue strolled the area too.

She was relieved that no one was pitching canvas tents, though hastily erected booths offering varied wares and food were sprouting everywhere. The owner of the inn, an elderly man named Simon Garver, who had once worked at Nonsuch, had told her that her presence had made the festivities larger than ever this year. In the springtimes when Dr. Dee had been abroad, old Garver the Carver, as she'd heard him called, had put up the Maypole, but without the display of the mirror.

Across the green from this lofty vantage point, they could see the Queen's Country Players erecting a scaffold of planks for an afternoon performance. Elizabeth was not surprised that they were here. Giles Chatam had claimed they'd gone from town to town in Surrey the last fortnight, but this was obviously the place to be today.

"There is quite a clear view of Dee's house from here," Cecil observed.

"Indeed. And before we join the others, what would you say to going one story higher?"

"But there's only the attic—ah, you mentioned that someone in that attic could have seen into Dee's garden, where Mistress Dee says she lost the mirror. And since only our male servants are upstairs for this night, and they should all be outside already . . ."

He followed her out into the hall. They could hear the voices of her ladies and yeomen guards downstairs in the common room, waiting to accompany their queen outside. The door to the attic stood ajar, and Cecil opened it farther. "Shall I go first, Your Grace? It seems bright enough up there in daylight that we don't need a lantern."

"Go ahead, since someone may yet be up there in half dress, though I warrant they are all outside. Despite the true reasons I have come to see this merrymaking with Dr. Dee's mirror, it will do everyone good to have a respite away from that lurking hunt park."

Cecil proceeded her up the creaking stairs and into the dusty-smelling garret with its crooked floor. He sneezed as they stood at the top of the staircase, surveying the slant-roofed, irregularly shaped single room, now cluttered with the pallets and gear of grooms, secretaries, and body servants. Jenks and Clifford were bedding up here, while Elizabeth had asked Ned to stay wherever his former troupe of players was this coming night.

"It's that one over there, I warrant," she said, and gathering her skirts closer, she walked toward the narrow window overlooking Dee's property. Each of the four thick-paned windows up here was set widely ajar. "Yes, a clear view of even the garden bench from here."

"And Mistress Dee is a comely woman," Cecil said.

"Rather like King David spying on Bathsheba at her bath, you mean? Hm, and was that why she was named *Bath*sheba?"

He merely shook his head at that lame pun. "We must inquire who had access to this room the day her mirror was taken."

"I already know. Simon Garver, our host here, mentioned that he had to turn out an acting troupe for a night to accommodate our men."

"Aha!" Cecil said, shifting to see the players' scaffold better. "Circumstantial, but—"

"There is more, Cecil. Floris told me privily the young woman—Katherine Dee—asked many questions about me when she was at Nonsuch. Evidently Katherine was taking a walk just after the Dees arrived while Floris was getting Kat some fresh air."

"Mistress Dee was walking near the hunt park or the tents?"

"Heading out of the palace, at least. Of course, Floris thought naught of it then. She also said that Mistress Dee asked Kat about me when she saw the two of them, and Kat told her that Elizabeth Tudor was not queen, but she hoped I would live long enough to rule someday."

Her voice broke. She crossed her arms over her breasts as if to hug herself.

"I know Lady Ashley's condition is a great burden to you."

"Much better now with Floris, at least. But I meant not to digress, because, my lord," she said, turning away from the window to face him, "our focus must more than ever be on our handsome, smooth-tongued itinerant actor—and on someone else, I regret to say."

"You think Mistress Dee could be in collusion with Giles Chatam about the missing mirror—and more? Despite her husband's skill with mirrors, you're thinking John Dee is clear of suspicion now? Might not the Dees be working together and Giles Chatam be a wild card?"

"I know only that John Dee seemed honestly shocked that his mirror was missing. Besides, Bathsheba did not resist King David's charms for long, did she? As for motives, Dr. Dee may want to be more trusted by his queen, and his wife may be desirous of making that happen. Perhaps one or both of them realized a strange murder would make me summon him. But she also craves attention for herself."

"From Giles Chatam?"

"From her husband, at least, she admitted that to me. And with that missing mirror, who knows what sort of plan she might haphazardly have concocted without her head-in-the-clouds husband's knowledge? She's very volatile, and as mentally dim as her husband is bright, I think."

"But, Your Grace, she was not at Nonsuch when Lavina's portrait caught fire."

"Or was she? It's only six miles, and John Dee gets so busy with his work he may not know where she is. And her maid, Sarah, told Jenks that Mistress Dee goes out and about a great deal."

"Then too," Cecil said, scratching his chin so hard his beard bounced, "if she's in league with Chatam, where was he then, eh? I can have Ned try to ask his uncle. Hell's gates, this is rather like picking at a loose thread on one's doublet, which then unravels in places you had not seen as damaged."

Elizabeth walked to another window. "Amazing, isn't it, my lord, that we are not even up to the top of Dr. Dee's pole, though I can see how he's rigged that big mirror from here."

Cecil shifted to her window, and they stared at the ingenious contraption Dee had fashioned to both keep the mirror attached to the top of the pole and maneuver it with a rope from below.

"If John Dee," Cecil said, "for some reason, had wanted to burn a tent with a mirror—and not so much as leave the ground, or perhaps even be too near the site—he could have."

"Granted. And when Kendale's tent burned, there was Dr. Dee, fortuitously just arrived at Nonsuch, available to be summoned and trusted by his queen. But if he was behind the fires, would he have helped us so much? I know only that we must consider as possible fire demons the Dees, Giles, and all three of my artists."

"You are resistant about Gil, of course. I know the boy has been a cause of yours, Your Grace."

She nodded, wishing that she didn't think of her own brother every time she beheld Gil. The facial resemblance wasn't extremely strong, and yet there was something that brought back Edward to her in the most disturbing way. Was it the fact that, however talented and glib Gil was, he lately seemed afraid of something or someone? Her brother, though beloved by their father, had feared him, and then, when Great Henry was dead, Edward had both adored and feared the powerful Seymour uncles who advised him. Was that the link between Gil and Edward in her mind? But who or what so frightened Gil?

"Is there anyone else you suspect in the slightest, Your Grace?" Cecil's voice broke into her agonizing.

"Only someone," she said, her tone sarcastic now, "who is powerful and hates me and who has been flaunting that hatred publicly in mirrors."

"That's no riddle. Your Catholic cousin, Queen Mary."

"I fear so," she said with a shudder. "She is like—like a ghost ever in the back of my mind, lurking there, wanting me dead and my throne for herself."

"But you don't think she could have sent someone to set the fires?"

"Sometimes, Cecil, I think so much that I don't know what I think. Let's go out to greet my people," she said and started toward the stairs. "Though this holiday has long had a reputation for being wild and free, I only pray the fire demon does not strike again."

Despite her anxiety, Elizabeth enjoyed the day. She always adored being among her people, and their love for her warmed her more than did the sun. Chatting with many, patting children on their heads, she strolled the impromptu fair with her ladies, examining fancies and fripperies at various booths, even buying a few things from awed vendors.

Traveling hawkers sang out the delights of feathered caps, scarves, and handkerchiefs on rickety tables or lying on bright baize cloths upon the grass. A fortune-teller's booth had appeared next to one selling succulent sausage pies. Ale and beer flowed freely from the inn. Piled ribbons and woolen thread made a pyramid of color near the players' stage, where the two lads who did the ladies' parts were giving a crude puppet show, crowded with children. And in the center of it all, the beribboned Maypole stood ready for the dancing and light show come eventide.

Elizabeth left her company behind, but for Clifford and Rosie, and walked around the makeshift stage while the crowd was entranced with the puppetry. As she had hoped, Giles Chatam was behind the scenes, sitting on a humpbacked trunk, reading what appeared to be lines for a play. He was mouthing his words, and occasionally gave a hint of a broader gesture.

When he did not look up, Clifford cleared his throat.

"Your Majesty, may I not fetch you a seat forthwith?" Giles asked, exploding to his feet to bow grandly and gracefully in that actors' style which could outdo her courtiers' any day.

"I am fine, Master Chatam."

"The real drama is later, of course," he explained, dazzling her with a broad smile that did not quite reach his startling blue eyes. "*A Surrey Spring Frolic* we've renamed it from an older piece set in France."

"I shall look forward to it. I regret my large entourage forced you and the players from your lofty chambers at the inn."

"We are glad to sleep elsewhere this night, Your Majesty. A haymow will do for the likes of us, of course, as, I must admit, I've slept far worse places than that. And far better, too, when fortune's star was in the ascendant for the Queen's Country Players."

"Isn't Ned with you? He said that for old time's sake, he'd like to spend some time with his uncle and you, of course."

"He was here but a moment ago. I can send him to you straightaway when he returns."

"That won't be necessary. So, how did you find the accommodations of the old Riverside Inn when you stayed there? I suppose the view is lovely from the top floor."

"Oh, it is—of the river," he said, smoothly masking what she read as surprise that she knew exactly where they'd stayed.

Other than asking him if he knew the Dees, she wasn't certain how to proceed. No good to tip off someone that she was watching him, especially an itinerant actor who no doubt had a hundred haunts to hide in.

"I'll be looking forward to the play," she said again, and went back to her circuit of the town green.

Floris emerged from the crowd with Kat, all smiles, trailing behind her. Her dear old friend had a tawdry red scarf tied on her sleeve, but Elizabeth could tell it pleased her mightily.

"Did Floris buy you that, my Kat?" Elizabeth asked.

"Oh, no, that young woman who has the same name I do gave it to me," Kat said, still fiddling with it.

"No, we did buy it," Floris whispered for the queen's ears alone. "She's referring to Katherine Dee. She's wandering around here somewhere, taking some food to her husband," she added with a quick glance over her shoulder. "Since you thought it best Kat and I not stay with her, I thought we'd just stop by to look around outside her place. And guess who was there at the door, personally inviting Mistress Dee to see their play about a spring frolic?"

Elizabeth's eyes widened. "Giles Chatam in the flesh?"

"In the flesh, Your Grace, a good way to put it," Floris said, rolling her eyes. "From what I saw, the two of them already knew each other, to put it politely."

"Did they see you?"

"Not me or Kat."

"Were they passionate?"

"More like familiar. And, I warrant, careful."

"Floris, you are priceless!" the queen told her with a nod. Though she was not used to Privy Plot Council members taking actions not earlier approved, this news was just what she needed. "I'll wager," Elizabeth added, "either Chatam took the mirror, or she gave it to him. Poor Dr. Dee."

"I'm afraid it only stirs the pot of possibilities," Floris said, shaking her head. "One thing I've learned over the years tending elderly folk like your dear Lady Ashley is patience."

"Of course, we'll jump to no conclusions. But we must watch young Mistress Dee and our clever actor even closer."

"I can help, and if Kat needs to go inside to rest, I'll get Meg Milligrew to be vigilant."

"I think," Kat said to Elizabeth, as if the lengthy whispered conversation between the queen and Floris had not occurred at all, "that Katherine is the same one your father married last. I don't want her to find out who set the fire in the tent, of course."

Elizabeth's insides plummeted. Kat was not only completely confused, but still tormented by the memories of the very fire years ago that haunted the queen.

"Kat, hush now," Floris said before the queen could speak. "That is just a bad dream you've had at night, and this is a lovely, sunny day."

As darkness descended, torches on poles set in a circle lit the village green, casting the May Day celebrations into flickering half shadows. But it seemed the festivities had only begun. The dancing around the Maypole was so lovely that the queen herself longed to join it. Songs from local musicians accompanied the interweaving of the dancers with their ribbons attached high on the pole, just below the mirror. She stayed among her people as she had all afternoon and evening, tapping her foot, clapping along.

Yet, like others in her band of observers, she kept close watch on those upon whom suspicion rested. John Dee was the easiest to watch, as he stood within the circle of dancers, next to the pole, working his rope attached to the mirror high above. He'd been fussing with it all day. So that her young artist was also in plain sight, Elizabeth had suggested that Dee literally show Gil the ropes. Ever in awe of Dr. Dee, Gil had been glad to act as his assistant.

Katherine Dee was doing nothing untoward; on the contrary, she had brought her mother-in-law to see the festivities in some sort of wheeled chair Dee must have rigged. More than once, Elizabeth had noted their maid, Sarah, darting hither and yon through the crowd. As for Giles Chatam, Ned was sticking tight to him, for both had managed to work their way into the dancing around the Maypole.

Meg had stayed close to Lavina Teerlinc all day, and told the queen that she had been making many swift sketches of these activities. Henry Heatherley, Jenks had said, spent his time drinking in the public room of the inn and boasting about who he was.

"It was worth a good laugh, Your Grace," Jenks had added, "that when the tosspot bragged of once working for Hans Holbein, none of these countrymen knew a fig about who Holbein was. 'Cept, that is, some rough-looking man with an I-tal-ian accent who'd been matching Heatherley bottle by bottle of wine. Heatherley may have gotten poor Will Kendale drunk the night he died, but no one can match the way HH himself downs that wine."

"Wait—you said a man with an Italian accent? And with enough coin to buy bottles of wine?" she mused. "Who did he say he is?"

"Didn't. And can't go question the I-tal-ian now, 'cause he's disappeared. He asked Heatherley questions about your artists, all of them, that's all I know."

"About Gil, too?"

"Oh, yes. Even about Will Kendale."

Elizabeth tried to tell herself that one stray Italian at this crowded English country fair meant naught, but she knew she should ask Heatherley and Gil about the man later.

Suddenly, she felt exhausted. Trailing two ladies and two guards, she went over to the entrance to the inn to sit on a long wooden bench the elderly Simon Garver and his dame had offered her earlier and now sat upon themselves.

"I believe I will take a respite," she told them. "No, do not rise, as I will sit with you. I find it quite agreeable to have the dancing and that magic mirror the center of attention for a while."

"Aye, Your Majesty," Simon said, and his wizened wife just smiled toothlessly and nodded. "I'm always glad to help set all this up, but it's John Dee's worry now."

"I understand the Maypole itself is yours."

"Oh, aye, one of the straightest trees e'er felled in these parts, much like the ones went for the interior walls at Nonsuch."

"I've always admired your fine work there."

Simon turned to his wife and bellowed, "Her Majesty admires the linenfolds at Nonsuch!" She nodded, and he turned back to the queen. "Had to have everything just right, your royal sire did, from the moment he tore down Cuddington."

"I regret the village's demise. Do any of the former inhabitants still live about these parts?"

"Some second generation over at Cheam, but most got dispersed, just lost. Why, it was twenty-seven years ago, you know." The queen and the old carver nearly shouted to hear each other over the noise of the revelers. "Even the Moorings got scattered and lost," he added.

"The Moorings?"

"The family what owned the manor house. Country gentry, relying on the bounty of the fields and local crafts to fill their coffers. Several fine timbered houses torn down too. The Mooring ancestors were buried in the Catholic church what got took down, but the family at the time was parents and two children. The breakup of the churches everywhere was one thing, but the entire village . . ." His voice trailed off as if he'd said too much.

Elizabeth recalled that Lord Arundel had told her he'd tried to talk the king out of razing the village, but Henry had refused to put his palace at the other end of the meadow. How greatly the local people, as well as the poor Moorings, must have resented the death—the murder—of Cuddington, the queen realized. She always took great care with people's feelings toward her, but her father had more than once let those be damned.

Though Elizabeth had been long schooled never to doubt or criticize King Henry VIII, she felt ashamed of his acts to build Nonsuch. "I regret the demise of the village," she repeated, more to her herself than the Garvers, "especially if it was anything like charming Mortlake. How old were the Mooring children then?" she inquired, remembering how devastated she had been to be sent away from court more than once as a child. She could not fathom losing not only her place in a home, but the entire home itself.

"Glenda!" old Simon shouted at his wife, who finally stopped smiling and nodding. "How old were the Mooring heirs when Cuddington went down? *How old?*"

"Not ten," she yelled, her voice as crackly as old paper. "Maybe the boy six, the girl eight. Never saw such white-yellow hair, like little angels! Died, I think."

"Both of them died?" Elizabeth gasped.

"Best left alone," Simon answered for his wife. "Oh, lookie there! John's got the mirror all rigged to get that firelight clear from Richmond Hill."

At least, the queen thought, there were no bonfires here. She rose to her feet, awed by the flash of flame that seemed to light the top of the Maypole, then reflect itself in a bright beam through the dark night. The crowd noise hushed, then became a huge "Ahhh!" as if from one throat. Next to Dr. Dee, Elizabeth could see that Gil was entranced, jumping up and down and clapping.

The dancers and musicians stopped as Dee worked his rope to tilt the mirror. From over two miles distant, it caught reflections of the bonfire on Richmond Hill and sent back the light in short bursts of flashes and pauses. Sometimes the glow from afar seemed to dwell within the big mirror itself and other times to leap from it to illumine the night. When Dee evidently moved the rope amiss, the beam would slash across thatched roofs, and once, even through the crowd.

The light show went on for nearly an hour until everyone's neck was ready to break from looking upward. Elizabeth had forced herself to scan the crowd rather than just watch these signals she knew Dr. Dee would discuss with her later, for he hoped to use the sun's light to signal from ship to ship in England's meager navy. But now she saw something below just as compelling as the events above.

Giles Chatam was standing next to Katherine Dee, who had moved several steps away from her mother-in-law's chair. And Floris, holding on to Kat's hand, stood watching, perhaps even overhearing the two young people, though if they were speaking, it was circumspectly, out of the sides of their mouths.

When Katherine finally wheeled the old woman closer to John Dee and Giles went the other way with Ned trailing him, Elizabeth hurried to join Floris and Kat. "Could you hear what they were saying?" she asked Floris.

"He told her that her husband might be good with reflected light, but he could ignite a blaze in her to keep them both hotter than fire."

Elizabeth nodded grimly. It sounded indeed like the sort of ornate speech that smooth-tongued actor would give. At least they had apparently not yet cuckolded Dr. Dee. But they knew each other, and so one or both of them could have committed mayhem with that supposedly stolen mirror. But exactly who and why?

Just to make their queen need the services of Dr. Dee or Giles and his players? Perhaps he—or Katherine, since she was on site that morning—had randomly selected a tent to ignite. When Lavina's at the edge of the encampment did not catch fire, the arsonist tried to burn the next tent and succeeded. No, it could not be at random, because Kendale's tent was tied shut from the outside. Or was that act disrelated to the fire?

"In case Kat is tired," Elizabeth told Floris, "there's a bench by the inn with the old couple who owns the place."

"Oh, no need," Floris said, squinting at the Garvers and shading her eyes even though the flashes of light hardly hit her here. "You're not tired, are you, Lady Ashley? If so, I can take you inside to bed."

"I never felt better," Kat declared, however fragile and feeble she looked.

Despite all the chaos and Elizabeth's fears, that was the best thing she had heard all day.

Notwithstanding her exhaustion, the queen could not sleep again that night. Too many people were crammed together at this inn. She kept drifting in and out of dreams, hearing creaking boards, no doubt one of the men upstairs getting up or shifting in his sleep. Someone somewhere was snoring in a muffled roar. And it was strangely dusty in this cleaned and painted chamber; the acrid scent scratched at her throat. Again as she pondered old Simon Garver's sad story of Cuddington, she heard his deaf wife's crackling voice, speaking of dead children.

Her mind had been in whirls, trying to think through who could be behind the fires at Nonsuch. It could not be Dr. Dee, not her Gil. And yet, how to prove it was someone else? The sweet spring sun had now become an enemy. She should pray for cloudy days to keep the killer at bay, should return her retinue to London, yet she could not bear to leave until she caught her deadly prey.

Her eyes began to sting and water. She rolled over again and stared into the gray, stale air in the room. Had fog or mist crept in clear up here? As she had earlier in the day, she marveled at the way the reflected light on the Thames threw flickering patterns on the ceiling. A full moon must have risen, which acted as the sun had earlier, but these colors were not silver or even pale gold. They were hot hues, something Gil would paint. And it was so bright out the windows of this room, suddenly even bright inside.

Smoke. It was thickening smoke!

She sat straight up in bed, her heart pounding. Flames! Flames close outside, crackling and throwing deadly light through the eastern windows. Had the thatched roof caught fire? What if the doors were locked, what if her people perished with her?

"Fire!" she screamed. "Fire!"

Chapter the Ninth

 ELIZABETH LEAPED FROM HER BED AND WENT PARTWAY to the window. The Garvers' thatch-roofed cottage next door was crowned with crackling flames. It took her a moment to realize that the inn was not afire—unless it burned too.

As her women woke, some hacked at the smoke, and several screamed.

"Listen to me!" the queen shouted, coughing herself. "Stop to take nothing with you. Rosie, go next door and wake Kat and Floris and see they get downstairs. Anne, run to the attic steps and scream the men awake. And tell them to come with me."

"To where?"

"Just see that everyone gets out! I'm going ahead."

Lest she found fire awaiting her downstairs, Elizabeth grabbed the sheet from her bed and dumped the two closest ewers of wash water to soak it. She wrapped it around her like a shroud from shoulders to knees and ran barefoot into the hall.

"Thank God!" she cried when she realized the smoke was

lighter here. The yeoman who should have been at her door wasn't there.

"I told the guard to go up and rouse the men!" Floris cried, coughing, as she led Kat from the room next door. The old woman looked frenzied, like a horse caught in a stables fire. She pulled back and cried, rolling her eyes. Floris could barely control her. Taking Kat between them, Floris and Elizabeth led her toward the staircase and helped her down it as heavy-footed men thundered behind, shouting to each other.

Blessedly, there was no fire downstairs but smoldering embers in the hearth of the common room. Yet Kat was still panicked, gasping for air and shrieking so that Elizabeth feared she'd collapse. "Kat, Kat, it's all right!"

"Your father and Queen Katherine will send me away, send me to the Tower for this."

"No, no, they won't!" Elizabeth promised, gripping both her shoulders to make the distraught woman look straight at her. "I'll tell them it was my fault. They won't send you away. I won't lose you."

"But you can't! They'll banish you again!"

"Floris," the queen cried, "you must see to her and keep her calm. I must go outside to help—to see . . ."

Pushing Kat into Floris's arms, she fled outside.

Though she was sweating from fear and exertion, the cold sheet made her chill and clammy. But, wearing just her night rail under it, she kept it wrapped around her.

The moment she was out the door of the inn, she saw that the Garvers' cottage flamed like a giant torch. Its thatched roof had evidently caught, and the flames were working downward.

"Are they out? Are they out?" she screamed as she ran to her men, who stood helpless amid the growing crowd of villagers watching the blaze.

Jenks dodged falling cinders and pieces of burning thatch to run to the wooden front door and pound on it with both fists. "Garvers! Master Simon! Fire! Fire!"

Someone put a heavy cloak around Elizabeth's shoulders— Robin. She nodded, but turned immediately back to the crisis.

"Your Grace," Jenks shouted through the roiling smoke, "the door latch is tied to the hinges with rope. It won't lift."

"Is it hot?" she shouted.

"Not very."

"Then the lower floor might not be in flames yet. Robin, have the men get the Maypole and knock the door in!"

Elizabeth moved slightly to the side. Even from here, in the blinding light and the wreaths of smoke, she could see the window shutters were also tied shut with rope. For the first time since this new terror began, she thought not only of her and her people's survival, but of the riddle of the fire mirror.

This blaze had been ignited at night; it could not have been started by reflected sun from a mirror, not even from Dee's signal mirror. That had been removed from the pole after it was taken down hours ago. But the marks of the mirror murderer were here: the flames had started on the roof after the escape route was tied closed.

She both sweated and shivered. "Jenks, get back from there!" she shouted as another clump of fiery thatch barely missed him.

To lift and move the massive pole, Robin worked with yeomen guards, villagers, and actors. She saw Cecil and Gil at the very back of it as they rushed toward the burning house. Dr. Dee appeared in the crowd with a disheveled Katherine at his side. She stood among the queen's women, the goodwives and children of Mortlake, her eyes wide but streaming silent tears. Elizabeth noted she was one of the few completely dressed and shod.

As if it were a Roman battering ram, the Maypole took down the front door. Everyone's gaze was fixed upon the opening, which now belched smoke. Inside, they could glimpse burning timbers falling from the cottage ceiling. The house was collapsing from within. The Garvers were doomed, she thought. No one could be alive in there.

She turned to see if Gil was still at the back of the pole. He was, but she glimpsed just behind him a child who must have bolted from his mother's care.

The small boy darted out of the crowd and ran headlong away. Someone else terrified of the fire, she thought. Even as the men moved the Maypole and her guards kept everyone back from the inferno, she stepped from the crowd to watch the boy.

Someone should comfort him, she thought, and wondered where his mother was. Was he terrified of the fire, like poor Kat? She must go inside to comfort her. But why did the child run toward the river and not to one of the houses here? Or could he merely have gone around to the other side of the burning cottage, which, like the Garvers' inn, backed up to the river?

"Clifford," she shouted to her yeoman guard, "come with me. There's naught that can be done to pull the Garvers out if they don't walk out themselves." She gestured for him to join her, and he and Jenks, who soon pounded along behind them, ran with her toward the Thames. The dewy grass was cold against her bare feet, but the dust of the river path felt warmer.

"You aren't thinking we can get river water on that fire somehow, Your Grace?" Jenks cried.

"I fear not. I saw a small boy run this way. He looked so desperate. I don't want him to run half crazed into the river."

"A boy running?" Clifford asked, his breathing ragged. "Short, kind of squat, all in brown?"

"You saw him too?"

"At least someone like that. But not tonight. It was in the hunt park at Nonsuch, in the distance when you sent me there after your portrait went up in flames."

" 'S blood, man, why didn't you tell me?"

"Just a child, Your Grace, and too far in the distance. The thing was, when he started to cross an open patch of meadow where the deer were feeding, he just disappeared—and I was looking for bigger game."

Silent now, they scanned the black width of the Thames, gilded by the house fire. Nothing. No sounds on the path, no one as far as they could see.

"Could he have run toward Dee's place or into the inn?" Clifford asked. "Your Grace, there's just no one here."

"I hardly imagined him—nor did you. We must go back and tell the mothers to account for their sons, so—"

A cheer went up from the green. They tore back around the inn toward the cottage. Bent over, blackened, his clothes and hair burned away, Simon Garver pulled his prone, unconscious wife from the roiling smoke into the yard, where others rushed to help them.

"At least," Elizabeth cried, "there is something good which came from this tragedy. Jenks, ride at once to fetch my physician from Nonsuch!"

Everything happened so fast the rest of that night. Dame Garver died of smoke in her lungs. Simon was burned badly on his limbs and kept coughing up black bile, even as the royal physician tried to tend him.

"Dr. Forrest says old Simon will live," Meg, poking her head in the door, reported to Elizabeth as the queen and Floris sat next to Kat's bed at the inn. Though Meg had dosed Kat with a powerful sleeping potion, she kept her voice low too. "But the doctor ran out of aloe, so I'll be sending back some of my alkanet-and-eglantine salve from Nonsuch for the old man."

"The question is," the queen said, whispering too, "since the method of starting this fire is obviously different from those at Nonsuch, was it set by the same arsonist-murderer?" She longed to put her head in her hands and sob, but she sat erect, becoming angrier by the moment. The entire village smelled of smoke and death.

"Your Majesty," Floris whispered, "I can care for Lady Ashley if you wish to rest. Maybe you should drink some of that powerful sleeping stuff—"

"Poppy-and-primrose cordial," Meg put in.

"I don't want to sleep," Elizabeth insisted, glancing toward the golden glow of dawn out the eastern window. "I have much to do this morning."

"Will we be heading back, or staying here to look into this fire, too?" Floris asked as Meg went on her way.

"I mean to survey the fire scene, but this large an entourage cannot remain at Mortlake, not long anyway." Her thoughts were slowing; she felt she was slogging through mental mud.

"Your Majesty," Floris said, "may I be so bold as to ask what passed between you and Lady Ashley last night about the fire she fears? Were you there then, at that other fire long past?"

Elizabeth leaned her head on the back of her chair and closed her eyes. "I was—nearly twenty years ago."

"If you would trust me enough to tell of it, I might be able to help Lady Ashley more when she carries on so."

"How things from the past can haunt us, Floris."

"Yes. Yes, I know."

"Like the fire tonight, it came at such a happy time. Late in his reign, King Henry had been triumphant in a French war and was coming home. Queen Katherine Parr had brought all three of his children together as a family to wait for him at Oakham Manor, the Countess of Rutland's fine home. The previous years I'd been banished from court, and I was delirious with joy to be with my brother again. I was but thirteen."

"And were you not glad to see your royal sister?" Floris asked when Elizabeth paused.

"The princess Mary never cared for me—the problem with our mothers and our different faiths—but I was glad to be with her. Even though I was still on edge from something I had done to annoy my stepmother, we were playing one afternoon in a bright pavilion—Edward, the male and heir, ever ordering his sisters about," she added with a tight smile as the scene took on detail and color before her. "He commanded that we build a fire to keep warm, and I fetched a lantern. Kat was the only adult with us for some reason. We could see the windows of the manor, where the queen met with her advisers."

"And somehow the tent caught fire?"

"Not somehow. It was Kat's fault, for she was appalled we had lit a small fire in the pavilion. She tried to snuff out the flames but only spread them. The tent became so quickly engulfed that we almost didn't get out."

"A tent fire that caught quickly, like the other day."

"Yes. It brought everything back."

"So Kat took the blame?"

"No. Only Mary and I saw who really was at fault, and Edward, all sooty, had fled inside to change his clothes."

"Like that running boy you told me of this evening—the ghost."

"Don't say that!" Elizabeth ordered, opening her eyes and glaring at Floris. "I saw that boy, and my yeoman Clifford also saw him, the day Lavina's portrait burned. He's a link somehow, and we must find him, but he is not a ghost."

"Yes, of course. But a child could not be behind these current fires, could he? So Kat was blamed for that early fire and has never gotten over it."

"Not so," Elizabeth said, slumping at last to put her head in her hands with her elbows propped on her knees. "Like now, I could not bear to lose her, the only mother I had ever known. And so, though I had been banished before and could not bear to be again, I said I'd spread the fire. For I knew Kat would be sent away for good, perhaps imprisoned, if she took the blame. Only my half sister Mary knew what I'd done, but she did not gainsay my lie, for she was glad to have me gone again."

"So poor Lady Ashley blamed herself for starting the fire and sending you back into exile."

"She was as relieved as I that we were not separated. I regret my lie, but not its intent or result."

"I understand, Your Majesty. Truly, I do."

———

When the sun rose above the housetops, the queen, Cecil, Dr. Dee, and Jenks examined the ruins of the Garvers' cottage. Town-folk had already reappeared to gawk, standing silently around the smoking pile. Elizabeth scanned the crowd for children. Quite a few had gathered, but none of them, she was quite sure, was the boy she had pursued last night.

Lavina Teerlinc was in the front row, sketching, and Henry Heatherley too, who looked as if he'd been through the mill. Pasty-faced and disheveled, whatever his state from swilling bottles of his favorite Bordeaux the previous night, he had pulled himself out of bed for this. He looked both curious, the queen thought, and angry. Occasionally, she overheard snatches of whispers as onlookers pointed to places on the green or the edges of other roofs where burning thatch had floated to darken but not ignite a spot.

"Thank God," Cecil said, shaking his head, "that there was no wind to fan sparks on other roofs."

"Mere sparks would probably not ignite good thatch," Dr. Dee put in, gesturing toward the roof of the inn as well as the burned ruins. "Densely packed, thatch is more likely to smolder than ignite, unless something like a strong-burning torch is put directly to it, or a flaming roof actually abuts another. It's one reason, Your Majesty, that London's roofs should be converted from thatch and shake shingles to tiles. Packed in as the city dwellings are, if one goes, many could."

She shuddered but merely nodded. For once, no one else so much as looked surprised at one of Dee's bits of random knowledge or far-thinking theories. Everyone knew they needed to keep to the task at hand.

"You did all note last night," Elizabeth said, "that, like the tent fire, the blaze started high and spread lower?"

"But," Cecil said, "it certainly wasn't the sun in a mirror that began it this time. Dr. Dee's mirror and the pole were down by then, and a bonfire two miles away could hardly start a fire through reflection as the sun's rays can."

"Indeed it could not!" Dee said. "By the way, Simon doesn't recall a thing that happened before the heat awoke him," he added hastily, as if to shift the subject. The old man was being nursed at Dee's house rather than at the crowded inn while plans were being made for his wife's burial in the graveyard next to Mortlake Church. "The old man said," Dee went on, "he thought he'd fallen asleep outside, and the blaze of the sun had awakened him—and then he thought he'd died and gone to hell."

They were all silent for a moment before the queen said, "I noted something significant from the window at the inn this morning. Though the torches for the Maypole dance were extinguished last night, most were left in their sconces—all but one, there, between the inn and the burned cottage."

"Indeed," Cecil said, craning his neck, "all the others seem yet to be in place. I suppose that one could have been taken during the fire, but it was hardly needed, since the flames illumined everything so brightly. Shall we theorize that someone relit and threw that missing torch onto Garver's thatched roof to start the fire?"

"If so," Elizabeth said, "the evidence has probably been consumed too—as have the ropes which tied the shutters over the windows."

"And tied the door shut," Jenks said, gesturing toward the big oak door the Maypole had battered down last night.

Elizabeth looked over at it, charred, broken amid the ruins. The ropes which Jenks had said bound latch to hinge were also naught but ash.

"Jenks," she said as a new possibility struck her, "even in the frenzy, do you recall if the ropes at the front door were laced in any particular way? From a distance, I couldn't clearly see the ones holding the shutters closed."

Everyone stopped and looked at the door, then back at Jenks. "Just wrapped haphazardly, I think," the big man said, closing his eyes tightly as if trying to picture it again. "But there might have been a sort of flat bow this time, too."

"Might have been . . . ," the queen repeated. "It's not just that you are picturing the lacings from Kendale's tent?"

"I don't think so, Your Grace, but it all went so fast that I'm not sure."

"About those ropes, Your Majesty," Dee said. "I surmise they were cut from the one by which I moved the mirror. After the Maypole came down last night, I left it behind, and I see it's missing this morning. Yet that fact doesn't point to any one person," he said, almost defensively.

Elizabeth wondered if her brilliant philosopher had finally inferred that he too—and his wife—could be under suspicion.

"But note," Dee went on, walking away from the ruins toward a pole with a sconce which still held a torch, "that the handle for this intact torch has a leather casing. And over here," he went on, striding to the pole with its torch missing, "this one has been pulled out with its leather holder. As you recall, Will Kendale's leather jerkin made it through the first fire, so we might assume we can locate at least the leather remnant of the death torch—if that is what began the conflagration."

"So you have been out already this morning, examining these torches?" Elizabeth asked Dr. Dee.

"I have."

She decided not to press him publicly on it, but wondered why he hadn't spoken of it sooner, especially when they discussed the torch. Though some of the embers still seethed, she and the others poked among the ruins with tree branches, occasionally turning up recognizable pieces of household goods.

"And what is this?" the queen asked, pointing to a diamond-shaped lattice which had fallen away from the blaze and was barely burned.

"Hm," Dee said, stroking his beard. "Perhaps Dame Garver's rose trellis."

"It's tall," the queen observed. "Even though the cottage roof was not far off the ground, where a torch could have been thrown atop it, perhaps the fire setter knew that good thatch, as Dr. Dee said, doesn't catch easily. So he climbed this trellis with the torch to start the fire in several places."

"Climbed like a tree in the hunt park," Cecil mused. "Yes, that's very possible, though this lattice wouldn't hold most men."

Elizabeth shivered. That boy running last night and in the hunt park . . . That boy who had simply disappeared—twice. But he couldn't have climbed a tree to escape Clifford's pursuit, for Clifford had followed him in an open meadow. She'd like to see the very spot herself.

"You'll have to ask Gil about tree climbers, Your Grace," Cecil added. "After all, he used to scale trees and buildings to get in windows."

"Since he broke his leg, he doesn't climb anymore," she insisted. "He even limps sometimes."

"Chatam pretended to limp in that play yesterday, and he's hale and hearty," Dee said quietly, glancing toward the actor, who had evidently just joined the crowd watching them.

Elizabeth felt doubly sick. She recalled that Gil had jumped up and down in excitement at Dee's fire mirror last night, and he'd hustled about fetching things for him earlier. Perhaps Gil was putting on a show about that leg. She'd best hie herself back to Nonsuch and set up a series of examinations there. And, again, she must include Gil.

"Look!" John Dee cried, and freed from the ashes a small leather handle that looked as if it had been tanned or petrified. "What did I say! Leather came through here, just as in the tent fire at Nonsuch. A different method was used to ignite this blaze, I surmise, but the very same murderer set this fire."

Two hours later, before her entourage headed back to Nonsuch, Elizabeth took Meg with her to visit Simon Garver. The Dees had made a bed for him on the first floor in their solar, where Dr. Dee had rigged a covering for modesty. It did not quite touch his burned skin, but was a tent of sorts over his naked, burned legs and arms. Though Elizabeth could tell he was in pain, he looked solemn and stoic as she stood over him.

"Near forty years wed," he whispered as Katherine Dee, who evidently was tending him personally, left the room. Just Meg stood with the queen, though Elizabeth didn't doubt that the Dees might be hovering outside.

"I am so sorry, Master Garver. I pray you will hold to the happy memories of your beloved helpmeet while you are healing at least your body if not your heart."

His eyes misted. "I'd like to live long enough—to carve her an oaken grave marker." He spoke brokenly, through puffy, blistered lips. "Wonder how long it would last—for both of us there—in the churchyard."

"Your work will be a lasting monument to you at Nonsuch."

"Least the inn didn't catch too."

"Simon Garver, I will be sending extra soothing salves and potions from my privy herbalist here, Mistress Milligrew. I will have prayers offered for you and personally keep in touch with the Dees to see you are being well tended, for which I am grateful to Mistress Dee."

"Aye, Your Majesty. A blessing to me, that she is."

She only hoped Garver's observation was true. But without accusing the Dees, how—and to where—could she have him moved?

"Never had children," the old man said, and began to cough. "Her only regret, she said—"

"Rest now. Katherine!" the queen called. Almost immediately, Mistress Dee came in with a drink in a cup to tilt to the old man's lips.

Elizabeth scolded herself for ever doubting the Dees, even Katherine. Didn't the young woman care well for her old mother-in-law and want her husband's approval and love? Didn't she nurse this old friend of her husband's with care and concern? Elizabeth lightly squeezed the young woman's shoulder as she left the room.

Dr. Dee was waiting by the front door with a book in his arms.

"I thought you might wish to take my mirror book with you, Your Grace, to peruse it in your own good time."

"Thank you, Dr. Dee," she said, taking it from him. "I shall do so, as I am getting desperate for any clues which will lead to this fire murderer."

"You know, Your Majesty, the Catholic Church—before your father led his realm to a better way—opposed all experiments with mirrors."

"Do not worry that I shall insist you stop your trials with them. But why were they once so feared?"

"The old belief in demon possession," he explained, his voice a mere whisper, though Meg had gone outside to await the queen in the yard. "Some thought a mirror's reflection could trigger a trancelike state. The gazer's attention was captured, blinded, turned inward—narcissistic behavior, in other words. And then a demon could snatch the soul."

"It is superstition that we of this enlightened age must never fear."

"But there is one thing I've especially noted for you in that volume," he added, pointing to a piece of red ribbon which protruded from the pages. "In light of what I told you about Queen Mary of Scots peering in mirrors and implying she wants your throne, I thought it might be of some interest, however arcane it seems. As you know, she's insisted that the symbol of England— the lion rampant—be quartered in her coat of arms when she has no right to that."

"That was reported to me several years ago. I believe she delights in tormenting me from afar. For now, I shall take the high road and merely keep an eye on her. Then, if she oversteps . . . but what is the information at this place you've marked?"

"It tells of the old legend, Your Majesty, that only a virgin holding a mirror is able to tame a unicorn. As you know, the unicorn is the symbol of Scotland as the lion is that of England."

"But what of that old tale? The widowed Queen Mary is no virgin, and since I am, I should be the one who tames the unicorn that is Scotland, not the other way around. But tell me straight what you are thinking, Dr. Dee, for you are speaking in riddles."

"Ah, there is a riddle which begins this book, Your Majesty, one about a mirror. But here is what I am theorizing. I had heard, though it made no sense to me before, that Queen Mary had lately ordered a huge painting for her throne room which depicts a lion bowing before the unicorn, tamed by a mirror in possession of, not a virgin, but that same triumphant unicorn."

Her heart pounding, the queen clutched the book to her. She was surprised how her voice trembled. "The insult in that painting aside, you mean, then, that she is fascinated by mirrors?"

"I do."

"And it might amuse her to send someone to torment me with mirrors somehow—as she tries to do from afar."

"We must not lose sight of the fact she is an avowed enemy, Your Majesty, however much she tries to cloak that behind her letters and Lord Maitland, whom you and Secretary Cecil evidently trust."

"Dr. Dee, I thank you for your wise counsel. As for my royal cousin, I shall continue to keep my eyes wide open. In dealing with Queen Mary, it is as the Bible says: 'Now we see through a mirror darkly but then face to face.' I shall be ever watchful and tread carefully."

But as she turned to leave, holding the big book, the queen caught her toe on the Dees' threshold stone and would have tripped had not Meg Milligrew darted close to catch her.

OTHER THAN HER GUARD CLIFFORD, WHO STOOD INSIDE the doors of her council chamber, Elizabeth faced her artist Henry Heatherley alone. Her entourage had been back at Nonsuch for barely an hour, but she intended to waste no time in pursuit of a villain. Nor were Giles Chatam and Katherine Dee off the hook, though Ned Topside had covertly searched the actor's possessions for the missing mirror and found only two old ones, which were unbreakable polished steel.

"Which, of course," Ned had said, with a dramatic roll of his fine green eyes, "doesn't mean the rogue didn't hide the stolen mirror or give it back to Mistress Dee for safekeeping. Or that the sun's rays concentrated on a plain polished-steel mirror could not ignite a fire as well as a concave one."

"You are my master player but not my philosopher," the queen had replied to Ned. "Best you only gather evidence and leave the theorizing to the likes of Dr. Dee and me. But I do intend to question that tosspot Heatherley soon."

And soon was now. Though the queen had meant to present a calm demeanor to her artist, the hot patch of late-afternoon sun streaming in the window on her skirts made her so nervous that she shifted into the shade of the table. She saw that her not having greeted him when he entered had disconcerted him even more.

"Your Majesty," Heatherley said as he straightened from his bow, "dare I hope you have summoned me to continue your portrait? So much time has passed since you first invited me to that honorable task, yet I have been working on it every moment I could spare."

"Every moment you could spare from drinking with Will Kendale the night he died and with anyone else in the Mortlake tavern last night?" she demanded. His countenance fell, but he swiftly cloaked his surprise at her words and tone.

"If I may reply to your implication that I waste my time and talents by spending too much time drinking, Your Majesty."

"Please do, Master Heatherley."

"Though I sometimes relish the pleasures of life, I do not believe my efforts have been unprofitable," he said, his voice sounding both hurt and haughty. "You will be pleased to know that I have successfully covered the scorch marks on your portrait and have much improved it since. Indeed, it is nearly completed, so I have brought it with me for your perusal. It is just outside."

"I shall see it later. You must know, I take a care about foreign spies lurking near my person and my people. So what can you tell me about the Italian man who was drinking at the Mortlake Inn with you last night?"

"Oh, him," he said, looking much relieved at her shift of topics. "He said his name wasn't of import, but I thought him a man of goodly learning and discernment."

"Because?"

"Because he was fascinated by the artists of our nation, Your Majesty, most impressed by my work, first under Holbein and now for you."

"Was he an artist himself then?"

"A patron of the arts, who heard there was a festival and came to see it."

"Then spent his time in a taproom, drinking."

"He was much disappointed in the rustic nature of the displays, a far cry, evidently, from what passes in his homeland. Oh, yes, his knowledge of wines was discerning too."

"And that rustic inn had in its cellars the Italian wines he favors?"

"Your Majesty, he favors drinking exactly what I like, French Bordeaux, which I had brought along myself. But he asked about your artists, and I told him of Will's tragic demise, not that he'd heard of him," he said with a sharp sniff as he tugged down the cuffs of his sleeves.

"He asked about your work and anyone else's?"

"Oh, indeed, Mistress Teerlinc's—though I told him you thought she painted faces too puffy and pasty, even a perfect face like yours."

"Forget the flattery, Master Heatherley. And Gil Sharpe? Did this nameless Italian patron ask about him, too?"

"He was interested that the lad had been sent to study at Urbino."

"So you told the man that Gil had been to Urbino?"

Heatherley looked blank for a moment. He frowned. She wondered how much of this was being resurrected through the haze of too much wine, or whether he was making it up as he went.

"Why, I'm not certain about that," he admitted, shaking his head. "Perhaps someone else had told him that, because I believe I said only that the lad had been to Italy but not where. The point is, Your Majesty, I have brought my beautiful portrait of you near to its conclusion. And since I have surmised that the need is pressing for a fine painting to be copied and sent throughout your realm, mine is ready to convey your power and presence to all. May I not fetch it in then?"

She stared the man down, wishing she could see inside his soul. Could his burning ambition have made him decide to eliminate his rivals, and so to attack either their portraits or their lives? Though she had seen no artist but Gil in the hunt park near the time the portraits were marred, Heatherley could have put scorch marks on his own work to draw sympathy, while he could easily repair that damage. Perhaps he thought it would allow him to leapfrog the others in the competition she had decreed. But would he go so far as to burn the Garvers' cottage just to confuse her? How unstable did this man become when he was drunk?

"I will see the portrait," she said.

He bustled to the door and brought it in, turning it to her with a flourish.

It was quite good, though he'd managed to make her look stiff and ponderous. Or perhaps it was simply that his style— Holbein's style—had an exacting yet flat quality compared to the suggestion of depth and movement in Gil's work.

"I know," Heatherley said, "you hate to pose, Your Majesty, and selecting this as the official portrait will eliminate the need for more of that. Once in your possession, this work will be safe from secret slashing or public burning by some demented person who wants to ruin all our efforts."

"Do the other artists know," she said, ignoring his clever ultimatum, "that you have worked on this not from life but from memory to outpace them?"

"Not yet, but whatever you decide—"

"Exactly. Then did you tell Will Kendale the night he died that you intended to race forward with your work?"

He looked instantly distraught again. "Why would I tell him or anyone, if I wanted to surprise them and you, Your Majesty?"

"Perhaps because you are too often in your cups, Master Heatherley, so that you brag and say too much and hardly recall what. And if you did tell Kendale, would he have been angry or threatened to tell me—or said he'd like to set your work afire or some such thing which made you very angry while you were very drunk?"

"Your Majesty," he said, gasping in a great breath on the word *"Your."* "You read in far too much. I only know, as an artist, I must protect my work at all costs—but never that way. Never."

"Best guard that portrait until I see the completed works from Lavina and Gil Sharpe," she told him, rapping her knuckles on the tabletop. "At that time I will judge which one I prefer. And I shall hope by then also to answer who is the one who shall be arrested and tried for Kendale's death, and perhaps for Mistress Garver's in Mortlake, too. On second thought, Master Heatherley, best guard yourself as well as your work, lest the mysterious fire demon put you in his sights."

———

Standing at his tall writing desk in his laboratory, John Dee hunched over the proposal he had written for his queen. Now that she'd seen his Maypole mirror work, surely she would listen to reason about testing signal mirrors on naval vessels. Now if only he had some excuse to ride to Nonsuch to share this with her. He'd told his Katherine that. She'd said he should simply go and volunteer to help with the queen's investigation into the arsonist's identity, but he'd told her he'd best not, with nothing new to offer.

"John!" He heard Katherine's excited but distant voice. She sounded happy, not alarmed, so he kept working. "John, guess what I found? You won't believe it!"

Does she want to wake poor, burned old Simon? Dee fretted. She'd said she would go mad if she didn't get out for a few moments, so she'd gone for a short walk. The queen's Dr. Forrest was resting, and Sarah was keeping an eye on the injured man. Perhaps Katherine has come across some patch of strawberries, Dee thought, or she's turned up some coins someone dropped at the fair yesterday on the green, something silly but sweet.

Dee stayed bent over his work, hastily putting the final touches on the diagram below the written section. It might take Katherine a minute to find him, a few more moments of peace. . . .

"There you are!" she sang out, standing in the door with her hands behind her back. "You will never guess what I found!"

"I don't like guessing games, my dear."

"You should! That's what you do all the time, guess at some wild theory, then set about to prove it," she said, pouting prettily, he must admit.

"All right, then," he said, straightening behind his drawing board, "what is it?"

"Look!" she cried, and held the missing mirror out toward him. "I couldn't believe it!"

"You had misplaced it in the house all this time?" he cried, rushing to her.

"No, I was walking toward the fields to get some sun and fresh air, and stumbled on it, hidden in a patch of violets, mirror side up so it caught my eye. I warrant whoever came over the wall to take it decided not to be caught with it and simply tossed or dropped it."

He took it tenderly in his hands. "Thank God, it did not break," he whispered, turning the mirror over to check its back, too. The frame and surface weren't so much as dirty or smeared, but perhaps Katherine had cleaned and polished them.

"So now," she said, her cheeks flushed rosy with the excitement of her great find, "I am back in your good graces, and you have a reason to visit the queen again. And I will gladly go along to explain to her. I shall tell Her Majesty that it's almost as if some magic hand put it where I could find it again, some sprite or guardian angel—"

"And not the evil one who spirited it away?" he said, a sharp edge to his voice. "Katherine, I must go to her with the mirror, but alone this time. You'll need to stay with our patient."

"Well, at least tell the queen that I am not there because I'm sitting with him and keeping company with Mother Dee. You know," she added, plucking at his sleeve, "all Dame Glenda Garver did was sit and look out her front window at people passing. I felt she was watching me all the time."

"When one is deaf, one's world shrinks, my dear."

"I suppose. But Mother Dee prefers her own kitchen and

hearthside. She has many memories of times long past, but she's not a busybody like Dame Garver."

"My dear, best not to speak ill of the dead, especially with her husband in our house. But I am grateful you brought me this precious mirror straightaway, for I believe one like it could have been used to burn that artist's tent at Nonsuch. Before all this happened, had you ever heard of such a thing?"

"Of course not, my lord. I know you have many ideas for mirrors like this, but it is of use to me only in my toilette."

He wanted to believe that Katherine had simply found the mirror. Its return did give him the perfect reason to ride to see the queen again. But it all seemed too easy, too—fantastical.

He studied her face; Katherine stepped quickly closer to embrace him. As he hugged her back, over her shoulder his eyes fell on the drawing of the signal mirrors he'd done for Her Majesty. He had to admit that in reflected light as in life, certain angles could create distortions—and then one couldn't read the signals right at all.

When Clifford reported that Gil Sharpe was in his tent in the privy garden, ailing—retching and puking, that was for sure, he said—Elizabeth ordered Meg to dose and keep an eye on him. Gil was not to leave his tent until he was much cured and the queen sent for him. Then, before the sun set, she went to see the patch of ground where Clifford had sworn that the running boy had simply disappeared. Leaving everyone behind but Jenks, Clifford, and Robin, garbed in hunting attire and riding her favorite palfrey, she set out through the hunt park toward the meadow.

The shadows of tree trunks slanted sharply sideways, making her blink as first sun, then shade shot past her gaze. "Start us exactly where you first spotted the lad, Clifford," Elizabeth ordered as they drew their horses up.

Robin reined in beside her and asked, "You don't really believe some strange child pops up here and there to set the fires, Your Grace?"

"I am pursuing each fork in the road—and there are many."

"I warrant," Clifford said, surveying the area, "it was nearly here. Though he was running away, I hardly reacted at first, set on looking for an adult."

"Could you tell if he had anything in his hands as he ran?" Elizabeth asked.

"Too far to tell, though I guess he could have hidden a mirror. Then, when I spotted no one else around, I rode through that break in the trees to follow him a bit, but he disappeared."

"Disappeared," Robin said. "If you were a good distance from him, perhaps he simply lay in the grass or ran down a hill. A child from one of the surrounding villages could have sneaked in to have a peek at the queen or court and then taken off when the hubbub began. Cheam lies on the other side of the hunt park, though it is a good four or five miles through thick woods and dales."

"I have thought of all that, Robin," Elizabeth said. "Let's ride anyway to the spot where you think he disappeared, Clifford."

They followed her yeoman guard out of the hunt park into a small meadow where grazed three of the fallow deer with which the park was stocked. The moment the animals heard the riders, they lifted their heads, froze for one moment, then bounded off.

"It makes me wish we had time for a hunt," Robin muttered.

The queen turned back to Clifford. "But you said that the deer did not flee when the boy ran into this meadow."

"God's truth, Your Majesty, they didn't startle or turn. It was as if he wasn't even there, and then he just went poof."

Despite the warm glow of the setting sun, Elizabeth shivered. She would not accept that the lad they sought could be a ghost. "Let's ride to the very spot," she said, noting well that the others had become nervous and quiet.

As they reined in about one-third of the way across the patch of meadow, Clifford whispered, "I think it was about here he disap—seemed to vanish."

Elizabeth stood straight-legged in her stirrup and braced herself one-handed on her sidesaddle to look around. "There!" she cried. "I see flat stones over there."

"Flat stones?" Robin said, craning his neck. "Oh yes, perhaps the remnants of some old building that was taken down when the village was razed."

They rode over to survey two layers of stones, roughly mortared still, barely protruding among the grass and weeds. Behind the stones was a hole in the ground, perhaps four feet square, also lined with mortared stones. Grass grew through the spaces and cracks of mossy stones that had, indeed, been here a while. Elizabeth saw no remnant of cloth or any sign of human life left behind.

"Aha!" Robin cried. "There's your answer. You should have ridden closer and you would have caught him, man. The boy knows the area well and hid in there, that's all."

As they dismounted and looked into the small hole, Elizabeth breathed a sigh of relief. Ghosts didn't need holes to hide in.

"But what exactly is or was this?" she mused aloud.

"I wonder," Jenks said, "how many deer have broken their legs in there. I'd best fill it in, lest we do have a hunt and someone's horse comes through here."

"Fill it in," Elizabeth echoed, neither giving a command nor asking a question. She suddenly pictured where she'd seen a similar configuration of stones: on top of the hillock where she'd spoken to Kat and Floris the day of the tent fire. And, come to think of it, on the rise just inside the hunt park. But neither of those elevations cradled a cavity like this.

"Yes, fill it in tomorrow," she said. "Men, we must find and question that child, perhaps more for what he could have observed than for what he himself did. Mayhap it was mere coincidence, not even the same boy that I saw flee at Mortlake. Jenks, ride back there, and if Simon Garver is yet able to speak, question him to see if he knows the purpose of the two hillocks on the west edge of the Nonsuch grounds—and this hole in the meadow. If he does not know, see if he can give you some names of others who might be able to tell us, however scattered he told me the former inhabitants of Cuddington are now. We are looking for any information we can find—any."

"Yes, Your Grace. I can be there by nightfall and return at first light."

The three men walked her to her horse. Clifford held the reins while Jenks linked his hands to give her a boost and Robin steadied her elbow until she was seated.

"But why bother to interview those who recall Cuddington?" Robin asked. "It 'died' nearly three decades ago."

Elizabeth gazed out over the meadow to the hunt park with the parapets of Nonsuch barely visible above the trees. "Perhaps because I feel sad about the ruination—the murder—of the place, that's all. But in this fire-mirror madness, nothing fits, nothing matches. The only connection I can fathom between why the Garvers and Will Kendale and the boy Niles could have been attacked is that Garver the Carver and Will the painter were once artisans who worked on the decor of Nonsuch."

"I was thinking, when you mentioned a ghost," Robin went on, "about a theory that the running boy Clifford chased is Niles's spirit, yet trying to escape the site where he met his fiery death."

Elizabeth gaped down at him. "Robin, ghosts do not cavort about in the open in broad sunlight, and why would Niles's ghost be six miles away in Mortlake?"

In truth, she had not thought of Niles as the ghost any more than she had considered him the intended victim of the first fire. She would not accept that the running boy was some sort of specter at all. No, the only kind of ghosts she believed in right now were ones that ran through her head, the memories of the fire in her youth and deep regret for what her father had done to Cuddington.

As dusk fell, the queen considered questioning the still ailing Gil Sharpe through his tent flap in the crowded privy garden, but soon gave up on that idea. Firstly, it always helped her to observe as well as hear those she interrogated. Secondly, since her courtiers were now crowded in such a small space, everyone would overhear her suspicions about Gil. And thirdly, if the boy was really ill, and Meg said he was, she didn't want to catch his condition herself.

"My lord Cecil," she told her master secretary as they sat at her council-chamber table that evening while she read and signed writs and decrees he handed her, "I fear my desired respite in the countryside has too much put the business of the kingdom to the side. I do not wish to leave here until we can solve these arsons and murders, but I cannot in good conscience remain much longer. 'S blood," she cried as another thought hit her, "I should have had Jenks bring back Dr. Forrest with him from Mortlake for Gil!"

"You don't think old Garver will live?"

"It's not that. Both Forrest and Dee believe he will, though he will be dreadfully scarred. But I need his opinion—Dr. Forrest's—on what ails Gil Sharpe."

"Speaking of good conscience, we must hope it is not a bad one making Gilberto Sharpino ill," Cecil muttered, handing her another decree to be signed and sanded.

"Do you believe, my lord, the boy is really to blame for any of this?"

"I only know, as you do, something he won't confess is eating at him."

"Granted, so—"

Clifford's loud knock sounded at the door. "Enter!" she called.

Her yeoman guard stepped in and closed the door behind him. "Dr. Dee has ridden in, Your Majesty, with good news, he says."

"I can use that. Send him in."

John Dee looked windblown and exhausted as he trudged toward them across the tiled floor and bowed. "Old Simon is doing as well as can be expected with those burns," he told them, out of breath, "yet I also have other fortunate news." He swung from his shoulder a saddle pack, which he placed carefully on the floor and bent to open. Within it lay the black tooled-leather box that used to hold his stolen mirror.

"The lost mirror has been found, Your Grace. Whoever took it must have abandoned it quickly, perhaps when he saw it had a glass which magnified and distorted rather than simply reflected, and didn't know the mirror's worth."

"I am delighted but surprised that the thief didn't at least sell it for its fine metal frame," she said, rising and walking over to take the mirror from his hands and examine it closely. Her reflection made her jump: she was all huge eyes and big nose. What would her preening cousin Mary of Scots think if she peered in this strange mirror? Elizabeth had half a notion to send her one like it.

"Or perhaps," Dr. Dee went on, "the thief feared being captured with it and so discarded it straightaway."

"And yet risked climbing a garden wall for it with people living in the house who could have seen him?" she challenged.

At that, the usually talkative Dr. Dee said nothing.

"Precisely where was it found and by whom, Dr. Dee?"

He cleared his throat. "By my wife, out for a brief walk—the strain of caring for Simon in such pain, you see. Precisely, she said, in a bed of violets not far from our house."

"I see. Quite a fortuitous turn of events."

"Ah, yes. Katherine herself said that."

"Not to change the subject, Dr. Dee," she said, "but perhaps you can help me with some local information about Mortlake. Someone told me of a strange boy running away from the fire at the Garvers' cottage. Dressed in brown broadcloth, perhaps even hopsacking. Rather broad-chested, I hear, squat in form, with short legs but ones that moved all too fast. He supposedly ran toward the river path and disappeared. Does he sound at all familiar to you?"

He looked at her wide-eyed, then shifted his gaze to the parchment he held in his hands. She could see his writing on it—not in code this time—and some sort of drawing with mirrors and dotted lines to signify angles. His tone wary as she glanced back to his face, he said, "Do you mean one of the village children?"

"I do not know but am curious to find out. Have you ever seen his like?"

"Not I, God's truth, but rumors say a few others have over the years. A man of logic and rationality, I don't give it much credence, but best you warn whoever saw that boy. I should have asked Simon if his wife had seen the apparition, for supposedly it appears only to those soon doomed to die."

Chapter the Eleventh

STILL HOLDING DR. DEE'S MIRROR, ELIZABETH MOVED TO the closest chair and sank into it. Cecil came to stand behind her; though he did not touch her, she felt his support as if he had clasped her shoulder. She stared down into the mirror again. This time it caught her mouth with her lips pressed tightly together but looking huge and trembling.

"Tell me more about this ghost, Dr. Dee," she said.

"May I inquire who saw the apparition, Your Majesty?"

"Just tell me more."

"They say, you see, the boy was one of many country folk who died in an early plague—not the Black Death but the sweat. Victims were buried in a mass grave on the edge of a farm, which is no longer there. As the site was not designated by tombstones, the name of the place became its only marker."

"The name of the place?"

"Why, Mortlake."

"Ah, *mors, mortis*—Latin for 'death,'" she whispered. "Lake of death."

"It was never really a lake, I take it, but a pond which the Thames evidently overflowed. I've read that the sweat carried off hundreds in the last century," he went on, his hesitant voice now taking on that tutor's tone he often fell into. "The addition to the cellar dug for the Riverside Inn about thirty years ago disturbed the old burial pit, according to my mother. Rumors of hauntings have been sporadic at best ever since, or I would have warned you not to stay there."

"I'm glad," Cecil muttered, "we didn't know we were sleeping above a plague pit."

"Dr. Dee," Elizabeth said, "since the hauntings began only after people learned a plague pit was there, could we not just as well theorize that the ghost is a figment of men's imaginations and not a specter whose bones have been disturbed?"

"I've always thought so, but someone once warned old Simon he'd be cursed for disturbing those bones." Dee gestured with his rolled parchment as if it were a magician's wand. "I asked him several years ago if he'd ever seen the running boy, but he said no."

"Dr. Dee," Elizabeth said, looking up steadily at him, "*I* have seen that boy, or one who could be so construed. He was running away from the fire at the Garvers' as if he had been burned."

Dee's eyes widened; he squeezed his parchment so hard it crinkled. "I thought at first you might mean you'd seen him, Your Grace, but I dared not ask. Running away as if—I suppose the plague pit could have extended over to the Garvers' cottage area."

She jumped to her feet. " 'S blood, that may be the first completely irrational thing I've ever heard you say!" she cried. "I heed not that sort of superstitious curse. Besides, my guard Clifford, the yeoman on the door just now, also saw such a boy running, and not at Mortlake. Here, at the edge of the hunt park, just after a fire mirror was evidently used to mar one of my portraits and incinerate another."

"But not after the tent fire?"

"Not that anyone reported, though we did not search the hunt park then."

"It may well be all superstition and happenstance," Dee said. "Can you tell me about the boy who was glimpsed here at Nonsuch?"

"He was no ghost—we've discovered that," the queen exclaimed, her voice gaining strength again. "His disappearance was made quite simple by a small stone cavity in the meadow, exactly where he supposedly vanished."

"A stone cavity?" he asked, frowning. "How small?"

"About four feet square," Cecil answered for the queen as she held her arms out to approximate the size. "And Her Majesty says there is similar stone work, though without holes in the ground, on two man-made hillocks at the edge of the palace lawns."

"Did you not pass my man Jenks on the road, Dr. Dee?" she asked, suddenly remembering him. She put both hands to her forehead. "I sent him to your house to question Simon Garver about those hillocks. After all, the old man worked at Nonsuch while it was being built and memories of Cuddington were still fresh."

"Ah, Jenks—yes. Those actors hailed him as they were coming back into town, and I saw him stop to speak with them, though I just rode on."

"He'd best ride on too. Tell me more then of how the old man is doing."

"Your physician's—and my Katherine's—care and the herbals your strewing-herb mistress sent have availed him some comfort.

Though he should recover, I fear he does not want to."

"I thank you for coming directly here with the mirror, Dr. Dee. Now if you would excuse us . . ."

"Your Majesty, you mentioned the old village on this site just now. Surely you aren't thinking there is some Cuddington curse after all this time?"

"Was there ever?" She asked the question of herself more than of these two brilliant men.

"John Mooring, the lord of the manor house there, according to my mother, cursed the king."

"My father. God's truth, I can understand why Mooring was angry enough to risk treason and death for such a curse."

"Before I go, Your Majesty," Dee put in, "this may not be the time, but I brought a plan to you for using mirrors on ships to signal, day or night, of dangers." He extended the parchment to her, now quite curled.

"You may leave it here, and I shall consider it as soon as I can," she told him. "Ship signals aside, this already is the time, day or night, of dangers. I need to see my dear friend, Kat Ashley, and get some sleep and try to think. My lord Cecil, will you see that Dr. Dee is well cared for this evening?"

Another of Clifford's distinctive knocks resounded. "Perhaps Jenks came back in the dark, though he said it would be tomorrow," the queen told them. "Enter!"

She, Cecil, and Dee gaped as Clifford opened the door, for not only Jenks but Katherine Dee stood there.

"Your physician did all he could, and I, too," the woman cried, even before she crossed the threshold and managed an unsteady curtsy. Her face was glazed with tears, her hair wild as if she'd torn at it. "He's gone."

"My old friend is dead?" Dee asked.

"Yes—gone," she said, her voice rising to a squeak as she ran to her husband's arms.

"I deeply regret Master Garver's loss," Elizabeth pronounced, fighting to keep her voice steady. "My kingdom can ill afford to lose the former generation of artisans, whose skills and knowledge grace our lives yet today. Jenks, did you have time to speak with Master Garver before he died?"

"So close but so far, Your Grace," he said, shaking his head. He looked as grief-stricken as she felt. "Mistress Dee said she'd go in first to decide if he could answer a few questions for me, but she gave a cry and said he was gone and I rushed in."

"An immediate cry," Elizabeth asked, "or did it take her a moment in the room, evidently to realize he was gone?"

"Well—quite soon she cried out, I guess."

Elizabeth's gaze snagged Dee's. Again she glimpsed an expression of stunned knowledge that his wife, at least, could come under suspicion. He looked away before the queen did as all eyes returned to the crying Katherine.

Apparently missing the tension in the room, Jenks went on. "Dr. Forrest came rushing downstairs. Surprised he was, but he said the old man lost his will to live and so gave up the ghost."

At the way he'd put that, Elizabeth again sank into her chair, for her trembling legs would not hold her.

The queen questioned Katherine alone at some length that night, thinking her emotional state might make her admit something. Though it seemed entirely possible that a badly burned man who was supposed to live could suddenly die—while only Katherine

Dee was with him and Jenks was about to question him—Elizabeth and Cecil were newly suspicious of the young woman's motives and deeds. But in the end, they decided not to detain her, so she returned to Mortlake with her husband the next morning to help make funeral plans for Simon Garver, too.

Exhausted and frustrated, Elizabeth took a stroll upon the rooftop the next morning rather than walking either outside or inside the palace. Even the beautifully painted and carved walls of Nonsuch were starting to make her feel as trapped as Whitehall had the winter before.

"The breeze is lovely up here, and you can see for miles," Meg Milligrew, who had accompanied the queen with Floris and Kat, said, and sucked in a deep breath.

"Yes," Elizabeth said, leaning both elbows in a cutout portion of the crenellated walls, "you can almost see the small meadow behind the hunt park from here, and over there, the spire of Mortlake Church, where both the Garvers will now be buried."

"It's the most beautiful view in the kingdom!" Floris gushed, thoroughly annoying the queen. She was glad Kat's companion had a sunny disposition, so she did not deign to correct her. But as lovely as it was here, her kingdom held many stunning views, and surely the woman who was nursemaid to elderly folk had hardly been all over to judge anyway. Such chatter was almost as presumptuous as Heatherley insisting she must choose his portrait because it was finished. But the queen scolded herself silently, for she was too much on edge with everyone. Each time she thought things could not get worse, they did, though she was not certain how any news could be blacker than Dee's blurting out last night that anyone who saw the running boy was doomed to die.

Elizabeth braced herself when she saw Lavina Teerlinc appear at the top of the staircase to the roof, which Clifford guarded. Ned Topside was with her, and, gesturing to Lavina to wait a moment, he hurried to the queen.

"Your Grace," he said, evidently out of breath from the climb, "Mistress Teerlinc says she must speak with you on most urgent business."

Elizabeth looked past Ned. Lavina was actually wringing her hands, and her expression was that of someone who has just sucked a lemon. Surely no one had managed to set fire to the portrait she was repainting, not here in the shelter of the palace.

"I will speak with her privily," she told her little coterie. "Floris, keep a close watch on Kat up here."

The queen walked to Lavina, and they stood about six feet from Clifford at the edge of the roof overlooking the hunt park. Lavina curtsied stiffly as the brisk breeze shifted her hair and skirts.

"You have something important to tell me?"

"Something dat's been eating at me for over a veek now, since the day of Vill's death, Your Majesty."

The queen caught her breath. "And what makes you tell me now?"

"Because I see him trying to trick you again, that's all."

"Him?"

"I know you favor him, Your Majesty, but your boy artist, Gil, he isn't telling you all he knows either. I thought he vould, since you seemed so—close. It vould be none of my affair if these dreadful things veren't happening—Vill's death, his portrait slashed, mine burned, even Henry's portrait of you marred."

"Lavina, what about Gil? He's holding back what? And, as you say, you have done the same."

"Dere, you see. Already you defend him."

"Calm yourself and start at the beginning. I assure you I am grateful for any help you can give me in solving Will Kendale's death—any."

Biting her lower lip, Lavina nodded. She glanced out at the hunt park and went on. "I saw Gil Sharpe sneak out of his tent and go into the voods—vit a mirror."

"With a mirror? Just before the tent fire?"

Lavina shook her head. "The next day—ven you vent to Mortlake to visit Dr. Dee for the day."

Elizabeth breathed again.

"I vas painting outside, a view of the palace. He came out of his tent and rushed into the voods. I'd seen Dr. Dee looking around there, drawing too, so I thought maybe you told the boy to make another sketch. I vas upset you didn't ask me to do it."

"I value your honesty. Say on."

"Vell, truth was, I didn't see the mirror at first because Gil had it hidden in his shirt. But ven he got into the trees in a bit of sun, he took it out and played it up and all around, catching the sunlight. He hoisted himself up in a tree and fixed the beam on my tent—dis vas before the tents vere moved."

Elizabeth had begun to tremble, whether with terror or rage, she was not sure. Gil had a mirror about which he had not told her. Gil had climbed a tree when he had said his leg now hurt him and he never climbed anymore. She had trusted and supported and cared for Gil, and like other men before him, he had betrayed her. She had let Gil's talent and her longing for her lost brother lead her astray to trust him.

"I only held dis back," Lavina was saying, "since I thought you vould hold it against me if I tried to put the blame on him. But I'm afraid now, afraid since my portrait was burned, that I'll be next, attacked like Vill."

"Lavina, you did well to tell me these things. I can't believe it of Gil—there must be some explanation. But I am grateful. You may go now."

As the woman curtsied and left her, the queen put both hands on the wall to brace herself. She must go to face down Gil now. He might even be lying about his illness; there were ways to make oneself vomit.

"Your Grace, are you quite well?" Clifford's voice came close behind her.

"No, I am not well, my man, and haven't been since that first fire came swooping from the trees out there."

"Forgive me, but I heard some of what Mistress Teerlinc said. I saw something that made me think the boy—your artist—hated Kendale."

"Tell me," she ordered, her voice hard. "This seems to be the time and place for confessions and accusations."

"It was just before that first interview you had with him in your chamber here at Nonsuch. He had to wait for you and Secretary Cecil to be free. And all he did was stalk up and down the staircase, muttering and glaring at those large paintings Master Kendale had done long ago. Made some obscene gestures at them too."

She hit the stone wall with her fists. " 'S blood," she cursed, followed by a few of her father's other favorite oaths. "Next the birds in the trees will be testifying against that boy. Clifford, come with me. Meg, attend," she called to the women waiting and watching across the rooftop.

Floris lifted both hands, palms up, as if to ask *What?* but the queen ignored her and stomped down the stairs.

Gil drank more of the spearmint elixir Meg Milligrew had brought him and lay back on his pallet in his tent. He had propped the painting of Dorothea up so he could see her. He'd hidden the mirror that was once hers under his single blanket at the foot of his pallet. He had to get up soon. Get up and face the queen. But he was terrified that she'd pry out of him the real reason he'd come home early, and then they could both be in danger. Elizabeth Tudor had always been able to search out his deepest thoughts, and that scared him witless now.

Besides, his ribs were as sore as his throat from retching. He hated to make himself throw up. It was a trick with a feather down the throat he'd learned from the other apprentices in Urbino. No one wanted to get too near a sick lad, and it was one way to get a day off from tasks too.

"Gil! Gil Sharpe!"

The queen? Here? Surely, in agonizing about her so much, he didn't only *think* he heard her.

"Gilberto Sharpino, get presentable and come out right now!"

"I am ill within," he called feebly.

"Not as ill as you will be if you do not get out here now!"

No, this was no dream. Not in his worst nightmare could he have imagined that tone. "Yes, Your Grace!" he called, and grabbed for his doublet.

She's found out, he thought. Someone had come after him from Urbino and told on him, demanded that he be turned over to them. No, they would simply have abducted him——or worse. He could not get over the thought that someone sent by Maestro Giorgio had focused a mirror upon the wrong tent and killed Will Kendale merely by mistake when the assassin had meant to murder him.

Gil opened the tent flap, trying desperately to smooth his uncombed hair. The area looked greatly deserted, yet a few folk were still about. The queen's big, burly yeoman guard and Mistress Milligrew were with her, but stood well back. He glanced into Meg Milligrew's eyes; no help there.

"I have need of a mirror, Gil," the queen clipped out, "and I suggest you get it for me."

His jaw dropped.

"And I swear," she went on, rhythmically wagging an index finger at him, "if you ask what mirror, you can spend the rest of the time here in the wine cellar with the other rats!"

He hadn't seen her that angry for years, and never at him. Her usually pale cheeks were almost as rosy-hued as her hair. He darted into the tent and, forgoing the urge to flee under the far side, unwrapped Dorothea's mirror and went back outside with it.

"This one, Your Grace? As you recall, I told you of Dorothea. This was hers, and she never asked for it back. Surely someone has not come looking for it or me——"

Her clarion voice interrupted him as she seized the mirror he extended and immediately read its inscription aloud: "'Complain not to me, O woman, for I return to you only what you gave me.' Well," the queen cried, now wagging the mirror at him by its handle, "I am complaining! And I expect you, my young man, as well as this mirror, which shines so brightly in the sun, to return what I have given you, namely kindness, care—and the plain truth."

He gaped at her, horrified that he had nothing else to hold her off with but the final confession. And that he could not give.

"All right," he said. "I more or less stole the mirror, but I could not bear to give it back to her. And in truth, as I said, she never asked for it before I left Urbino."

"Dorothea?"

"Yes, Your Grace."

"You fled Urbino two years early and came back here because you took a mirror which was not yours, but belonged to your master's mistress? In other words, because of a woman?"

"Well—yes, Your Grace." His knees were weak as grass, and he locked them to stand. The queen herself had given him another way out of a full confession.

"And why then were you in the hunt park on the hillock up a tree and shining sun from this mirror on Lavina Teerlinc's tent shortly after Will Kendale's had been burned with him and his boy in it?"

Gil stood stunned again. He prayed that he would not have a double murder pinned on him if he clung to this new excuse for why he'd really fled Urbino.

"I—yes," he stammered. "I went out to test the mirror to see if it could catch the sun's rays and project them on a tent. I thought you meant to include me in the search for a murderer as you had in times past." He lowered his voice. "I must admit I overheard Dr. Dee's theory about a fire mirror setting off the blaze. It wasn't easy for me to get up in that tree anymore—which hurt my pride more than my leg—but, yes, I scaled it, just to the lowest big crotch, and tried to see if I could flash light on the tents with it."

"And was it possible? To focus your secret mirror to catch the sun and train it on the tents?"

"Yes, it was," he admitted, feeling naked before that sharp-eyed Tudor gaze. "But," he went on, head down, "I couldn't tell you without letting you know I had that—that mirror."

She looked into the reflecting glass even as he spoke. The light off it even here in the privy garden illuminated her fine face. Thank God, Gil thought, her high color was abating and her tone was tempering.

" 'S blood, it's as good as raining mirrors lately," she said. "Dee's many mirrors, this one, the one in your painting of your lost Dorothea, my cousin Mary's, and whichever one lit the fire to murder Kendale and the boy Niles—if it was none of those."

Gil held his breath, uncertain whether he was still under a cloud or not. Suddenly the queen thrust the mirror toward him, stiff armed, so he was gazing right into the glass. "Did you use this mirror to start any sort of fire, Gil Sharpe?"

"I did not. Instead it was used by a woman to begin a fire in my heart."

She sighed, and her arm went limp as she lowered the mirror. "I must take this for a while, for safekeeping."

"Yes, Your Grace."

"You sound like a parrot Kat Ashley used to have, 'Yes, my lady, no, my lady.' " She took one step away, then spun back. "Are you sick in the body, heart, or soul, poor Gil? You know, you must get over your Italian lady. I assure you, it can be done."

"Yes, I—I shall heed your advice, Your Majesty."

"And that reminds me, find Henry Heatherley and have him describe to you the Italian man who was asking all about my artists—including you—in the inn at Mortlake. Gil, you've gone pale again," she said, stepping toward him. "Clifford," she cried, turning back over her shoulder as the big man rushed up to take his elbow to steady him.

Despite his trepidation that the queen would cast him out for the dangerous secret he still kept from her, Gil felt a greater fear. The next time Elizabeth of England confronted him, he would have nothing left but the terrible truth. The remnants of his strength fled, and he could barely nod as Clifford helped him back into the tent.

Maestro Giorgio Scarletti and his artists' guild had indeed sent someone after him. He felt his heartbeat accelerate as he collapsed on his mussed pallet. They meant to silence him. To kill him. Should he try to flee to draw his pursuers away from the queen? But if he ran, she might suspect him of the fires here. It was obvious she already did.

"Don't leave this tent until you hear from Her Majesty again," Clifford ordered, and went out. Gil just rolled up into a ball, wishing he could die, preferably in Dorothea's sweet, round arms.

The queen's exhaustion had finally caught up with her. Wearied, worried . . . in the late afternoon she sat with Kat and Floris in her bedchamber window, half nodding off, watching her women lace long-stemmed daisies into necklaces. In the privy garden below, Elizabeth could hear the buzzing blur of men's voices raised in some sort of argument.

Her people were too packed in down there, too nervous about

another fire, she thought. Their tempers were tightening too, like those ropes on Kendale's tent flaps, the rope controlling Dr. Dee's big mirror, those holding tight the shutters and doors of the Mortlake death trap.

As much as she hated to admit it, she needed to head back to London, even though she would be greatly hampered there in the murder investigation. If only she could stay a few more days, ride the area incognito, even back to Mortlake to talk to others about the running boy, or to the little village of Cheam on the far side of the hunt park. After all, the boy might have fled in that direction. But duty called . . . duty and sleep and London, where a forest of chimneys trailed their smoke into the sky. . . .

Her head jerked, but she thought she fell asleep again. Her eyes had nearly crossed signing papers lately, listening to her advisers talk and argue policy . . . agonizing with Cecil about Mary of Scots' marriage and a possible uprising in the northern shires.

The fresh air and sweet sun felt so very good as they sat here. They'd played cards earlier; she'd let Kat win. Strange, how Kat could remember how to play cards but not what year it was or who was on the throne—even when that person was right in front of her. Floris had told them about her last employer, a wealthy old man who had known Lord Arundel's father. Arundel himself had recommended her for a job with Elizabeth Tudor's beloved Lady Kat Ashley. Yes, Kat was beloved. They had clung together through shifting times to get the throne, to outlast Elizabeth's worst enemies, enemies who had always been her family. But Kat was her family now; even Cecil, Robin, Meg, Jenks, and Ned were closer now than her father or sister, even Edward, had ever really been. . . .

Somehow the sun flashed past her eyes, illuminating her closed eyelids so they went bloodred. Elizabeth dragged them open and blinked. There it was again. And then she saw the beam of light slicing straight through the window at a sharp downward angle, where it sat like a brilliant spider on the skirt-covered knees of the sleeping Kat Ashley.

Kat's gold damask skirts had begun to steam—no, to smoke! But how did the beam come so high into this second story? No tree was that tall. The roof?

Elizabeth knew she could sneak to another window or even to the roof to see who shone a mirror this way. With enough time, she could trace the beam and trap whoever was at the other end of it, but then she would give herself away, and Kat's skirts might be in flames. A picture of poor Garver the Carver's burned body popped into her mind. Kat was so afraid of fire. . . . And the terror had now come inside the palace!

The queen stood and yanked one heavy drapery from the window and threw it over Kat's legs. "Floris, wake! Get Kat— everyone—away from that window!"

Instantly alert, Floris leaped to her feet as the other ladies in the chamber started and screamed. Flowers, playing cards, and lapdogs dropped to the floor. As the dogs yipped in protest, the queen stood in the window and tried to follow the shaft of light.

Suddenly it leaped into her eyes as if to blind her, flickered, and disappeared. Though that last flash still made pulsating dots before her gaze, she pushed past her ladies and ran for the council-room door, pulled it open, then rushed across the room to the hall door.

"Someone has a fire mirror on the roof and just tried to burn Kat Ashley!" she shouted to her yeomen guards as she raced down the hall toward the stairs. "Up, straight across from my windows! We've got to trap him there!"

Her guards went for their weapons and pounded after her, but she was quicker as she lifted her skirts, opened the door to the roof, and tore up the stairs.

Chapter the Twelfth

 AT FIRST GLANCE, ELIZABETH SAW NO ONE ON THE BROAD expanse of palace roof. Suddenly the crenellated walls reminded her of widely spaced teeth in a huge, open mouth. The culprit could be hiding behind those distant decorations or the ornate chimney stacks.

Buffeted by the rising breeze, she shaded her eyes to scan the roof areas accessible from here. In the shape of a large, squared letter C, they encompassed both wings of the palace and were linked by a walkway wide enough for three men abreast. She saw no one on this first section of the roof above the royal apartments. But the beam of light had come from the other side, across the courtyard.

Clifford and three other guards bounded up and joined her, pikes at the ready and swords drawn.

"Where?" Clifford shouted. He pointed to the staircase itself and lunged around the enclosure. "No one back here!" he cried.

"Look all around—and over the sides!" she ordered. "The flash of sunlight came from over there!"

With the guards, who stopped occasionally to look over the sides, she rushed across the connecting walkway. From this side of the roof, she could see the windows of her apartment. Yes, someone could look into her bedchamber from here. An icy shudder racked her, and the breeze cooled her damp skin.

She shaded her eyes and gazed across the courtyard again. The sun had evidently come in on the perfect slant for this time of day. The person with the mirror could have hidden behind these raised sections of wall and held out the mirror in the aperture between. Although in London Elizabeth usually kept all draperies of her chambers closed at night, at Nonsuch she had kept them open to catch spring breezes. Had someone been spying on her, just waiting for an opportunity to start a fire, perhaps to trap and burn her?

"Over here, Your Majesty," Hammond, a yeoman guard, shouted, and pointed over the side of the walls facing the hunt park. "A dangling rope someone could have climbed down!"

"And climbed up," Clifford said as they pressed into the two nearest openings to observe the slightly swaying rope. She saw it was actually several knotted together. The knots were at equal distances; she counted three of them, which meant four ropes. The top one was looped around and secured to an ornate drainpipe. Did the ropes yet sway, she wondered, because someone had just gone down them, or was the breeze moving them?

She shaded her eyes again and scanned the grassy area below, where the tents had first been pitched, then the park itself with its newly leafed trees hiding whatever moved beneath. She could not quite see the meadow with the stone hole from here.

"Hammond, take a contingent and scour those woods and the meadow beyond, including a small stone hole you will find there.

Bring to me anyone—even if it is a child—whom you find lurking in or running through that park."

"Yes, Your Majesty," he said, and headed back around toward the staircase at a jog.

"So," Elizabeth muttered to herself as much as to her three remaining guards, "our prey can scale more than trees, but how did he get up here to tie those ropes on in the first place? I smell a plot. Clifford, fetch Secretary Cecil for me at once."

"Aye, Your Grace."

As he hurried away, she moved closer to the massive stone drainpipe, one of a matched set of four that cleared rain from the corners of the roof. Each was adorned with the carved stone faces of forest animals which were hunted here, deer, fox, and, in her father's times, wild boar. The top rope was secured around the head of a fox, but that was not what caught her eye. The rope was not tied haphazardly but knotted in a flat bow. And that bow was similar to the very type Floris and Kat had been using to lace flower stems the day of the first fire and just now.

"Leave those ropes exactly as they are, but one of you stay to guard them—and this roof," Elizabeth ordered. She went as quickly as her skirts would allow toward and down the stairs, where she met Cecil, who was coming up.

"Your Grace," he cried, "I hear the mirror fire ignited your skirts and you beat the flames out with your bare hands!"

Despite her haste, she almost laughed. "I am astounded how quickly tales become embellished at court, even one in the countryside. No, it was Kat's skirts, which did *not* ignite, and which I smothered with a *drape*. My lord, go up on the roof to view the ropes above, then come down to me. I must speak with Floris Minton."

"Ropes above?"

As their gazes met and held in the dark stairwell, she nodded. "The wielder of the fire mirror may have an accomplice," she said, "one in our midst with access to the roof."

"You know the old adage 'The better part of valor is discretion,' Your Grace. We must leave Nonsuch for London, where you—all of us—will be safer."

She nodded. "Come down to the council room when you've seen the ropes," she said, and pushed past him on the stairs.

The women had dispersed from her chamber, and Elizabeth sent the rest of her guards except Clifford to join the chase. But for the drape she had pulled down and some scattered, wilting flower necklaces, nothing looked amiss. She stooped to pick up a daisy chain and examined the knot. Was it the same? And so what? Had she overreacted?

Pushing the half-completed necklace up her sleeve, she went out in the hall and to Kat Ashley's chamber. Quietly, she opened the door.

Kat lay on her bed, still clothed but curled comfortably, asleep. Floris stood near her, leaning against a bedpost, just watching. Kat looked peaceful, but Floris's face was wet with tears.

When the nursemaid saw her, she swiped at her cheeks and came on silent feet around the bed and to the door. "Step out," Elizabeth mouthed before the woman could curtsy. They stood in the corridor, and Floris quietly closed the door behind them. The queen saw Clifford was back on her own door, but ever watchful of his queen.

"Your Grace," Floris said, using that less formal form of

address for the first time the queen could recall, "I beg you not to blame me."

"Blame you," she said, her tone neither questioning nor condemning. The queen's heartbeat kicked up, and not just from her fear and physical exertion in the last half hour. What was Floris going to confess?

"I should not have fallen asleep like that in your chamber, even if Kat and you did," Floris began, gripping her hands across her waist. "I should have been more watchful, for I know how much she means to you—to me, too, now, I swear it. And to think that after her fearful memories of that other fire where she could have been sent away from you for good . . . Your Grace, I beg you not to send me away from Kat for failing to keep a good watch on her. That is no doubt the crime she would have been punished for years ago when she tended you."

"I cannot hold what happened against you, Floris, for I never suspected the fire demon could reach us inside the palace or that my very bedchamber was not safe."

"But I fear I've disappointed you terribly. I was so honored to be helping you to look into these dangerous events, to be trusted. Protecting Kat is my main concern, and I know I failed in both things, Your Grace, but just as you kept Kat near you when she began that fire long ago—"

"But you did not begin a fire."

"I did not imply that. And I don't mean to sound like a madwoman loose from Bedlam, but I could have died when I woke and saw her skirts smoldering. Do you think the murderer meant to harm Kat, or just show his power to strike—or could he have thought it was you whose garments he ignited?"

"Yes, I fear that's possible."

"The thing is, we were all so close in the window together, with the sun on all our lower bodies but not on our faces so someone could see who was who."

"I know only that the mirror murderer is getting closer and closer, coming inside, nearer to those I care for—and so to myself."

"But that's dreadful, so dangerous for you. Then we'll be heading back to London where we can escape him?"

Floris was bright, that was certain. And, of course, she wanted Kat to be well tended, for several reasons. Elizabeth had no doubt of Floris's affection for the old woman—and, on a practical note, if anything happened to Kat, there would be no more reason for Floris to be so royally tended herself.

"London, soon, I think," Elizabeth said. "Very soon."

"And you will not send me away?" Floris went on, gripping her fingers so tightly they went white as sausages. "Your Grace, Kat reminds me so of my own mother, whom I nursed and then lost. I cannot bear to lose Kat, too."

"Nor can I, so we are sister spirits in that. You have been most careful and kind with her. And to think that when all of this happened," Elizabeth mused, "we were simply playing games and chatting and making these." She reached up her sleeve and pulled out the wilted flower necklace. "Wherever did you learn to do such designs with the stems?" she asked, hoping she sounded nonchalant.

"The lacings and ties, you mean? My mother was a seamstress in Bromley who made lovely busks and corsets and bum roles— all undergarments. She tied them like that. I've known many others who make their knots that way, including Kat, who has no doubt dressed you from time to time."

"You're right, of course," Elizabeth said, placing the partial necklace around Floris's neck. "This has taken so much out of me of late ..." Her voice trailed off as she realized she was coming to think of this woman not only as a trusted servant, but almost a confidante, as she did Meg.

"You were reared in Bromley, then," Elizabeth said. "It is but a day's journey from here. And you lost your mother young?"

"I was young, but she had borne me when she was older. Perhaps it's why I've always felt honored to nurse the elderly, and having Kat in my care is a little like having her back—a silly thought, I know."

"Not silly at all," Elizabeth assured her, annoyed she was so suspicious of everyone lately. Next she'd be accusing Kat of something dire.

Down the hall, she saw Cecil striding toward her chambers. "I have work to do, but I hope you too will rest for a while, Floris. I was just thinking that your name means 'of flowers,' so perhaps your mother loved flowers to name you so."

"She did, Your Grace," the nursemaid said, her eyes misting again. "Especially spring daisies just like these."

The queen gave the orders to pack for London, with the news that they would be leaving first thing in the morning. The hubbub began, especially in the privy gardens below, where people were crowded into tents.

As evening came on, the queen paced in her council chamber while Cecil stood at the window. They spoke of plots, of the diabolical ingenuity of this one with mirrors and fire.

"And with Queen Mary using mirrors to try to frighten or

threaten me," Elizabeth said, "I cannot rule out that it could be a political plot."

"All plots near a monarch are political one way or the other, Your Grace."

Clifford's knock on the door startled them both. "Enter!"

"Your Majesty," her yeoman cried as he opened the door, "your guards have found someone in the forest, someone known to all!"

"Who is . . . ?" she got out as two of the tall guards dragged Giles Chatam to the door. "You!"

"I've done nothing wrong, I swear it!" the actor cried, trying to shrug off the big, burly guards. "I was simply off by myself, walking along at sunset, learning my lines. Your Majesty, you do not believe I or the others in the company would be poaching in your hunt park?"

"The other actors," Hammond said, loosening his hold on Giles, "were camped at the edge of the palace property closest to Mortlake. But this one was in the woods itself, and that's what you wanted delivered here, Your Majesty—man, woman, or child."

Once the guards had unhanded him, Giles swept her one of his embellished bows, although it looked a bit shaky this time. He had leaves and soil ground into the knees of his stockings, and pieces of leaves or grass even stuck in his mussed hair.

"Did you try to flee from or resist my men?" she asked.

"Only at first, when I thought they were ruffians. It's getting dark in the woods, Your Majesty, and robbers could be plentiful."

"Why, then, are you and the Queen's Country Players in the darkening forest when you should be safely back in your attic rooms at the inn?"

"None of us are sleeping there one more night, not with the innkeeper's cottage burned next door and a vengeful ghost on the loose."

That took her aback, but she recovered quickly. "From whom did you hear about the ghost? It must have been recently, or you would no doubt have earlier found yourselves a better place for the night than the forest floor."

"I—yes, we heard just today."

"And you were told by . . . ," she prompted, getting angrier by the moment. She had just recalled a play she'd seen Giles in once, where he'd climbed to his lover's balcony up a tree made of nailed and painted planks while carrying a looped rope over his shoulder so he could help his lady love escape her prison. And he'd slid down it handily while spouting verse in iambic pentameter!

"I believe I heard it in the common room of the inn, Your Majesty. Dame Garver's funeral was today, and everyone was greatly impressed with the mourners and meal you paid for, so perhaps word spread there, too. In short, everyone knows the queen herself saw the ghost of some boy and what it could import."

The queen spun her back to Giles and mouthed to Cecil, "Katherine Dee! She was a chatterbox before and is again."

"Am I under arrest, Your Most Gracious Majesty?" Giles dared.

"Do you own ropes, Master Chatam?" she countered, turning back to face him.

"Half a dozen at least," he said with a slight shrug. "We tie boxes shut with them and secure them to our carts. We use them in certain plays."

"Hammond, detain this clever actor in the guards' quarters,

then take torches and ride to find his fellows at their encampment. After inquiring first from Wat Thompson exactly how many ropes they have, search through their things and bring me every one—and whatever mirrors you find too."

"Your Majesty," Giles said, his usually stentorian voice now shaky, "you don't mean this has something to do with the mirror that caused the fire in a tent? Surely that cannot be linked to the Mortlake fire—or was there another fire here?"

"That is all for now," she told Hammond, ignoring Giles. And then another ploy struck her. "Wait!" she said, and walked toward Giles as her guard began to pull him away. "Do you know why I think you could be tied to a fatal fire, man?" she demanded, her face close to his.

"No idea in the universe, Your Majesty."

"Because last winter when you were at court, I heard that when you were a boy, your parents died in a strange fire which you conveniently escaped. Is that right?"

For the first time under such scrutiny and duress, he seemed to crumble. "I—yes. I try to carry on, but it was the most horrendous thing ever in my life," he said, his voice a mere whisper. His blue eyes were wide as if he saw the conflagration even now. He seemed to look past her, through her. He began to tremble. "It's why I would rather be anyone else—to play anyone else's part in life—for I lived and they did not. But it was not my fault, only that I fled without going back into the house for them, and that has—haunted me."

His tearful gaze locked with hers. She read terror there—and truth, or so she thought. And she felt a bond with him because of the fire of her youth, which was not half as horrendous as his. The clever player might be guilty of consorting with the flighty

Katherine Dee, but Elizabeth had more important things to solve than that possibility.

"Take him away for now, but keep him comfortable," she said, still frustrated and furious with everyone and everything.

It was late that night before her guards delivered to her six short ropes, none of which was of the same length or composition as the ones which had hung from the palace drainpipe. And they reported that Wat Thompson had claimed six ropes were all they had. Her guards also brought her two steel mirrors from the players' trunks. Though the metal was polished, reflections in them were quite dull.

"'S blood," she said to her Privy Plot Council members as they examined the collection of ropes and mirrors she had laid out on the council table, "nothing matches, not mirrors, ropes, clues, nothing."

Meg sat between Jenks and Ned; Cecil was directly across from the queen, who had the center chair. Lady Rosie sat to her left. The queen had asked Clifford to join them, though he stood just inside the doors to the hall. She had been undecided about whether to invite Floris again, but decided that the nursemaid should stay with Kat, and so did not tell her of the meeting. She did not want Floris to think she didn't trust her. If she hadn't, she would not have left Kat in her care for one moment more. As for Gil, he was being watched by one of her guards, as was Giles.

"When we return to London, we can test whether these steel mirrors of the players' troupe will ignite a fire," Cecil said, putting down the one he had minutely examined. "I'm sure we can replicate Dr. Dee's experiment without him."

"Good," Elizabeth said, feeling alert again, as though she had fought her way through exhaustion to get a second wind. "By the way, since we have not one real shred of evidence to hold Giles, I'm going to release him."

Ned's head jerked up from his perusal of the ropes. "But he's a traveling player, Your Grace. He could disguise himself, pass as nearly anyone, and just disappear."

"I swear, I wish this whole thing would just disappear. No, Ned, I think not. He wants above all my good favor, and I just pray he did not seek to obtain that by causing chaos he and his company could calm with their plays—or that he is not a habitual fire demon. I intend to tell him he must stay in this general area until further notice, and that he should stop by Dr. Dee's from time to time to discover if I have further need of him here or in London."

"Yes, he might bite on that, ambitious as he is," Ned agreed, making faces at himself in Dr. Dee's magnifying mirror.

Meg said, with a side glance at Ned, "Giles is stuck on his comely face too, I wager. Probably looks at mirrors in the middle of a meeting."

"Enough," Elizabeth insisted. "Though I like to conduct our meetings at a roundtable, where everyone may freely give and take, I've actually asked you here this late at night to tell you what I plan to do."

"Here or in London?" asked Rosie, who seldom said a word in these meetings.

"Both. And I want no Katherine Dees among us, that is, no one who cannot keep something I say in private kept private."

She stared them down individually until each acquiesced or nodded. Cecil looked upset, but then, he knew what was coming.

They had argued it out already, but she had prevailed. The others looked merely curious; Ned, perhaps, expectant.

"I am returning to London with everyone on the morrow," she announced, "but I am staying only a day or two to accomplish some business and make some public appearances, including posing for my artists again—inside. Then, with Clifford, Jenks, and Rosie, I am coming back here incognito to look further into this fire-mirror matter. I don't want to leave Kat, but I will make the trip in less than a day, spend, hopefully, just one or two days away, and so return to London in a total of two or three."

Rosie's mouth gaped in an O. Ned fumed, no doubt because he hadn't been included. Cecil looked grim, but he'd already argued himself out. It was Meg who spoke first.

"Disguised as me, Your Grace? We haven't traded places for ages, but I suppose I'll have to be ill and stuck in my bed again if I'm to be queen."

"Well," Ned exploded, "do you think she'd have you giving speeches at Parliament or dining with the court?"

"I said earlier, enough!" Elizabeth cracked out, and smacked the table with the palm of her hand. "Yes, I will be garbed as you, Meg, and you will keep to your bedchamber at Whitehall, with a severe head cold—and with Secretary Cecil's help. Rosie, as soon as we return, you will supposedly leave for your home for a few days."

"Does Dr. Dee know all this?" Jenks asked.

"No, and he is not to," the queen clipped out.

"Will Floris Minton know?" Meg asked. "Why is she not here, since Kat's probably sound asleep?"

"That is the sticky part. Because I see her and Kat so often at close range, Meg as me would never fool either of them. I will probably take Floris into my confidence. Still, I could send orders to them that I do not want them near, lest Kat catch my cold. Yet I fear Kat would want to tend me as she often used to, and she'd drag Floris along, and then they'd know I was gone anyway."

"And what will we be doing," Rosie asked, "if we come back to Nonsuch?"

"We will not stay at Nonsuch or at Mortlake," Elizabeth explained, "but find a place at Cheam and hope no one there saw me on May Day."

"Your Grace," Cecil spoke at last, "I must again counsel that I deem this a rash and dangerous plan."

"I cannot let all of this simply pass, my lord." She turned to him and tried to keep her voice reined in. "I fear that my portraits, my people, and my person are not safe until there is a stop to it. I've passed as Meg before, and she as me, and I'll have Rosie as companion, let alone the two best guards in my kingdom, if not all of Christendom. I am just praying that this fire-mirror plot does not have my cousin Mary Stuart behind it."

"Or Dr. Dee," Cecil muttered. "We need him, both here and abroad."

"You know, Your Grace," Ned said, calmer now, "Giles Chatam could have been in the woods not to practice his lines, but to await a tryst with Mistress Dee. That part of the hunt park stretches within a few miles of Mortlake."

"I know, Ned. It's one of the many threads of this . . . this twisted rope," she said, picking up the end of the long, knotted length which had hung from the roof to the ground. "But I am hoping that if we pick away at frayed ends like this, the entire thick thing will unravel."

"But can't we just stay here and you can sneak out dressed as Meg?" Ned questioned.

"The element of surprise will be in play if our arsonist thinks we are back in London."

"What if he follows you there?" Ned asked.

"Ned, all of you will be much better protected at Whitehall. Before Kat was nearly burned, I wanted to stay here longer. Indeed, the fire demon may have believed he was trying to burn me. I must do this before I have no one left to trust—but all of you, of course. I regret the inward working of my suspicious mind, for that can grow as ugly and deformed as . . . as reflections in that mirror of Dr. Dee's."

"Sadly, Your Grace," Cecil put in, "a suspicious mind must go with being monarch—if one wishes both to thrive and to survive."

"As I do and shall!"

Chapter the Thirteenth

 THOUGH THE QUEEN KEPT HERSELF BUSY, THE WEEK'S
end loomed long. Saturday she spent time amid her
courtiers and worked diligently with Cecil and her
other advisers. On Sunday, she went to church in a
great procession to Westminster by river, nodding and smiling to
all—and feigning to cough and sneeze and blow her nose from
time to time. That afternoon, she put out word that she had a
severe spring cold and would take to her bed for a few days.
Meanwhile, preparations went on apace for her secret return to
Surrey.

"I still have to cinch in your garments," Elizabeth teased Meg
after she'd donned her walnut brown traveling attire early Monday
morning. "I guess I'd better begin to eat more." She carried a
cloak with a hood which she could use to her advantage, should
they be in a crowd of people. She and Meg waited in the queen's
council chamber for word from Clifford that Jenks had the horses
ready. They would be meeting Rosie Radcliffe at the Ring and
Crown just outside the palace walls.

"If you wear those fine kid boots of yours," Meg countered, "someone will spot you sure."

"I still can't mimic your speech the way Ned taught you to do mine," Elizabeth said. "And the boots stay. All I need is blisters on my feet to match the ones on my heart from this fire-mirror plot—for I'm convinced we are in search of more than one conspirator. And I must find out the *why*, because then, I vow, I will have the *who*."

"Your Majesty," Cecil said the moment he came in, "I'm afraid Kat Ashley and her maid Floris are insisting on tending your cold. They're just outside in the hall."

"Tell them my physicians and herbalist will see to me," she said, frowning as she tugged down the too-short sleeves. "No, never mind. I've been fretting over what to do about them. I was going to just hope you could hold them off from Meg, but I must see Kat again. Send Floris in alone first, if you can manage it."

After Cecil stepped back out, she heard his voice through the door. Clifford opened it and whispered, "Horses ready," just as Floris popped in under his arm. Her jaw dropped when she saw how the queen was dressed.

"Your Grace," she managed, and dipped a quick curtsy.

"Floris, I am trusting you with more than Kat's comfort the next few days. I am riding back to Surrey to pursue this matter of the murderous fires."

For once the unflappable Floris looked stunned.

"I will be back soon, and you are not to tell Kat."

"No—of course not. I was simply surprised at the garments— and that you would take the risk. You go with guards, I pray."

"Do not fret. As for Kat, I don't want her alarmed. Indeed, I don't want anyone alarmed or suspicious. Will you vow to keep my secret, Floris?"

"I swear it. And I shall guard Kat doubly well, lest the fire demon has come back here in your entourage. I will keep her from sitting in sunny windows, and—"

"I have the roof and main corridors well guarded. Things are much safer here for all of you. No one shall be a prisoner of fear in my palace in my capital city."

"I ask but one thing then, if I may."

"Say on."

"That you will let us know the moment you return, so that we may greet you and know you are well."

"Meg," the queen said, turning to her, "you will tell Secretary Cecil he is to let Floris and Kat know the moment I return."

"Then shall I take Kat away?" Floris said as she curtsied and backed toward the door.

"No, send her in. I am always glad to see her, and will say a fast—but not a last—farewell."

Floris almost said something else, but nodded and went out.

"Oh my, you're going hunting," Kat declared the moment she saw her. She did not curtsy, so Elizabeth assumed she didn't recognize her, at least as queen.

"Yes, my Kat, as a matter of fact I am."

"And taking that girl with you?" she asked, nodding toward Meg, who stood a ways apart.

"She will remain here, as you must. I bid you farewell until later."

"Is your father going too?" Kat asked as Elizabeth went slowly closer. "I wish we could get you back in his good graces, my girl."

Kat has scrambled years and crowns again, Elizabeth thought. She had to leave now. Her people and their mounts were waiting.

"Kat, will you give me a hug good-bye then—just for now?"

"Of course, lovey."

At that familiar childhood endearment, tears stung Elizabeth's eyes. They embraced; the old woman felt so frail and fragile.

"I shall see you soon, my Kat," she said, stepping back. She gathered her cape, whip, and riding gloves from the table and nodded to Meg, who must now retreat to the royal bedchamber until her return.

"Let's just not worry anymore about that fire they blamed you for," Kat whispered as the queen reached the door.

"All right," Elizabeth said, turning back with a forced, bright smile despite the tears still matting her eyelashes. "Let's not worry about a thing except having a good hunt."

Gil had heard the queen was sick in bed. He didn't doubt it, as little as she'd slept lately, as tautly strung as she had been. But since he had not worked the day before on the Sabbath, he needed to stop worrying about Elizabeth Tudor and get back to painting. He opened the pane of his slitted single window, the type they used to shoot arrows through, though decorative now. The chamber he'd been allotted here at Whitehall was much like a tiny cellar. It was damp instead of sunny and airy; the smell of his paints and oils disturbed him. Damn, but this window gave no good light to work by either, as dreary as the section of palace was, hard by the smelly kitchen block.

He stomped out into the narrow, dark corridor, took two lanterns from their wall hooks, and brought them back in. He lit them with his flint; their glow helped some. Leaning Dorothea's portrait against his low bed where he could see it best, he went back to work on his painting of the queen.

The royal portrait was going well, despite the chaos of his life—the entire court—of late. The painted version of his adored queen seemed to breathe, to move as she turned slightly beneath those sumptuous robes of state. The ladies of Italy—all but one—could eat their hearts out, but they'd never match this queen in the fabulous fire which emanated from her.

He shook his head; best not to think of it that way, linking queen and fire. But energy and emotion did blaze from her, and he could not ignore it in his art.

He worked intently until his stomach growled and cramped. Maybe that's why he was feeling weak, for sometimes he forgot to eat. And it was nearly midday, so he could go downstairs to the great hall and get something. He'd been placed on the bouche, the list of people allowed to eat there, though those of rank could have their allotted drink and meat delivered to their chambers. Yes, he'd just go get something quick and come back to paint.

He stopped to clean his hands on a rag. "'Complain not to me, O woman,'" he recited the words from Dorothea's mirror, which the queen still kept, "'for I return to you only what you gave me.' And that goes for both of you, the loves of my life," he added as he bowed to the queen and stroked Dorothea's painted cheek before he turned away.

He shook his head again. What he'd just declared sounded rather grand, as if it should be something Ned Topside or Giles Chatam recited from the stage. But it was true.

He went out and hurried down the corridor to find food to fill the hole in his belly, though he knew that nothing could help fill the one in his heart.

Riding fast without the royal entourage, the queen's party made it to Surrey in four hours. They went straight into the little village of Cheam on the eastern side of Nonsuch Park. The town, which she'd glimpsed through the years on hunts, was a bit bigger than Mortlake. It sat not on the river but amid fields the people worked, most coming in to town at night as if it were a walled medieval village with dangers lurking outside. The four of them reined in at the only hostelry in town, the Black Swan, which looked newer but dowdier than the inn at Mortlake.

"Jenks, I shall have you settle the horses, then bring the saddle packs inside. Clifford, Rosie has some coins to get us two rooms, so take her inside with you while I wait out here."

Her three companions froze, darting looks at each other.

"Go on then," she urged. "I'll not wander off, even if I see the running boy. Rosie, fetch me when you have the rooms."

Elizabeth stood back under the hanging eaves of the three-story inn—its roof was tile, not thatch, she noted with relief—and watched the sporadic passage of carts or hay wains. Driving a flock of geese with a long stick, a girl went by, so intent upon her task that she did not look up. What is her life like? Elizabeth mused. As much as she loved being queen among her people, she was always awestruck by going anonymously among them. How different her life, and her desires and dangers, would have been had she not been born Elizabeth of all England but simply Bess of Cheam.

Half-timbered houses both small and large stared at each

other across the town green, on which grazed black-faced sheep. A small church, but one sporting a spire and well-tended graveyard, stood across the way. How far from danger this rural setting seemed, but she would not let herself be lulled into complacency. Somewhere here were answers to her questions, and she meant to find them.

She turned back to discover what was keeping her fellows and saw Rosie peering at her through the thick-paned window of the inn, as if Elizabeth were a child out at play who must be watched. Jenks soon scurried around the front of the building, and Clifford popped out the door to announce they had the rooms. Such good people, she thought proudly, so vigilant for her safety and well-being.

"Are the horses being fed and watered?" she asked Jenks, who nodded. "Now that we are established, I plan to chat with the innkeeper about where we can find someone who lived through the demise of Cuddington and recalls the building of Nonsuch."

"I already found out one person who was at both, Your Grace," Jenks told her. "An old man named Beeson, at the blacksmith shop out back. It's his son what runs the stables."

"'S blood, I knew it," she muttered, slapping her gloves on her palm. "I should have come to Cheam the first time Dr. Dee mentioned that some who'd worked at Cuddington might still live here. And did this Beeson work on the art or decorations at Cuddington?"

"Seems Beeson was only a groom for the Mooring family there, Your Grace," Jenks said, shuffling his big feet, "so I'm not sure how much he'll know."

"If he knows half as much as my trusted friend Stephen Jenks, who began as *my* groom," she said, patting the big man's arm, "he may know a great deal."

Gil had laid into a good joint of mutton when he heard the hue and cry: "Fire! Fire in the kitchen wing!"

Since such an event was not uncommon, a few kept eating, but those who had been to Surrey with the queen jumped up and ran, either away from or toward the kitchens which adjoined this banquet hall. Because Gil's chamber was in that direction, he ran with those going to help or to gawk.

He scented smoke before he saw it. Damn, but it looked as if the men rushing with buckets were heading down his very hall! He made his way farther, through a makeshift bucket brigade composed mostly of kitchen staff. He tried to dart around the bystanders, then pushed his way through.

It was his chamber! And they were heaving bucket after bucket of water into it.

"Stop!" he shouted. "You'll ruin everything!"

"Too late for that," a voice cracked out. Cecil. Secretary Cecil himself stood here, watching, maybe organizing things. It was Cecil all right, even though he was holding a handkerchief over his nose and mouth.

"My lord, that's my chamber!"

"With your portrait of the queen, which has gone up in flames, the last of the bunch!" Cecil said, then started hacking.

Gil gaped in the door and beheld devastation. But he'd been gone only a quarter of an hour. Granted, he'd left the lanterns burning, but they had been on the table—nowhere near the bed, where they lay now. They had hardly leaped across the room!

He was desperate to explain to Cecil, but he went as mute as he had been as a boy. Someone had come here to burn him out. The bedclothes had caught. It looked as if both the queen's and Dorothea's portraits had been thrown on the bed to be incinerated, and water damage had completed that destruction. He was not sure if his tears were for his loss or from the smoke.

"I—is the fire setter here?" Gil choked out. "My work—the queen."

"Arrest him," Cecil said to someone, and two big guards—the queen's yeomen—seized his arms. "You figured you'd best sacrifice your things to save yourself, didn't you, lad, but left the chamber first?" Cecil demanded as other guards cleared onlookers from the hallway.

"No—I—no! I swear it!"

"You were seen bringing the lanterns in here, and that's what started the blaze. You've been holding things back all along, and that's the same as lying to Her Majesty. Now you can cool your heels under lock and key until she can question and deal with you later. Take him upstairs to one of those little rooms high above Sermon Court and keep him locked in and guarded."

Gil wanted to protest, but he knew better. His own half-truths had done him in. As he was hustled past Cecil, Gil overheard him whisper to a guard, "At first light tomorrow, you'll ride with word of this to the inn at Cheam, then, if need be, on to Dr. Dee's at Mortlake."

Gil's mind raced as fast as they were forcing his feet up the back servants' staircase. He could understand John Dee being informed of this fire, for it was obvious he'd been helping Her Majesty look for the fire setter through logical deduction. But who was staying at the inn at Cheam?

————

Paul Beeson, called only by his last name, was a wizened old man with a bird's nest of white hair and a face that looked as if it were tanned leather. The queen thought it ironic to find him by a belching farrier's fire with leather bellows. She thought too of Dame Dee, sitting by her hearth fire, for this seemed not to be Beeson's place of employment but retirement. It turned out another of Beeson's sons worked this forge, just the way one owned the stables.

"Greatly honored to make your acquaintance, milady," Master Beeson said more than once, nodding his head, when Elizabeth introduced herself as Bess Smythe from Coventry. The old man had evidently decided on his own that she was a lady, and she didn't correct him. She saw that he was nearly blind; one eye was cloudy, and the other never focused on or followed her.

"And I am honored to meet you, Master Beeson. I dare say your hoary head and wrinkled visage bespeak not only many years but much local knowledge."

"Used to tend horses at a great house near here, I did, 'fore its fall."

"Its fall?" she prompted as the old man walked her away from the heat of the forge and the huffing hiss of the bellows that fanned it. He did not pick up his feet when he walked, but shuffled. Yet he moved as if he had the placement of everything memorized. She hoped she was dealing with a sword-sharp mind.

"Aye, the Moorings' manor house at Cuddington," he explained. "You've heard how it was torn down, manor, church, and town, I warrant."

"Oh, yes. You knew the family?"

"Knew the sire, Master John, who loved to ride and hunt. Like everyone else, admired from afar Mistress Malinda, a rare beauty. But taught young Master Percy to ride, I did," he said, thrusting out his thin chest.

Elizabeth's heartbeat quickened. "But even after Cuddington fell, as you say, you stayed in these parts while the palace was being built?"

"Nowhere else to go, and had family here," he explained as they paused between the blacksmith shop and the inn. Chickens scratched and scurried about their feet, but she ignored them. From here she could see into the public stables, where her horses were being curried by local lads, perhaps Beeson's own grandsons.

"My good man," she went on, "do you know of anyone in these parts who worked to adorn Nonsuch—painting, carving, and the like? That would have been anytime after 1538."

"Hm, how many years ago is that?" he asked, stroking his chin. "Must admit I sometimes pay no heed what year or month it is, though I still got my memories, that I do."

"It would have been just over twenty-seven years ago."

"Damned Tudor king, and most folks in these parts still feel the same, e'en when the young queen comes calling across the hunt park," he groused. Both Clifford and Jenks stiffened at that, but she shook her head at them. "Well, milady," the old man went on, "I can think of two who might have suited, but they're both dead and buried."

"Of old age—natural causes?"

"Tell you true, both of unnatural causes. Old Friar Rolland— he wasn't no friar, but wore his hair like that, you know, milady, cut in a tonsure—he fell off a roof. He was a tiler, see, but no one knows how he slipped, 'cause the roof he was doing then, just down the way there," he added, gesturing vaguely, "wasn't that steep."

"At least it wasn't a fire," Elizabeth muttered to Rosie, who stood beside her.

"Now, how'd you know that," Beeson countered, " 'cause Will Croydon worked on setting them Roman emperor's portraits into the walls of the inner courtyard of Nonsuch. And got hisself kilt by a hearth fire what spread to his bed clothes one night and burned him to death in his own bed, it did. Always said I'd like to die in my own bed, but not roasted like a pig in a poke."

Elizabeth shuddered. The pattern and possible motive for the attacks on Will Kendale and Simon Garver matched these deaths. Someone was killing, mostly by fire, the artists or craftsmen who had worked to adorn Nonsuch. And had those vengeful acts then spread to attacks on other artists—her artists? Or on the queen's ladies and the queen herself?

"Master Beeson," she said, trying to keep her voice steady, "can you tell me anything about the two strange hillocks which are to the east side of Nonsuch?"

His eyes widened as he seemed to regard her anew, though his vacant gaze looked slightly past her. "You hain't been staying in Nonsuch, have you?" he asked, his voice shaky.

"I am simply interested in this area," she assured him. "It is very beautiful and the local history fascinating."

"Best not be riding onto Lord Arundel's land and what's still a royal hunt forest, e'en though they say the queen's gone back to London," he warned. "Trespassing at best, poaching at worst."

"I'll remember that," she said, taking two gold crowns out of the pouch she wore on her belt.

"The Moorings were formerly a Cath'lic fam'bly on the

climb," Beeson said. "I don't know for sure, but I think that was another reason—besides the fine prospect of their land—that the king good as beggared them. Supposedly, they were compensated," he said with a derisive snort, "but it wasn't nothing like what they lost." Elizabeth listened raptly, holding the paltry coins in her perspiring palms before she slipped them back in her purse. "Proud of their manor and the church and little town what sprung up around, they were. And of their two fine children."

"I noted well your pride, too, when you mentioned how you taught the heir, Master Percy, to ride," she said. "Can you tell me what happened to all of them when they had to move elsewhere?"

"Bitter and broken, all of them. But Master Percy never had to turn his back on his birthright and ride away like the others. You asked, milady, 'bout those hillocks, aye, man-made, they were. I helped haul in the soil and pile it up."

"For watchtowers or hunting platforms or blinds? I note there are remnants of building foundations there, and something once made of the same stones in the meadow."

"Who are you really, then, milady?"

"Someone who regrets what happened here and wants to be certain such never happens again."

He nodded and started to walk again, past the inn, out toward the high street through the village. Elizabeth, trailed by her trio of companions, hurried to keep up.

"Once we reach the green, you'll have to steer me the rest of the way," Beeson declared.

"Where are we going then?"

"I think it's time, milady, you paid a visit to Master Percy."

———

This tiny room might as well be a prison cell, Gil thought as he rolled over on his lousy, sagging bed. He hadn't had lice for years, but he would now. Still, he lay there, fingers linked under his head, staring up at the ceiling.

He felt he might as well have burned up in that fire too. He'd lost everything he valued, the painting which was his past and the one which was his future. His very supplies, Italian, costly. His clothes, but for these work ones on his back. The queen had his mirror, and could even have his life when she returned.

He figured she'd gone back to Surrey to oversee an investigation of the murders, for he'd seen her do such before, leaving Meg Milligrew in her place and just shutting her doors to everyone but Cecil and Lady Ashley for a day or two. If he could only get to her, plead his case, tell her the truth—and warn her that the fire setter was here at court but was not the person the zealous Cecil had locked away.

Gil groaned and sat up. He had to get out of here. His eyes still stung, not only from the smoke, but from the sight of his beloved Dorothea blackened, and the queen, so regal and so real, gone up in flames, as had the works of Kendale, Lavina—but not Heatherley. Oh, no, that braggart had repaired his well enough! If Gil had to pick someone to blame, it would be that blackguard with his grandly scrolled HH on each portrait that might as well mean his idol Hans Holbein as well as his own name. A good thing Holbein was dead so he didn't know what leeches artists could be to copy another's works by hook or by crook! Heatherley was as bad as the Italians, mimicking others' works, though they did it with their damned mirror tricks and not a pack of lies.

Gil forced himself to his feet and stood on tiptoe to look out the single, high window of this tiny room. It let in light but no breeze. If there hadn't been a guard on his door, he'd have broken the glass and risked his neck trying to get up on the roof. But everyone knew it was guarded now, lest the fire setter walk freely here as he had at Nonsuch.

He heaved a huge sigh and fiddled with the window latch. In olden days, before he grew so tall and broke his leg, he would not have feared going out that window, grabbing the roof tiles, and getting himself out of here.

To his surprise, as if it were a sign, the latch lifted and the window shoved easily, silently outward. Sweet air and the late-afternoon sun came streaming in like a beckoning finger. He tried to shove the single chair under it so he could look out, but the legs grated against the stone floor. He knew a guard was on his door. And if he heard a sound or came in, Gil had no doubt that Cecil would take an escape attempt as a sign of further guilt. So he lifted the heavy chair to move it silently. Climbing on it, he saw he was not under the eaves but on the next story down—the one, he could see, that had the narrow decorative ledge running under it.

He closed his eyes and prayed hard, not in Italian, as he had done when he was in Italy, but in good, solid English. *Oh, Lord God, if you could just get me out of here and spirit me to the queen, I could set everything right . . . let truth and justice prevail . . . warn her that her palace and people are in danger here. I could keep her throne safe for all Christendom. Please give me a sign if this is what I should do.*

He sensed no answer, and stuck only his head out to look down at a ledge the old Gil would have danced along in delight. That is, he sensed no answer until a lark flew into the nearby ivy, fluttered its feathers, and sang him its sweet song.

"Those heavy ivy vines run all along this side," Gil muttered. "I'll just walk on the ledge and hang on to the vine, and hope the roof guards don't look down or across the court."

With nothing but the clothes on his back—and frantic fear in his heart—Gil glanced around the room, then lifted himself up by the lintel above the window, and got his feet out first. He writhed through the small rectangle, wishing he were little Gil again. Turning over, belly down, he held on to the sill with his legs and backside dangling and felt with his booted toes for the ledge beneath.

How far below? Where? At first, his feet windmilled nothing but air. Cecil would think him a double liar now for claiming he never climbed anymore. There! One toe on it. If only his old skills—and old courage—would come back.

His shoulders got stuck, and when he tried to wrench them free of the window, he nearly fell backward away from the building. He grabbed for the thick vine. Twigs and ivy tore free from the brick; the lark darted and protested, as if he were after its nest. But he held tight.

And then he made the mistake of looking down. Three stories below lay the patterned pavement of Sermon Court. The black and white diagonals seemed to waver, the corners to round and shift. He closed his eyes tightly, then looked up and out over the thatch, shake, and tile rooftops of London toward the broad river.

That steadied him somewhat, and he made himself a vow. He was going to get down from here and to the queen or die trying.

Chapter the Fourteenth

GIL PRESSED HIS BACK TO THE IVY-LACED WALL, ARMS straight down to grab the thicker vines behind his bum, and shuffled along the narrow ledge high above the pavement. Several courtiers walked below, even two of Cecil's scriveners, earnestly nodding in conversation. He thanked God that none of them glanced up, nor did he see the queen's guards on the opposite roof.

His bad leg began to ache, then to tremble. No, he was shaking all over. If he got caught, he might as well have fallen. Cecil considered him guilty of the fire murders. Worse, Gil knew that he'd used up all his favors with the queen. And now that his portrait of her had been destroyed . . .

He gulped as he came to the corner which would take him around to the Kings Street gatehouse. This would get him outside the bounds of the palace proper, but it presented two problems. More people would be on the street below to see him. And the ivied wall was about to be left behind.

However would he get down from this height to the public

thoroughfare to make his final escape? He could never manage a flying leap to the nearby trees. And then, without a farthing to his name and looking like the street urchin he once was, how could he get all the way to Cheam or Mortlake to throw himself upon the mercy of the queen—if indeed she was in Surrey?

The corner terrified him, when he would not even have slowed for it years ago. He and his mother, Bett, had been the best of anglers, crawling in second- or third-story windows to steal or at least survey what to steal later with their long angling hooks. Now he held to the last of the ivy vine for dear life and managed to turn inward to the building to chance the corner. He scraped his face and chest as he went around it. Yes, the thick mat of ivy ended here; he was on his own with just a ledge barely as wide as his painter's palette.

Old advice he'd heard as a child from other anglers came back to him. Don't tense up. Don't look down. Remember to breathe. If only he could find a window open at this height. Otherwise, sliding down that distant drainpipe would be the only option.

The late-afternoon traffic in the street below began to make him dizzy. Foot travelers, carts, horses, wagons, people with supplies for the palace, streamed by. Down the way he noted the guards on the palace gate where Cecil had gotten him in when he came back to London with high hopes just a fortnight ago. Now he was high, but his hopes were—

"Look! A lad up on the gate! Look, Evan!"

Others gazed up, gawking, pointing, calling out to him. Their voices blurred. Were they saying "Jump" or "Don't jump"? The guards on the gate looked his way. Though they didn't leave their posts, he assumed they would summon someone, and soon Cecil would have him caged again. He tried to anchor his back and shoulders to the wall to risk motioning the crowd away, but their noise and numbers grew. Did they think he was performing for their pleasure?

And then he saw a man looking up at him from the sea of faces. It was the one he'd been sure was after him in Dover, even in London. A swarthy man—perhaps the Italian in the Riverside Inn at Mortlake—staring up with a smirk that seemed to scream, *I've got you now!* Could he be the fire-mirror murderer, meant to torment and threaten Gil to silence—or kill him—and he'd simply missed so far?

"But you said young Percy Mooring died," Elizabeth protested as old Beeson led her around the edge of the town green toward the church.

"Aye, but you can still pay your respects," he told her. "He's in here, his mortal remains at least, and a lot can be read from that."

"His tomb, you mean?" she asked as Jenks leaped ahead to open the church door Beeson headed for. "With an epitaph perhaps? How did he die, Master Beeson?"

"When you see it all, I'll tell you all," he said, and shuffled inside.

It was dim within the church, lit only by natural light from narrow windows. A chill seemed to seep from the cold stone bones of the arches and pillars. Creeping in from somewhere, a draft breathed in their faces to stir hair and garments. She saw few memorials carved into the paving stones to signify crypts beneath, and fewer effigies on graves above the flagstone floor.

But one ornate and grand tomb stood out. In finely carved stone, it was the life-size effigy of a boy, lying on his back and staring upward with his hands stiffly pressed together in perpetual prayer. As with many of the fine tombs in St. Paul's and Westminster in London, the figure was painted in lifelike colors. A long Latin inscription snaked around the big black stone casket on which the effigy lay as if it were a bed.

"That," Beeson said, and his voice echoed strangely as they approached the tomb, "is how much they loved him."

"'Percival Mooring, departed this mortal life at ten years of age,'" she translated the Latin script. "'Died defending his home which was under attack'? A mere boy defended Cuddington, Master Beeson? Will you tell us the story you promised?" she asked, gripping the ornate iron rail which encircled the monument.

"You asked, milady, 'bout the man-made hillocks and remnants of stones. The lad loved to play gallant knight and soldier. So his father built him three small stone towers, he did, two on gentle rises and one in the meadow. Master Percy pretended to guard Cuddington manor house—this was e'en before they knew the king would take it. And on the very day the king's men rode in to tell the Moorings all must be swept away, Master Percy threw stones at one of the royal surveyors striding around the grounds."

"The king's men surely did not hurt the boy!" she cried.

"Of course they did, though not the way you mean. See, in throwing stones, he tumbled down and broke his neck. I think that broke Master John's spirit to fight back, though he cursed the king, and Mistress Malinda threw her mirror at them and cursed them too."

"Threw her *mirror*?"

"Oh, aye, bad luck, curses on them, you know. She was the loveliest of women, though my wife used to say all she did was comb her long hair in the sun and look into that mirror."

"And the mirror broke to curse the king?"

"No, saw what happened myself, I did. It landed in the grass and didn't break at all."

"But all the Moorings are dead now, are they not?"

"So's I heard. The daughter not so long ago, maybe two years, the others earlier, and none of them but the boy buried here. Should have been interred in the church at Cuddington, course, but that was . . ."

". . . To be torn down," Elizabeth finished as if in chorus with him. She gripped the metal railing around the monument even harder. "Such tragedy," she whispered.

"My lady Bess," Jenks said, his voice somber, "you don't think the so-called running boy in the woods could be related to this dead boy Percy do you?"

"I told you, we are putting stock not in ghosts but in reality, man."

"What running boy?" Beeson asked. "Never heard of no running boy ghost round these parts. If there be ghosts, they're over there at Nonsuch, on the site of the old Cuddington church with its graves disturbed. Read more of those Latin words there, milady."

With a shudder that was not from the physical chill of this place, Elizabeth read the rest of the script on the tomb, translating it aloud for everyone: " 'Beloved son, not even to lie with his ancestors in the Cuddington church to be torn down.' Oh, look," Elizabeth said, "they've carved a dog at his feet on this side." She turned the corner of the rectangular monument. "And who is this little boy here at Percy's feet opposite the dog—his playfellow?"

She had to squeeze her skirts between the church wall and the monument to see better. It was so dim here, yet even as the others pressed closer, she recognized what the carving depicted.

Both hands flew to cover her open mouth. What a fool she'd been! This was not the statue of another boy. Why hadn't she thought of this possibility?

"If you mean the dwarf," Beeson said, edging around behind her, "that's the children's playfellow, Dench Barlow. I know I told you to keep clear of Nonsuch forest, but Dench lives out there somewheres, has for years. Never was quite right in the head since young Percy got kilt and Cuddington ripped down. No one's seen him much in years, 'cept recently."

"You've seen him recently?" she blurted before she realized she should not have put it that way.

"I heard," Beeson said, "he played a drum and cavorted for a few coins with a traveling players group what's been in the area off and on."

Gil froze in fear. Master Giorgio *had* sent someone to silence him about the way he and some other Italian artists rigged mirrors not only to copy paintings but to create realistic portraits from life. Their secret was to have been shared with Gil only after he took a blood oath never to reveal it to others, but he'd fled before that, and—in trying to overhear information for the queen—he'd seen how the so-called camera obscura with its mirror and darkroom worked. And so this man must be an assassin sent after him.

At that instant, as the swarthy man began to push his way through the crowd, a hay wain, probably carting its pile of feed for the royal stables, passed under the gate. It was going the wrong direction, but Gil saw it as his only chance.

Feet extended, he threw himself out and jumped into it.

Despite the amount of hay, he landed hard on his back. He sucked in a huge breath of chaff and dust. Trying to ignore the pain in his bad leg, he rolled out of the wain and bolted back the other way, pushing through people, though the gate. Behind him, some laughed, some cheered.

He turned toward the river, for the crowd coming up from the public landing was thicker. He plunged through them, hoping, if the man gave chase, to lose him. The Thames could take him upstream to Mortlake if he could find a boat to hide on.

Panicked, he darted into a narrow passage between two buildings near the public-landing stairs and threw himself behind a large wooden rain barrel, his heart nearly beating out of his chest. At least it would soon be dark, one hour, two at the most.

He caught his breath, and his heartbeat slowed. The sounds of the street were muted here, so this would make a good place to stay until night fell. Some small craft plied the river at night with lanterns on their prows. He'd try to catch one heading upstream toward Richmond and hope he could tell when they passed Mortlake in the dark, lulled by the river, rowing on and away. . . .

He jerked awake. He must have dozed, how long he didn't know, but it was sometime between dusk and dark. What had awakened him? Surely not just the distant cries of ferrymen tying up for the night or the thinning rush of passersby. He stretched his aching legs and arms and back.

Then he heard a shuffling sound nearby, coming closer. He stopped breathing. Whatever it was, it was not a rat or some stray cat, but bigger. Wishing he had a weapon, he felt behind the barrel but touched naught but grit and grime. Nothing nearby, not even a stick. He could jump up and bolt again, but the passage

narrowed beyond and might even lead to what scared him most—
a dead end.

The moment they returned from Cheam's church, Elizabeth had
Clifford order partridge pie, cheese, and bread sent up to her and
Rosie's chamber at the Black Swan. But so far only Clifford and
Jenks were eating. She and Rosie were both so nervous they could
barely stomach even the sugared wine the innkeeper had sent up
gratis. But the cider was so far out of season, it would have
knocked them all on their ears. Indeed, Elizabeth felt so shaken,
she might as well have been as drunk as Henry Heatherley.

"At first light," she told her crew, "we're going into the hunt-
park forest to find this Dench. He could well have a motive for
revenge. And I want to take Beeson with us, even if he can't see
farther than the length of his own nose. We will describe the ter-
rain to him, and if we can find Dench, having Beeson with us may
keep him from trying to flee."

"We get anywhere near him, we'll get him this time, Your
Grace," Jenks vowed, his mouth full of food. "Can't get far on
those little legs."

"He has before," she countered. "I can't believe, *cannot believe*, I
didn't realize that the running boy could be—especially with
those squat legs—a dwarf! I've seen dwarfs at court, especially
those my father favored."

"Well," Clifford put in, "I saw the running boy and didn't
think of a dwarf either. And if he's been working for Giles
Chatam—"

"Exactly," Elizabeth said, hitting the table with her fist so hard
the pewter plates rattled. "Even if Dench lit one or more of the

fatal fires, it doesn't clear Giles of collusion. And if Giles is possibly linked to Katherine——'s blood, I shall forgo this disguise and question Giles and Mistress Dee tomorrow too."

"And what about that magic mirror of Mistress Mooring's?" Rosie put in.

"It was hardly a magic mirror," the queen chided.

"It didn't break when she threw it," Rosie protested.

Elizabeth just shook her head. It reminded her of Dr. Dee's tale that Katherine had found his stolen mirror lying unbroken and unscratched in a patch of violets, no less. Oh yes, she was surely going to question both Giles Chatam and Katherine Dee again.

"Clifford and I," Jenks said, spearing another chunk of cheese with his knife, "will be taking turns sitting outside your door in the hall tonight, Your Grace."

Still mired in her own thoughts, she merely nodded. "I wager that dwarf Dench has been playing with fire, though at whose urging we are yet to determine."

"And if he thought he was playing with fire, he's not seen nothing yet," Jenks said. "Not with Lady Bess Smythe and her folks on his tail, I'll tell you that."

Ordinarily, the queen would have laughed, especially since the plain-minded Jenks had turned a clever phrase. But even though they now had more answers, a knotted web of possibilities was yet to be unraveled.

Gil figured he couldn't afford to wait to see who peeked around the barrel and trapped him here. He shoved himself to his feet and tensed to run or fight.

Just a bulky form at first, but yes, the swarthy man! How long had he been searching for him?

"Stop, Meester Sharpino!" he cried in English heavy with an Italian accent. "I will hide you from zee queen's guards. I have message and money for you from zee maestro!"

He also had, Gil could see, a dagger in his hand.

Hoping in this dry stretch of weather that the rain barrel might be nearly empty, Gil managed to tip it and roll it toward the man, who went down like a bowling pin. Trying to keep to the far wall, Gil edged past him and fled toward the street, even as the man tried to grab his leg.

No, he was cut—his ankle bleeding on his bad leg. It pulsated with pain, hot, then icy cold, as he ran toward the waterfront. Good thing it was dark, for he might be leaving a crimson trail for the man to stalk him like a wounded deer.

But he was determined to get to the queen. If he died bleeding at her feet, maybe she'd at least know he was no fire murderer.

Gil knew supplies for the palace came day or night to this landing, some surely from the upstream countryside. And at night, they must make their way back to reload. Dragging his leg, trying to swing it forward with both hands at each step, he looked desperately for any sort of craft which seemed to be setting out. He dared not even take time to look back.

The big horse- and foot-ferries were moored for the night, but barges and wherries still had boatmen in them. Yet it seemed nothing was setting out, or even ready to cast off. Yes, there, an empty lighter that unloaded the large barges. And the boatman had unwrapped the mooring line and was ready to pole out from the landing while two younger, big-shouldered crewmen hunched over, awaiting his orders to row.

"Help me, I beg you!" Gil cried. "A thief robbed and cut me and means to kill me—back there...."

As he glanced behind him, he saw that the swarthy man was close. No knife in sight now, but the look on that foreign face must have decided the bold English boatman. In an instant, the lighterman lifted and swung the pole to send the Italian tumbling into the Thames with a splash.

"I kin see yer bleeding, my boy," the boatman cried. "Shall we summon the constable or a leech then?"

"I just want to go home—to Mortlake in Surrey!"

"Come on then, climb aboard."

The pain in Gil's leg was so excruciating he almost couldn't manage the climb, even with the boatman's help. As he sank to his knees on board and clung to the side of the lighter, he scanned the inky Thames where his pursuer had fallen. Nothing but ripples, soon erased by the wake of their craft. He wondered if Italians could swim, for he saw nothing else but black water, and then nothing at all.

For the first time in weeks, a spring storm rent the Surrey countryside. Elizabeth and Rosie awakened to the rumble of thunder and flash of lightning.

"'S blood," the queen muttered as they hastily dressed, "we're going after Dench anyway. This has got to let up."

The worst of the weather had retreated as they set out, though without Beeson, who had said he wasn't well. But he'd come to the door of his son's house to give them some parting advice. "His place won't be easy to spot. It's always deep in the woods, though he moves about from time to time, he does. So can't really tell you where to look. Closer to Nonsuch than to Cheam prob'ly, always was."

"Is it a sort of hovel?" Elizabeth had asked. "Partly underground? One greatly disguised by trees or sod?"

"Not Dench," Beeson had said, rather proudly, she had thought. "Strange, you know, but you'll have to look up to find him. Little as he is, he has more in common with the squirrels in the trees than with the foxes in their dens. He'll be off the ground a ways in a sturdy tree, a little place built with boards and ropes."

"With ropes . . . ," Elizabeth kept muttering to herself as the four of them rode into the damp, dripping forest, where she'd been on many a hunt before. She could not believe that a dwarf could climb trees, or palace walls, but perhaps with help from ropes—and someone else.

"He'd be easy to flush out in the winter without all these leaves," Jenks observed as they scanned the trees above. "We ought to send to London for your yeomen, surround this place, and flush him out."

"From treetop level?" Elizabeth challenged. "He'd just stay put. And why didn't he strike at us before this spring, if he's lived here for years? We've had tents in the meadow every time we've come to Nonsuch. Perhaps I should leave the two of you to search for Dench, and Rosie and I should ride to speak with Katherine Dee and Giles—if we can find him and his troupe. I'll bet that night my yeomen guards found him in the forest here, the rogue had been meeting with Dench." She halted her horse and sucked in a breath. "Clifford, do you recall that the yeomen guards who brought Giles in for questioning that day mentioned he was in the part of the forest nearest to Mortlake?"

"That day he was supposedly practicing his lines? Right," Clifford agreed. "And we now know that Dench was in his employ as a drummer by then. Let's try that section of forest. At least it's on the way to Mortlake, where you would question Mistress Dee."

Despite the hope of that lead, they were a sodden, sorry group after they'd scanned the thick trees for another hour. Rain dripped off their noses and down their necks. And then Rosie pointed up and cried, "What's that? If he's living like a squirrel, that looks like a big squirrel's nest!"

"Keep your voice down," the queen ordered as she rode closer to get the same vantage point Rosie had. "Yes, I warrant that is it."

Despite her desperation to find Dench, a glimmer of sympathy shot through her. To be so small, to have to look up to everyone, except one's playfellow Percy, and then to lose him . . . Her brother's face flashed through her mind. How she had missed him when he died, and still did. That longing for him had made Gil even dearer to her, as if she could have Edward back to help and encourage.

"Your Grace, what shall we do now?" Clifford's question shattered her agonizing.

"Let's surround the place as best we can," she whispered as they clustered together; "then one of you go up. There must be footholds on the tree, though I have no doubt now he is very adept with ropes, so he's probably pulled them up after himself."

"I'll go up," Jenks said. "I'm built a bit more for it than Clifford."

"But I don't want him to surprise you twenty feet above the ground," she argued, more with herself than Jenks. "You must be careful, for I won't have you hurt!"

Gil's cut leg was crudely bandaged, but it hurt terribly, more than any other pain he'd ever felt—except having to leave Dorothea.

And his heart pained him now, losing so much with Cecil, perhaps the queen.

He stirred stiffly and opened his eyes. It was morning. He lifted his head. The rhythmic thrust-pull, thrust-pull of the two rowers' oars had rocked him to sleep for hours. The queen's Richmond Palace was just coming into view, so Mortlake wasn't far.

"You 'wake, boy?" Lem, the boatman, asked. "I think you got a fever. Here's beer if your whistle's dry."

"I'm grateful," Gil managed as he accepted a proffered tankard and took a swig.

"From Mortlake, you say? I know the place, not far now. Who's your family there?"

"Dees," he said. At least, if he blacked out again, maybe this Lem would deliver him to their door.

"The magician?" Lem said, his voice awed. One of the rowers turned around and stared, though he didn't miss his next pull.

"Just a wise man. Yes, Dees, Dr. Dee."

He guessed he did have a fever, but he wasn't out of his head. He handed the tankard back before slumping back down on the deck in utter exhaustion. Though he tried to picture his dear Dorothea, all he saw in his jumbled dreams was that drowned Italian, holding a magic mirror spewing fire and death.

"I'd like to go up there with Jenks," Elizabeth muttered under her breath as she, Rosie, and Clifford watched him climb. He had found no footholds on the trunk of the massive oak which supported the small, ramshackle house in the tree, but had climbed a nearby chestnut with more limbs, trying at least to see into the makeshift structure.

He looked down, shaking his head and shrugging, for Elizabeth had told him not to call out, so they could surprise and capture a still sleeping Dench Barlow. Either he could not get a glimpse inside the little place or could tell no one was there. The queen was thoroughly frustrated and lifted both hands, palms up, to convey her uncertainty about how to proceed.

"I don't see how he gets up and down with no footholds and no ropes visible," Clifford said. "I fear you're right that he must pull them all in behind him, so I'd say he's up there."

"And watching us, perhaps," Rosie added.

"Cheam must have a thatcher or tiler who owns a long ladder," Elizabeth said. "Clifford, if you think you could manage bringing it back on a single horse, ride to borrow or rent one while the three of us stay here. And bring back some ropes."

"But with Jenks up there and me away, it's not safe for the two of you," he protested.

"This must be done. Nothing worth a risk is really safe, my man. Go!"

As Clifford rode away, Elizabeth gestured to the puzzled Jenks to stay put but hidden. Rosie tied the three remaining horses a slight ways off, and they settled in to wait. The forest smelled rich and dank, for the sun popped in and out, flashing shards of light, then shadows all around. Tired of standing, her neck sore from looking up, Elizabeth sat on the large trunk of a fallen oak. The wait dragged on; how long had passed she was not sure. She almost dozed, until a shrill voice resounded from above.

"Am I to be honored you've come calling, eh? I know she didn't send you!"

Elizabeth jumped to her feet and looked up. Jenks was so shocked he barely kept from falling off his perch. No one was visible at first, but then she saw an angry face peer over the edge of the wooden planks high above.

"Good day to you!" the queen called, though her heart was pounding and her voice shook. "Dench Barlow, I presume? I've come from Giles Chatam with some coin for you and a request. Could you not come down?"

"You think I don't know who you are, eh? After watching all of you for the last few weeks ere you betook yourselves away."

"Who do you say I am?" she demanded.

"Spawn of the king who murdered my prince!"

He did know who she was, and was not only not impressed, but sounded dangerous, maybe demented. But would someone who helped to burn people alive not be so? Beeson had said he was not well in the head.

"I have deep regrets about the Moorings and your childhood friend Percy," she called up to him. "I wish I could make it right."

"Liar!" he screamed, so loud his high-pitched voice seemed to echo off the tree trunks. "You wish to get the land back from Arundel! All you Tudors lust for land and pretty things and power. You wish to have your likeness painted so all can see the grandeur of the Tudors! You want to enslave those of us who are left, and we will not let you!"

She fought to keep calm. "But who is 'we'? Who is the lady you don't believe sent me?"

"The lovely and the lethal," he said with a sharp laugh. "One of the few who have been kind, always kind to him, of course."

"Kind to whom? Is she a lovely lady from Mortlake who is kind to Giles?" she threw out wildly, hoping for a response. "I only want to talk—"

"Liar! You mean to trap me!" he screeched. "I see your man in the next tree, eh, I do!" he cried, pointing to the spot where Jenks tried to hide himself. "And that one there with traps and snares!"

She turned to see Clifford returning with a ladder balanced on one shoulder and ropes coiled about the other. When he saw or heard them, he spurred his horse faster, though she tried to motion him away.

"You plan to catch me and torture me to tell!" Dench accused, "but that will never be. I will never betray the one who will be the death of you, too, even of your people and places! And it's already too late, so be prepared to suffer. I hear you thought I was a ghost, and I shall haunt you from my death to yours!"

"Please, just calm yourself and come down so th——," the queen began, then gasped with the others when Dench stood to his full height at the edge of his lofty home. He unhooked a rope from somewhere, leaped into air, and swung directly down and at them—at her.

Rosie screamed, Jenks shouted, and Clifford dropped the ladder and leaped from his mount, but they were all too late.

Chapter the Fifteenth

 THE ROPE WAS NOT LONG ENOUGH TO BRING DENCH TO the ground. To everyone's horror, pumping his little legs to give himself more speed, he swung with great velocity up in a huge arc, then back toward his tree, where he intentionally rammed himself headfirst into the trunk.

Rosie screamed. Stunned, they stood stock-still at the sickening sound of Dench's cracking skull rising above the rustle and twitter of the forest. He fell straight to the ground and lay motionless while his rope bounced, then swayed above him.

Elizabeth ran to him, hoping she could save him, have one last moment to ask him who were the "we" and "lady" he had referred to. But the moment she saw his bloodied head and grotesque sprawl, she knew that he was gone. He had taken so much with him, including the truth of whom he'd been working with.

Gil felt hot, then cold. He wasn't sure where he was, but the woman who washed his face was not his mother and not Katherine Dee, nor one of the queen's servants, either.

"Where am I?" he asked, but his voice came out a mere whisper.

"At the boatman's home, poor lad," the plump woman said, and lifted a tankard of something to his lips. Beer. Cool beer, or else he was burning up. But he had to get to the queen.

"Bit of a storm come up last night," she went on cheerily. "They put in at our landin' rather than takin' you the rest of the way."

"Got to go—Mortlake," he said, then went back to gulping the beer she held to his mouth.

"Just a mile away. We can send one of the boys to tell your mother. You rest now."

But the moment the kindly woman left the small room, Gil rolled to his side, swung his good leg over the bed, and lifted the other one down with both hands. He saw he had a new bandage on his ankle, though blood had seeped through that, too.

When he tried to stand, the entire room seemed to tilt and sway. But he could surely walk one mile. He'd just ask which way to Mortlake, to Dr. Dee's, then step carefully on his cut leg, which burned now like the very pit of hell.

Already panting from his exertion, he stopped only to guzzle the rest of the beer. Wishing he had coins to leave for the kindness he'd been shown—and for the lighterman's knocking that Italian assassin in the river—Gil made a vow. He'd see these people were rewarded if the queen took him back.

He started out the door into the wan afternoon sun, dragging his bad leg and hopes behind.

———

With the possibility of questioning the "running boy" gone, the queen acted quickly. She sent Clifford back to Cheam with Dench's corpse and money for Beeson. Clifford was to thank the old man for his help and to see that Dench was buried, perhaps, she suggested, in Percy Mooring's tomb. Jenks, meanwhile, was to accompany her and Rosie to the Dees' house, then track down the acting troupe in local villages and bring Giles to her. Elizabeth and Rosie would question Katherine Dee and perhaps Dame Dee, to see what the old woman had observed of the death of Cuddington and birth of Nonsuch.

But after Jenks had ridden off in search of Giles, the queen and Rosie discovered that Katherine wasn't home. John Dee himself greeted and escorted them into the solar while Elizabeth explained about Percy Mooring and his dwarf Dench.

"So, the puzzle begins to fit together, yet the very corner pieces are still missing," he said, stroking his beard. When their serving girl came in with a tray of goblets, he added, "Ah, yes, Sarah with wine. But to see you suddenly here like this, Your Majesty, nearly unattended and thusly attired . . ."

"I could not leave these fire murders alone. No one is safe until the perpetrator is caught."

"You recall the Roman emperor Nero, who fiddled while Rome burned, Your Majesty."

She shuddered involuntarily. The mere idea of her capital city going up in flames made her sick. "Semantics and stories aside," she said, "I must speak with your wife the moment she returns."

"But you do not think she has aught to do wi—"

"Of course not, but I thought she might have observed Giles

Chatam. Since we have witnesses who say Dench worked for him in one way, we might assume—"

"Ah, indeed. Might assume that this demented Dench worked for Giles to set the fires, too. But why?"

"One possibility is that when Giles and his players came to Nonsuch just after the second fire, he said he thought they could calm the court."

"As in that old adage 'Music can soothe the savage breast,' which so many erroneously believe is 'soothe the savage beast.' Only this time Giles must have hoped you would believe that comedies and romances soothe the distraught court—and queen."

"Exactly," she said, admiring his perceptive nature again, yet wondering if it hadn't occurred to him and Katherine that a fire would also make their queen need Dr. Dee more. After all, it was exactly how she had reacted, both to Giles and the Dees—keeping them closer and bestowing benefits.

"But surely," Dr. Dee said, "my Katherine cannot help you with information about this Giles Chatam fellow."

"Has she ever mentioned him?"

"Only that she thought he was quite wonderful at the May Day festivities. I was so busy with the Maypole mirror that day— Ah, I think I hear her."

Elizabeth stood and put down her goblet of untouched wine. "Let me greet her," she said, holding up a hand to halt his rush, "and explain my need for her help."

He nodded, but the queen could tell that he was worried. Perhaps he had put together the puzzle he had mentioned and found his dear Katherine was very possibly a missing piece.

Elizabeth left the solar and walked toward the young woman in the front hallway. When Katherine saw her, she gasped and dropped her basket of strawberries. They were so ripe that everywhere they bounced, including against the hems of both their skirts, they made crimson stains.

"Is my husband quite well?" Katherine cried. "I'm just startled to see you suddenly back here, Your Majesty, dressed so plainly."

Elizabeth recalled that Katherine had dropped meat pastries at her feet the first day they met. She didn't seem clumsy otherwise, so was such agitation the outward sign of a guilty heart?

"Come with me into the garden," the queen said, and surprised Katherine even more by indicating she should precede her.

In the kitchen, Dame Dee was asleep, her mouth agape, her head cocked against her high-backed chair. In the walled garden, Katherine spun to face Elizabeth, the empty basket clutched in her hands before she threw it down.

"Whatever brings you back here so soon, Your Majesty?" she asked before Elizabeth could speak again. "And dressed—well, in disguise, I take it?"

"I am trying to learn all I can about the itinerant actor Giles Chatam, and thought you could help me."

"Giles Chatam?" Katherine cried, not cloaking her surprise. "You think he has some part in this—this fire problem?"

"I don't know yet and wish to accuse no one without proof. Katherine, as I have no patience for circling around what I need to know, tell me plain your relationship to Giles Chatam."

Katherine gasped again, a quick little intake of breath. "Why, I've seen him, of course, and thought he was quite wonderful and told him so."

"You've been observed in intimate conversation with him."

"What? By whom? It's a foul lie!"

"One of my own servants observed you in most earnest, privy conversation with him nearly on your front doorstep the day of the Mortlake fair."

"Your Majesty, I swear your servant is mistaken."

"And I have it on good authority that you were listening to his romantic whisperings the night of the festival. How did you respond to his claim that he could make you hotter than your husband's fire mirror that night?"

The young woman looked truly aghast. Her palm over her mouth, she collapsed on the bench where the two of them had sat before.

"Katherine," the queen said, sitting and leaning closer, "this is all deadly serious. Have you been lying?"

Her hand still over her mouth, like a child, she nodded wildly.

"Who first came up with the idea of the fires, you or Giles?"

"No—not that," Katherine whispered, now gripping both hands between her breasts. "I did not speak privily with him, nor did he speak such fiery words to me. I lied only about losing and finding my husband's Venetian magnifying mirror. Oh, forgive me, Your Majesty, but I wanted you to need my advice, and to invite him to court more—myself, too—and perhaps pay him more. That is how I lied—only that. I wanted to make you think he might be in danger because someone stole his mirror, so you would want to protect him more...." Tears soaked her thick lashes and splattered on her flushed cheeks each time she blinked. "I hid the mirror, then pretended to find it. Oh, now I've ruined everything!"

"You claim you had no improper, intimate relationship with the actor Giles Chatam?"

"I swear it!" the young woman whispered, looking straight into the queen's eyes.

Elizabeth's voice rose in frustration. "Do you deny you ever so much as met him at your front door and stood whispering to him on most intimate terms during the May Day festival?"

"I not only deny it, but defy anyone who says different!"

"Your Majesty," Dr. Dee called from the inside the house, "your young artist Gil Sharpe has just arrived, and he's been hurt!" Dee stepped to the door. "We're tending him. I know you wanted privacy, but I thought you should know."

The queen and Katherine ran into the kitchen, where Dame Dee had been roused. Though she was still seated, she dabbed with a wet cloth at Gil's infected-looking ankle. His leg was extended on a bench on which he sat, with his back propped against the hearth near Dame Dee's chair. He looked flushed, filthy, sweaty, and bedraggled.

"Gil," Elizabeth cried, leaning over him, "what happened? What are you doing here?" She squeezed his shoulder and bent closer as he groggily opened his eyes.

"I didn't do it, Your Grace. I escaped but didn't do it. My lord Cecil says I did, but I didn't."

"His cut's infected," Dame Dee said, her voice raspy. " 'Tis the fever talking."

They heard a horse outside, coming fast. Dr. Dee ran out, then back in. "It's your man with Giles Chatam," he announced.

"Dr. Dee and Rosie," the queen threw over her shoulder as she hurried out, "I trust you will remain here to help Katherine treat Gil." Surely, she thought, Katherine Dee could not escape, even if she was guilty—but the thing was, Elizabeth was coming to believe that she was not.

She wondered if Jenks would have Giles tied, but the handsome actor sat easily, gracefully, behind him on the same horse.

"Look, Your Grace," Jenks called out. "Met him with his fellows on the road just outside of town."

Giles lifted a leg up and over and slid off as Jenks dismounted. "Your Majesty," Giles said with another of his exquisite bows, "I am amazed to see you looking so countrified, but the effect is entirely charming. I hear you have need of our troupe again?"

"Need of you at least. I want to know flat out with no thespian flourishes or spouted lines, what in heaven or hell is your relationship to Dench Barlow?"

"The dwarf? I can probably get him to come with us if you'd advance me some money, though he's a bit addlepated. I've had him merely beat the drum for us off and on to draw a crowd in these rustic rubbish piles where we've had to play, but I could teach him to act the fool at court if you wish."

"And what is your relationship to Katherine Dee? Have you ever tried to sweet-talk her, to put it politely, man?"

He frowned and tapped his index finger against his lips as if he were actually trying to recall, but then he'd probably left a line of swooning women in his wake. "She's fetching, I'll admit that, but I'd never dawdle with the magician's wife, if that's what you imply."

"You fear him?"

"No, for I warrant he's all noise and show in his performances," he said, gesturing broadly. "In a way, he's an actor like myself, with his own brains behind the effects rather than someone else's script. But I want to keep him on my good side. Someone who's that brilliant with winches and rigged ropes to fly scenery and mirrors and lights for special effects, why—" He stopped speaking for one moment. "What about Katherine Dee? She told me she thought I played a wonderful role on May Day, but—Your Majesty?"

Though she was dealing now with a consummate actor, unlike Katherine Dee, something told Elizabeth that the rogue, too, was telling the truth. Not that she had not been hoodwinked by liars before, for she had. But Giles Chatam believed he could get by on his looks, charm, and sweet speech, so why would he ever turn to murder? And he had seemed so honestly distraught when he had confessed to her that he was an actor because he wished to be anyone but himself after his parents died in that tragic fire in his youth, a fire he passionately claimed he did not start. Then too, his version of events matched Katherine's down to the least detail: she had used exactly the same word—*wonderful*—to describe how she'd praised his performance.

"You two wait here," she said, and ran inside. Her heart was pounding, her mind racing. If they weren't lying, she suddenly feared she knew who was.

"How is he?" she asked as she rejoined the others in the kitchen tending Gil.

"Resting better," Katherine said. Gil's leg had been rebandaged, and the young woman had taken over wiping his feverish brow.

"Dame Dee," Elizabeth said, "could you tell me what you recall of the Mooring family of Cuddington? The heir Percy died—I've seen his tomb at Cheam's church. But are the other Moorings indeed deceased too?"

"I heard so," the old woman said, trying to stand. Dr. Dee helped her to her feet. She made a shaky bow to the queen, then went on. "'Tis said the master of the manor, Lord John, drank and wagered away what means they had after the demise of their estate. I do recall hearing that. He took sick and died. That left Mistress Malinda and her daughter on their own. Some say they took in washing and stitchery, that beautiful woman and that golden-haired girl," she said, shaking her head.

Golden-haired girl. Her words echoed in Elizabeth's brain. But the hair of such towheads often turned nut-brown as they aged. "And the girl, Malinda's daughter?" she asked Dame Dee.

"Why, I heard she died about two or three years ago. Flavia, I think her name was. Forgive me, Your Grace, but however good my old ears and eyes are, my legs hardly hold me anymore."

"Yes, please sit," Elizabeth urged, and reached to help her.

"No, that wasn't what I meant," Dame Dee protested, though she sat anyway. "I must admit I heard you questioning our Katherine about speaking on our doorstep with that actor Giles during the May Day festival. The only ones I saw outside here that day were two women peeking round the corner of the house, and neither of them Katherine. 'Twas your Lady Ashley with that friend of hers who tends her."

"Floris Minton," Elizabeth stated, instead of asked. Her pulse pounded harder; her stomach knotted. It couldn't be. But if Katherine and Giles were telling the truth, then it must be Floris who'd been lying. Perhaps it was no coincidence that both Floris and Flavia had the initials F. M. Dear God in heaven, their ages would be about right, their hair color could be . . .

And Elizabeth had always sensed how deeply Floris had loved the land around Nonsuch. *It's the most beautiful view in the kingdom!* she had gushed from the castle roof. And, too late, she feared, the queen now recalled how, on the grounds of Nonsuch, Kat had once claimed that Floris had told her she used to live there. Since Kat was confused about places and people, Elizabeth had ignored that, evidently at her peril.

"Can you recall anything else about little Flavia Mooring?"

Elizabeth asked, bending over the old woman. "Anything at all?"

" 'Twas said she wasn't a very proper young lady. Didn't want to learn stitchery or embroidery but wove together chains of flowers for everyone." The old lady laughed, though no one else did. Dr. Dee, his face in a puzzled frown, leaned intently closer. "Instead of proper feminine amusements," his old mother went on, "I heard she used to play with her brother and climb trees and—"

The queen cried out as if she'd been struck. Everyone turned toward her.

"Dr. Dee," Elizabeth said, "do you know anyone near who has a watercraft? It will cut my time back to London by half."

"No, but there must be someone who—"

Gil seemed to rouse himself again. "Send Jenks to a house a mile east of here, ask for Lem, the lighterman. He brought me this way, and you'd be with the current—"

"I'll ride there with Jenks," the queen cried.

"Your Grace," Gil's voice cut in again, "Cecil thinks I set the fire that burned my chamber and your portrait, but I didn't, I swear it."

She turned back momentarily at the door. "I know you didn't, and I know who did. Everyone puts too much emphasis on the male heir, but it's sometimes the sister who is strong."

She ran from the house and, using the stone mounting block, was up onto her horse before Jenks could react. "Leave Giles and come with me!" she shouted. "We're heading back to London now, though we may already be too late!"

Chapter the Sixteenth

BY THE TIME THEY SET OUT ON THE THAMES FOR LONDON it was late afternoon, and each moment seemed an eternal agony. The sun sank swiftly behind their backs, but at least the current and stiff breeze were with them.

While Lem steered, Elizabeth and Jenks sat in the front of the small barge, which was rowed at an even faster speed by two oarsmen. The lighter crew did not know who she was, or if so, did not let on. Perhaps the expression on her face or the gold crowns she paid kept them from asking questions as they bent to their tasks. Staring into the quick current, Elizabeth went over everything in her mind again.

She was indeed dealing with a sort of ghost, she realized, a haunting from the past. Flavia Mooring had evidently returned from the dead—her demise, no doubt, her own intentional fiction—and had resurrected herself as Floris Minton. Through fakery and fortune, she had managed to become caretaker of her hated enemy's beloved Kat. Worse, she no doubt meant to make Kat and

Elizabeth suffer as Flavia's own family had been, as she saw it, tormented by the Tudors.

Elizabeth had no doubt that Floris had been building toward a grand, ghastly finale, all the while secretly reveling in the queen's mounting frustration and fear. Floris Minton had seemed so skilled with Kat that Elizabeth hadn't seen or sensed the woman's sick motives. With a perverted passion, Flavia, alias Floris, hated Elizabeth and those the queen loved or merely employed. If people could be burned to death because they had once helped to adorn Nonsuch, what would Floris do to her beloved Kat?

More than once, Elizabeth had played into the wily woman's hands. She had so wanted to take Floris into her confidence and her inner circle, while all the time she was, indeed, being taken in by Floris. Even worse, she was terrified that Floris meant to harm not only Kat. For if Whitehall Palace caught fire, it could spread to the entire city, especially with this brisk western wind.

"At least it's been a cloudy day and dusk is falling," she said to Jenks as she frowned into the turbulent Thames. "Floris won't be starting any fires with her precious mother's mirror today."

"No, my lady," he said, "but it was night when the Garvers' cottage burned. But see," he said, pointing ahead, "the city's in view. Coming back so fast like this, we'll surprise and stop her."

"But she's already set that trap for me too," Elizabeth told him. "At her clever request, I made Meg and Cecil promise to tell Floris the moment we returned, so she and Kat could greet us. But I fear she intends to greet me with my chambers—or Kat's— in flames as she flees."

"So we're going to sneak in?"

"I will have to send you in, since guards on all the doors report to Cecil—who is supposedly with the queen. They might send word to him the moment they glimpse me. Besides, I don't need everyone to know about my disguise and deception."

"We could put in at the palace's royal barge landing so I can go up the back staircase into your apartments by that privy door your father built. Bet I could surprise Floris that way."

"I ordered it locked and guarded. Besides, she asked me who was going with me, so if she so much as glimpsed you . . . No, I'm afraid you're going to have to get in by going around through the kitchens. Then you must get to Cecil by the servants' stairs and back halls and have him seize Floris—and be careful Lady Ashley is not hurt. I want to be there to confront Floris myself, but I can't bear to have Kat so much as vexed. If she sees a fire, I don't know what she'll do."

As the outskirts of London, then the spired silhouette of Westminster slipped by, her voice and thoughts merged with the rush of the river again. Her nursemaid, her governess, her first tutor, Kat had tended her through thick and thin. She could not recall a time without the dear woman who had gone to the Tower once for her and once with her. How Kat used to fret when the princess Elizabeth was given cast-off clothes and a paltry allowance. How much it meant to Elizabeth when she was crowned to have a fine, warm wardrobe for them both and to put Kat in charge of it all as mistress of the royal robes and first lady of the bedchamber. Kat had become her confidante, her friend, almost her mother. But now, old age and mental ailments had made Kat slip away, like this river.

As dusk deepened, they put in at the crowded public dock just west of Whitehall Palace. A fine mist floated in the air; scattered puddles from an earlier rain dotted the cobbles. Surely this weather could help fight any fire that tried to spread. As Jenks gave her a hand to disembark, she pulled her hood up over her head.

"I'll be waiting under the Kings Street gateway," she told him. "Come for me yourself if you can, or send Cecil, but see that you catch Floris first at any cost—and keep her away from Lady Ashley no matter how much either of them protests. Mistress Minton is skilled at convincing lies, so trust her not!"

He was off at a run, darting around the last of people and carts on the street. Elizabeth paid the bargemen the rest of their fee and walked briskly to wait under the arch of the gate which spanned the street. She pressed her back against the carved stone and let the mist which was not quite fog cool her face.

How calm and solid and safe her palace and her city looked as darkness slowed its pace. Thank God, that demented, vengeful woman had not lit the palace as she had feared, not yet at least. If only they could surprise her before she did more damage or killed again.

It seemed to take Jenks forever. Shadows blackened before torches were lit along the street and on both sides of the arch. Their flickering flames turned the puddles to pools of light like eerie mirrors. The torches bothered the queen, but she could hardly step forward and order them put out. As it was, a few folk stared at her, though most just pushed past, hurrying home, some pulling children along.

Her stomach knotted tighter. She shuddered as she pictured Dench swinging on that rope to kill himself against a tree. How loyal the little man had been to Flavia and her brother.

She gasped when she saw a figure rush past as if hurrying away from the palace. Even in the fitful light, she saw it was Lavina

Teerlinc: there was no mistaking her yellow hair, height, and form. Elizabeth peeked around the edge of the arch. Gilded by torch-light, Lavina paused before the Ring and Crown Inn just down the way. She looked nervous, almost furtive.

Then, from the other direction down the street, came Henry Heatherley with his unmistakable swagger. Elizabeth knew he lived near Whitehall but not where; she was hardly surprised he frequented a tavern—but Lavina, too? As the queen squinted to see better, their silhouettes merged in a crushing hug.

"Hell's gates," she swore as her two artists, arms around each other, went into the Ring and Crown. Surely those two had not been in collusion all this time, and she was somehow wrong about Floris. And what was keeping Jenks? At last she saw him darting toward her through the traffic.

"Did you catch her?" she cried the moment he was within earshot.

"You won't like this, Your Grace," he said, out of breath. "She's gone, but she left you a note."

"And Kat?"

"Missing too. Some of your women said Kat walked some-where with her, but that happens all the time. Secretary Cecil was going to have the palace and grounds searched, but a guard said they walked out into the city."

Elizabeth almost wavered on her feet. Jenks touched her elbow to steady her. Her hands were shaking as she took the note. As soon as she read it, she would send Jenks to hold her two artists in the Ring and Crown for questioning.

"Secretary Cecil said," Jenks told her as she broke the wax seal and opened it, "whatever Floris wrote, you're to come inside by the back privy staircase. He'll unlock it, but meanwhile he's gathering guards."

She turned her back to a torch on the gate to read the bold script:

> O GREAT AND MIGHTY AND WISE QUEEN WHO SITS FOR ROYAL POR-
> TRAITS——WHICH THEN EXPLODE IN FLAMES——COME <u>ALONE</u> UPSTAIRS TO
> THE RING AND CROWN. WE ARE WAITING FOR YOU, AND THERE WILL BE
> ONE FEWER——AMONG MANY OTHERS——IF YOU DO NOT HASTEN TO
> OBEY.

Elizabeth's insides cartwheeled. The Ring and Crown? But Heatherley and Lavina's meeting but a moment ago had seemed a lovers' tryst, and it was Floris who had walked out with Kat. She'd never seen the handwriting of any of them, so that gave her no clue. Surely this could not be a larger conspiracy than Floris and the dead Dench.

As she skimmed the letter a second time, Elizabeth fought to keep her face calm so she would not alarm Jenks, for she was determined to go alone. The mocking inscription in this note—it could have been written by Floris or Heatherley, if he was drunk enough. *We are waiting for you* could mean Kat and Floris, or it could mean two illicit lovers who had been so angered by Gil's inclusion among the royal artists that they had staged all this. No, she would still wager her very life that Floris wrote this—but had she brought the artists into her conspiracy?

"What does it say?" Jenks asked.

"That I may reclaim Kat tomorrow, tied to a tree in the hunt park, while I watch Nonsuch Palace burn," Elizabeth lied. She hated to mislead Jenks, but for once she needed her loyal man to desert her. "Run back to tell Secretary Cecil," she ordered, "that I'll be waiting at the privy door as he suggested."

"But I can go with you. He'll have it unlocked by now."

"No, you go ahead. Tell Cecil I'm coming. No, wait. Just so you feel better about your queen being on her own for a few minutes, let me have your sword and dagger."

His mouth and eyes opened wide. She actually thought he would argue or defy her. But he unsheathed and handed her his sword and then his dagger. He started to say something, then turned away. Assuming he'd look back once, she feigned starting toward the river. When an empty cart passed between them, she stuck the knife in the back of her belt and secreted the sword in the folds of her riding skirt. Then she darted down the street and into the covered doorway of the Ring and Crown.

What memories this old place held, for it was here she had first found Gil and his mother, Bett, trying to steal goods with a long angling hook. But now it looked only brooding and foreboding.

She glanced upward again to assure herself that what she recalled was true: yes, the roof of the old inn was stone shingles. And, unlike canvas or thatch, they would not burn.

Elizabeth hesitated just inside the door. The smell of the place hit her before the noise: smoky hearth fire, cooked meat, onions, stale beer, too much humanity packed tightly in the common room. A raucous laugh came from inside. Holding her hood tight around her face, she scanned the twenty or so in the common room—all men. Heatherley and Lavina were not among them, so they must have gone upstairs. *Come alone upstairs*, the note had read, but someone meeting for an illicit lovers' rendezvous could be upstairs too, where the private chambers were.

Before someone saw her, she hurried up the stairs she'd once climbed to pursue Gil and his mother. But she'd had others with her then, and felt so naked and alone now. For no one else in the kingdom but Kat—or Cecil—would she risk this.

She assumed Kat's captor or captors waited in one of the upper rooms and would make her bargain for the old woman's life. Worse, Kat and the queen could be locked in while the inn was set afire. If it was Floris, perhaps she would demand a public promise that Nonsuch be torn down and Cuddington rebuilt. Her quest for revenge had obviously driven her to the depths of desperation. But if her artists were in collusion . . .

A stair creaked; the queen jumped so hard she tripped over the sword and almost fell backward. Steadying herself again, she felt behind her back to be sure Jenks's knife was still stuck in her belt.

A lantern with a cheap tallow candle nearly gutted out hung at the first landing, and the flame from another lantern wavered in a draft of air at the top of the narrow stairs. Yet that wan light in her eyes almost blinded her. She hesitated. Should she start to knock on chamber doors, or call out for Kat? She had no illusions that she could simply surprise her enemy. She—or they—may have been watching out a window and would want some sort of elaborate show, one preferably with fire. She had to find Kat quickly and—

"We're up here," someone called from down the dark hall. The falsetto voice seemed almost disembodied; she wasn't sure if it was a man's or a woman's. The queen saw no door open, no one in the hall. The nape of her neck prickled.

"I've been watching you," the voice called in an almost childish singsong, "and it is good you came alone. You like heights, so come on up."

Elizabeth squinted down the black length of the corridor. Did those strange whispers belong to Floris?

"Where's Kat?" the queen demanded, her voice stern and strong despite how she was shaking. "I want her freed now so this can be just between us."

"Come up or go away," the voice said, making Elizabeth shiver again. Fresh air suddenly wafted down the hall into her perspiring face. Had someone opened a door to the hall? A window?

To free the hand which didn't hide the sword, she thrust the note up her sleeve; then she unhooked the lantern near her. Rather than lifting it close to her eyes, she held it low. In the dim hall with its shifting shadows, which seemed to jump each time she moved the lantern, she saw that the doors were indeed closed. But at the very end of the hall a rectangle of gray light fell onto some strange, shapeless form on the floor.

Surely not Floris hiding there, and never a ghost, though that's what popped into her mind. Could it be Kat in a huddle of her skirts and petticoats?

Holding her breath, gripping the sword handle and lantern so tightly her fingers cramped, Elizabeth moved down the hall. She saw no rope stretched here to trip her.

Prepared to swing the sword, she lifted the lantern. A pile of linens was heaped here, probably waiting for the laundress. But the gray shaft of light that illumined them came from the ceiling. Through a square hole above, she could see racing clouds trying to obliterate the stars.

Then she saw the ladder, leaned against the wall. So Floris must be on the roof and had called down through this hatch. Staring up, Elizabeth pressed her back so hard against the wall that the dagger at her back pricked her skin through her garments.

"Show yourself and Kat!" Elizabeth called, still not climbing the ladder.

"Coward, come up at once," Floris ordered, her voice now her own. "If not, Kat will be gone and then I myself—only I shall go across the roof, not fall from it."

She meant to kill Kat and escape across the roofs of London? Starting with this inn, buildings did abut each other clear into the City itself, so if she started a fire, it could spread. Her pulse pounding in her ears, Elizabeth hooked the lantern over one elbow. Slowly, she climbed the ladder, then lifted the lantern through the hole to the roof. If Floris meant to cut her down, she'd let that take the worst of it.

"Can't you see the stars up here?" Floris asked. "Put that thing out, or you might accidentally start a fire."

Annoyed at being taunted but not wanting to vex Floris until she could save Kat, Elizabeth pinched the candle wick out and set the lantern down on the roof. She still did not poke her head through.

"I want proof Kat is up there."

"Too bad, for she's not saying much."

Elizabeth peeked and saw Kat trussed and gagged, wide-eyed, bound to one of four brick chimneys, each of which was slightly smoking, the main one over the hearth below most of all. Floris stood defiantly, arms folded over her breasts, against a chimney about ten feet from the queen. She was garbed all in black with skirts so narrow she must have taken off her petticoats.

"Release her at once!" Elizabeth ordered, and climbed partway up and sat on the roof, still hiding the sword in her riding skirt. She longed to face Floris at her own height, but stayed seated, her feet still on the top rung of the ladder.

Beyond, under the stars, lay the rooftops of London. It gave her heart to see that not only was the entire roof slate shingles, but there was a flat area in the midst of the various gables and slopes. And, thank God, Floris seemed not to have any source of fire, though she did hold a mirror in both hands as if it were a bouquet.

"I will release Kat," Floris said, "only after we've had our talk—our final meeting of minds. You know I have the upper hand, or you would never have risked coming alone."

Slowly, keeping the sword in the folds of her skirt, Elizabeth climbed up the rest of the way. She prayed she'd have the chance to rush this woman. Kat, who seemed dazed and perhaps not even aware of the situation, was tied by a long rope to the chimney. The queen yearned to cut her loose and get her down the ladder.

"Cecil told you I was back?" she asked Floris.

"No, but I saw your man Jenks knock on your council-room door and rush in quite disheveled and out of breath. I immediately took Kat from the palace, and we entered the inn from the back street. I've had everything arranged here for weeks, even before our jaunt to Nonsuch, when I'd thought never to see the area again. But isn't this a lovely night?" she said, stretching her arms over her head as if lifting the mirror to the heavens. "I can almost believe I'm back at Cuddington."

"Perhaps on the little hill where your brother had his boyish forts built and where he died so tragically? People just don't realize, do they, that women are sometimes stronger than the men around them."

Elizabeth and Floris stared at each other, yet the queen addressed Kat when she saw the old woman had roused to her voice. "Do not be afraid, Kat, for I am here. Floris, why wasn't it enough for you to make me pay—since you don't seem to know my father from myself, and your argument must be with him. Why burn those others?"

"You know the answer to that," she insisted. "Did the power of the Tudors torment me only, or did it crush everyone at Cuddington, not just my brother and parents, but all our workers, retainers, and servants? You are your father's legacy, and I must deal with that."

"I deeply regret what happened to Cuddington, but I had no part in that. I am not my father."

"Just look at you!" she cried, thrusting the glass of the mirror at her, though the distance was too great to catch a reflection. "His hair, his wit, his power and ambition! My mother should have burned all his spawn alive in that tent at Oakham years ago!"

"Your mother . . . saw the fire at Oakham I told you of?"

"She didn't start it, because evidently Kat did! But she'd followed you there, hoping for justice on your father when he arrived. She said she saw the three of you playing in the tent, and hoped for the chance to ignite it to kill his son, his heir, in return. And then, before she could bring the king to justice, fire sprouted and you all escaped, and she dared not stay around watching after that. We've lain in wait for years, all the time I nursed her in her final illness, and the day she died, I told her I'd take care of it. And then I saw you ordering that your face and form be painted so that your prestige and power would be spread abroad. And I remembered all those artists of your father's decorating Nonsuch for the Tudor dynasty's pleasure and glory, where my home and life had been."

The queen saw that Kat was now not only terrified, but in deep distress, breathing hard, trying to buck against her ties. Sometimes her eyes were closed, other times open and rolling in wild fear. Stepping carefully across the flat center area, going slightly uphill, Elizabeth edged toward Kat. If she could only slice through her ropes with this sword or the knife without hurting her, then get her down through the hole in the roof. That little fall would be better than the three-story one to the cobblestones below. And all the while, she tried to keep a conversation going with Floris.

"You can't pull this off," Elizabeth told her. "Whatever you think will be your final revenge will not work. Dench has given you away, and—"

"Do you think any of that matters to me? No more than my brother's death mattered to your father and his people."

"I visited Percy's grave at Cheam. I will see that you are buried there too someday."

"Someday, like tomorrow, you mean? You'd like that, wouldn't you? But you are lying again, for Dench would never betray me. He'd die first and never mention he helped me burn your portraits and your people."

"Is that your mother's mirror? It has no power now, you know, for the curse is spent and done."

"I suppose you don't see a bit of fire up here, so you feel safe," Floris said with a loud sniff. "Didn't heed the message when Garver the Carver's cottage went up, did you? Or is it just that you believe you live a charmed life—that no one can conquer you? But I know you fear that your cousin Mary means to claim your throne. At least you will go out in a big blaze, one that will welcome her to claim your kingdom."

Floris threw the mirror. It hit Elizabeth's shoulder, bounced off, and smashed into a thousand shards against the slate roof. Floris moved from her spot for the first time, backing away.

As Elizabeth knelt to cut Kat's cords with the knife, the entire area leaped to light. Where had that been hidden? Then she saw Floris had produced, as if by sleight of hand, a torch.

Floris heaved it sidearm at them. Elizabeth tried to kick it away, but it caught Kat's skirts. The queen stomped out the flames while Kat bucked and moaned through her gag. She should not have cut Kat loose until she had beaten Floris.

She only had time to pull Kat's gag away to let her breathe better. Hefting Jenks's sword with both hands, knees bent, she advanced on Floris. Not for the first time in her life did she wish she had been tutored in the manly arts as well as in her book studies.

The woman scrambled away. For one moment, Elizabeth thought—hoped—she might fall off the roof, but she pulled out yet another torch from a smoking chimney. Elizabeth gasped when she saw that it had been suspended within by wires and was capped with an iron hood with holes poked in it. Floris knocked away its hood against the chimney, then waved the smoldering head, which burst, like magic worthy of Dr. Dee, into bright flames.

Floris swept this one too in a broad arc toward the queen, then came at her. Elizabeth swung the sword; it cut into the head of the torch; sparks flew like fireworks. Holding the queen at bay with the torch, Floris pulled out yet a third one from another chimney.

Each fighting for firm footholds on the shingles, they feinted and parried, sword against the torches. Despite the wind, the mist finally had risen to this height; the slate was slightly slippery underfoot. Elizabeth's arms were exhausted, yet fury stoked her strength.

"There, on the roof of the inn!" came a man's cry from below. Jenks? "Fire—figures! See, my lord?"

"That's them!" another voice echoed, Cecil's she was sure. "Get men up there and clear the building!"

Elizabeth shuffled nearer the edge of the roof to see who had gathered. "Up here!" she screamed, not taking her eyes from her enemy. "You see, Flavia Mooring," Elizabeth goaded, hoping she'd step to the edge, "you've done me the great favor of summoning my men."

"Then I shall do myself the great favor of permanently separating them from you."

Elizabeth thought Floris would rush her with her double torches again, but instead, she dropped one down through the roof hatch. Almost instantly, flames leaped up to cut them off from the hall below. That pile of linens, Elizabeth thought. Had she even put those there? Through the hatch she heard male muffled voices, but could the men beat out those flames? Again, the fire-mirror murderer had started a blaze at the top, and it would burn both up and down.

"This roof won't ignite!" Elizabeth shouted as Floris came at her, swinging the last torch. The shards of her broken mirror gritted under her feet as she charged the queen, screaming, "You will burn in hell with all the Tudors, and I've one more torch waiting to burn all Lond—"

Elizabeth dropped to her elbows and knees upon the roof. Torch flaming in her hand, Floris skidded on the broken glass, hit Elizabeth, then toppled over her. It seemed as if she threw herself into the starry sky. Black skirts flapping like strange wings, she simply disappeared. She did not cry out, but Elizabeth heard a warning shout below and then the thud as she hit the cobbled street.

But she had no time to look over the side again. Not only did the tongues of flame vault up through the roof hatch, but smoke now belched out the two nearest chimneys. Soon the wooden trusses and beams holding up this heavy slate roof would burn, and all of this would collapse into one roaring inferno.

She ran to Kat, who had huddled in a ball when Floris had begun swinging her torches. She was trembling, but breathing, as Elizabeth grabbed the rope with which Kat had been tied. As best she could, she made sure it was secure around the chimney, then tied it under Kat's arms. They both hacked from the smoke. The slate shingles were getting hot. She feared the rope wouldn't reach the ground but it was the best—the only—escape they had.

In a sitting position, pulling the terrified old woman after her, she slid to the edge of the roof, then quickly pulled her feet back. Flames were roaring out of the second story windows; she heard glass shattering, and smoke obscured the view of her men below.

"Jenks! Cecil!" she shrieked. "I wanted to let Kat down on a rope, but these second story flames . . ." She quit in a fit of coughing even as she sliced Kat free from the rope holding her to the chimney.

"No ropes will work!" Cecil shouted. "We're getting a wagon with hay for you to jump in! They tell me that's how Gil survived a fall, and it's all we have—"

"But I can't see anything! I can't see you!"

Behind her the slate roof buckled, then settled and began to fall in with huge, shattering bangs. She gripped Kat to her in a side hug. Even if they died together, there was no one else she'd rather hold to.

"You're queen," Kat suddenly spoke, her voice amazingly calm. "You're queen now, and you must save yourself. You survived to be queen, lovey, and I'm so proud of you."

Elizabeth burst into tears. To have Kat back at the last moment amidst this smoke, the flames . . .

"There's a big hay wain here!" Jenks's strong voice shouted.

"Jump to my voice because I'm right beside it. When you jump, sit down in the air. Jump now, my lady!"

Dear Jenks, still carrying on the charade. Though she had loved her family, they had never really loved her, except maybe poor Edward. But it was these loyal servants—and her people— she cherished.

"Doesn't that boy know you're queen now?" Kat asked, holding even tighter to her.

The queen almost laughed in her hysteria, but Kat's heavy head hit her shoulder, spurring her to action.

"Kat's coming first!" she cried. "Keep talking!"

"Right here. We're right here. Lots of good soft summer hay, sweet smelling, right here . . . ," Jenks's voice went on.

"Do it now before this damned hay burns!" Cecil shouted.

Elizabeth hugged Kat hard and shoved her. But Kat clung, and they both went down through the flames and smoke together. They hit hard and bounced, then the hay wain was pulled away to fresher air. A fine mist was falling like tears, but Elizabeth was sure she could still see burning stars.

Afterword

"HERE IS DOROTHEA'S MIRROR BACK, GILBERTO SHARPINO," the queen said, handing it to him as she joined him in the privy garden at Whitehall Palace nine days later. She also greeted Cecil, Dr. Dee, and Jenks, whom she'd summoned to meet her and Gil here this morning.

Already from over the palace walls and down the street, they could hear workmen pounding iron nails into boards to rebuild the Ring and Crown Inn, which had burned to its cellars. Only one nearby thatch-roofed edifice had caught floating cinders and ignited, so the plan of Flavia, alias Floris, to kill the queen and burn London had ended with her own death, a flaming torch still in her hands, on the cobbles of the street.

Gil was busy setting up the experiment he had explained in his written confession of why he'd lied to his queen more than once since his return from Italy. Cecil had forgiven Gil for his escape from custody when he'd learned that the lad had gone to try to warn the queen that the fire-mirror murderer was in London.

"Will the mirror be a keepsake of your first love, Gil, or will you use it to make copies of your art?" she asked as the lad merely glanced into the mirror, then laid it aside on the ground.

"I did adore her, Your Grace," he admitted. "Still, she was not the first woman I adored, but the second. And that other paragon has told me I can recover from this lovesickness, so I shall."

"That paragon has learned the hard way that we must all recover from dreadful losses in our lives," Elizabeth intoned. Then deciding she sounded too somber for this lovely day, she sat on the bench outside the tent which had been pitched for Gil's demonstration.

Though they were all nervous to be near tents and mirrors on such a sunny day, Gil had written that he needed such to show the secret he had nearly died for and thought he was protecting her from. *But there is power in knowledge, dear Gil,* Elizabeth had written him during her period of grieving Kat's death, *so I wager it is best if I know all.*

Now their eyes met and held; for the first time since Kat had died, a small smile lifted the corners of the queen's lips as she nodded her encouragement to him. Cecil and Dr. Dee both moved to positions behind her, while Jenks kept a watch over them all. Gil—using Dr. Dee's now famous concave mirror— kept popping in and out of the tent.

Her men were obviously not certain whether to make conversation or not. She had taken the loss of Kat hard, despite the fact that she had been preparing for it for months. Kat had lived through the terror and fall from the burning roof, but had slipped into a coma and died the next day without another word. But at the end, she had known Elizabeth was queen, and that was some solace. Although the queen considered Kat to be Floris's victim too, she had still ordered the murderess buried on Nonsuch land, under the tree where Dench had died—but without a marker on her grave.

Still, but for sending out written instructions the week before, the queen had emerged only once for her brief appearance and briefer pronouncement at Kat's memorial service in the palace chapel: "Katherine Ashley," she had declared in her clarion voice, "was like a mother to me and will never be forgotten by her friend and sovereign, Elizabeth Tudor. Queen Anne Boleyn gave me life, but Kat Ashley gave me love."

And that was all. She had returned to her royal apartments as soon as the service ended. She had not even seen Cecil, but had communicated to him only through writing. To take courage from the past to prepare for the future, she had simply needed time in silence and solitude. Mary, Queen of Scots, whose name Floris had invoked on the roof, would not go away, but perhaps, with care, she could be kept at bay.

It amused Elizabeth to see Dr. Dee staring in awe as Gil set up the demonstration, checking angles and distances for his mirror and other equipment. She announced to everyone, "Just as the artists' guild of Urbino takes a secrecy oath to protect this so-called camera obscura, the five of us shall not speak of this beyond these walls, even if we decide to use this technique to replicate my official portrait.

"And Gil," she added, rising and stepping closer to watch him adjust the chair his subject would sit in, "I'm expecting you to get busy on your new portrait of me, as close to the lost original as possible. My two remaining artists got burns on their hands in the fire at the inn, meeting as they must have been," she said, lifting her eyebrows, "to confer about painting the human form or some such."

Shaking his head, Cecil said, "They came tearing out of there like scalded cats, half dressed. That will teach them not to burn with lust, I wager."

"I've already begun to repaint the portrait, Your Grace," Gil said as he motioned Jenks to the chair. He would pose outside the tent, in which had been cut a square window. "All right, Jenks," Gil went on, "don't move."

Looking more nervous that he would have in combat, Jenks settled himself. Gil indicated the rest of them should step into the tent.

They went inside and gasped. On a piece of parchment Gil had positioned inside the tent was Jenks's living picture, in color, though upside down. When he sneezed, it sneezed. Gil explained how the image was reflected through the window cut in the tent and bounced off the mirror to the opposite side to the parchment. Moving the mirror or parchment could make the image come into clear focus or blur and fade.

"You see," Gil said, "if I were doing Jenks's portrait, all I would now need to do would be to sketch what I see down to the last detail, rather than painting if from just looking—from life."

"Why, the perspective is perfect," Dr. Dee said, bending close to the image. "Once the outlines are sketched in, of course, it can be turned right side up. But it reverses everything, just like a mirror, so that right-handed people—say, holding a pen or paper— would be made left-handed."

"Or their hair would be parted on the wrong side," Cecil put in.

"But no one cares," Gil said, "not when they see how exacting this is. It's made some Italian fortunes. And now that I realize how detailed even Hans Holbein's portraits are, I wonder if he hadn't learned of it somehow."

"Wouldn't that unsettle Heatherley even more?" the queen cut in, and even Gil, as nervous and engrossed as he was, had to grin.

"*Camera obscura* means 'dark room,'" he explained, still evidently relishing lecturing Cecil and Dee, not to mention his queen. "Of course, the darker the artist's area, the better."

"But in a way," Cecil said, "this is cheating—a falsehood, for the viewer and owner of the portrait believe it is all the artist's inherent, God-given skill."

"And so it becomes a secret," Elizabeth said, "one some misguided men will kill for by sending an assassin after *my* English subject, the lad *I* entrusted to their court to learn to paint. The damned Catholic plotters. Why, I'll take raw English talent over fancy foreign fripperies any day!"

"As I said before," Gil replied, nodding, "Maestro Titian doesn't use it. But I tell you, it still takes great skill to fill it all in. Each detail is needed to complete the whole."

"Much like solving any puzzle," Dee said.

"Or crime," Cecil added. "But if we keep working at it long enough, it comes into view, even shading and shadows."

"Exactly," Elizabeth said, unwilling to dwell on all they had just been through. "Gil, will you also paint me a portrait of Kat Ashley, one from memory?"

He followed her out of the tent, where she motioned to Jenks that he could stop posing. "Of course I can," Gil vowed, hurrying to keep up with her. "I can paint her from heart."

"From heart, that's good. Just remember that working that way is more important than reflecting someone else's talent, however much you admire that person. Even when life becomes fearful, always paint—and live—from the heart."

She dismissed him and the others with a simple gesture and walked the sharp angles of the garden paths alone.

AUTHOR'S NOTE

QUEEN ELIZABETH I WAS ONE OF THE FIRST RULERS TO USE PORTRAITS of herself, grand and symbolic, as what we today call PR. Her and Cecil's brilliance to use art this way was part of the inspiration for this book. She had not yet begun to use all of the symbolic Gloriana and Virgin Queen imagery she employed later, but the impact of her propaganda began at this time. The portraits of previous English rulers recorded how they looked and were displayed in the homes of royalty or nobility; Elizabeth Tudor meant for her portraits to speak of her virtues and power to a much broader audience.

The summer I was writing this book, which also happened to be the four hundredth anniversary of the queen's death, I was able to revisit London and see a marvelous exhibition on her life at the Maritime Museum on the site of the long-gone Tudor Palace of Greenwich. The treasures on display included the queen's original poem that begins this novel ("No crooked leg . . .") in her own hand; her gift to Katherine Parr, the translation of *The Mirror of the Sinful Soul;* and many items about Dr. Dee.

The brilliant Dee was one of the wonders of the Elizabethan age and did sign secret notes to the queen with his 007 sobriquet. Some say that author Ian Fleming used that as partial inspiration for his character James Bond, who served in another Queen Elizabeth's "secret service."

Cuddington's cruel fate under King Henry VIII is fact,

although the Mooring family is my fiction. Mortlake and Cheam are charming towns yet today. Fabulously decorated Nonsuch Palace is no longer standing (the site was excavated in 1959), but the vast hunt park, now called Nonsuch Park, remains. Elizabeth regained the palace in 1591 from Lord Arundel's heir, Lord Lumley, and spent several weeks there each year through much of her reign. The palace on the cover of this book is Nonsuch from the north gate, though the artistic grandeurs of the palace lie within.

When I began to research this book (the seventh in the Queen Elizabeth I Mystery Series), I found that between 1550 and 1650, mirror titles abounded in English books. In his book *The Mutable Glass*, Herbert Grabes calls the mirror "the central metaphor of a literary era, especially in Elizabethan England." I could not pass up mirrors, or "glasses" as they were sometimes called then, as a hook for a book, especially when I found an old engraving from a 1488 manuscript in which a man holds a mirror up to the sun to start a fire.

The subplot about Gil Sharpe's forbidden knowledge of the camera obscura is based on a recent fascinating and controversial book called *Secret Knowledge* by artist David Hockney. It is also true that some of the Italian Renaissance craftsmen's guilds took secrecy oaths which could be enforced by pain of death. And so I included an early "mafia hit man."

Titian's paintings *Woman at the Mirror* and *Venus of Urbino* actually exist as described in this story. The painting of the queen on the cover of this book is from the title page of Christopher Saxon's *Atlas of the Counties of England and Wales*, 1579, though I like to imagine it is Gil Sharpe's painting of his queen. Lavina Teerlinc was a real artist who painted miniatures at court, before the genius Nicholas Hilliard eclipsed her later in the queen's reign.

The queen's beloved companion Lady Katherine "Kat" Ashley did indeed die "greatly lamented" in 1565.

Katherine Constable was the first of Dr. John Dee's three wives. Little is recorded of her but that she was the widow of a London grocer. She herself died in 1575, only ten years after this story, but Dee's second wife lived barely a year before he married a third. Hm, do I scent a story there?

Karen Harper
December 2003

The Fatal Fashione

WHITEHALL PALACE, LONDON
OCTOBER 21, 1566

 "IF THE MEMBERS OF PARLIAMENT ARE HERE, THEY MAY cool their heels for a while!" Elizabeth Tudor a nounced the moment William Cecil, her trusted se retary of state, was admitted to her withdrawing room. "They have come to urge me to marriage and motherhood, but I know what they are thinking even beyond that impertinence."

"That if—when—you refuse," Cecil said, "they will urge you to name your cousin Queen Mary of Scots as your heir, even if she is a Catholic?"

"Exactly. And I'll not play into their hands."

"They do await your presence, Your Grace. But you sent for me?"

Though she had been attired in her bedchamber, her ladies were still arranging her large neck ruff and long strands of pearls. Yet she'd wanted to see Cecil before she faced down the men who forever tried to tell her how to govern. At least Cecil merely advised.

"I cannot abide their audacity," Elizabeth went on, flinging gestures despite her women's attempted ministrations. "They think because my cousin Queen Mary of Scots has wed again and produced a son, that I must wed posthaste and go to breeding, too. They believe they have me trapped. For if I choose not to wed and name Mary my successor, I risk my safety, for my death would place her on the throne. 'S blood, my Catholic shires to the north could rise in open rebellion. And my Parliament is one step from that, I swear they are!"

"Yes, Your Grace, but I believe their concerns about the succession have some validity and merit, and their words to you—"

"Were rude and rash so far." She took the last loop of pearls from Lady Rosie's hands—Rosie always panicked when her queen raised her voice—and finished the job herself. Leaving her ladies behind, she strode toward Cecil with her huge black satin skirts swishing.

"You saw what they dared write to me!" she told him. *'It sets a fatal fashion if a young queen does not wed, and endangers the realm.'* I set the fashions here, my lord, not only for garments and ornament, such as what they are calling these 'pearls of the virgin' set off against my favorite black, but for manners, behavior—even morals."

"I understand, Your Grace."

"Do they think I am some green girl or schoolroom dunce to be lectured and set aright? I'll not be preached to about suitors, foreign or domestic, nor about who should get my throne if I departed this earth. For I do not plan to do that for years, God willing!"

He seemed to have no retort to that or else he realized she needed to vent her ire and would calm down if he but listened. Yes, she and Cecil knew each other well after all these years working together, first to attain the throne and then to preserve and use it well for her people. Elizabeth knew she had been the cause of most of the lines on his long face and the gray hairs in his shovel-shaped beard which made him look older than his forty-five years.

She heaved a sigh and turned to glance in her new Venetian looking glass. Good—her appearance was startling, even stark, with the black bodice and skirt and the huge white satin and gold-embroidered sleeves. Her starched neck ruff was so stiff and large it almost looked as if her red, bejeweled head were on a platter—which her enemies, and there were many, would love to see.

With a decisive nod to Cecil, the queen preceded him out. The two yeomen guards at the door fell in behind. She might be a woman, Elizabeth thought, a *mere* female as her father had said more than once. But she still—thanks to a good and gracious God—looked young and strong at age thirty-three after eight years on England's throne. Graceful, tall for a woman and slim with sharp dark eyes and gold-red hair, she was still what her court favorite, Robin Dudley, called *fetching*.

Yet, though she never told even her closest friends and advisors such, not even Robin or Cecil, she intended to live and die unwed, but for her marriage to her country, of course. From her toddling days, she'd seen at too close range what dreadful things men could do to women, even their wives—even queens.

Flanked by her crimson-clad guards, Elizabeth Tudor stood beneath the scarlet canopy of state on the dais before her throne, facing sixty parliamentarians, thirty from the House of Lords and thirty from the House of Commons. The nobility had donned their best attire for the occasion; even the others wore their best. The few Puritan members, led by Hosea Cantwell, were in their somber black and white, as if following her fashion, when in truth all they did was carp about it.

She had expressly forbidden the speakers of the two houses of Parliament to attend, for she meant to do the speaking on this day. If they thought her so-called weaker sex would make her entreat or retreat, they were much mistaken. Did they not know she had learned—though sometimes from afar and under fire—from her sire, Henry VIII, that talented builder and terrible destroyer?

"Lords and men of England," she began, in turn staring directly at each man in the front row. "You write to me of my 'fatal fashion' of not wedding and pronounce it dangerous to crown and kingdom. And so you try to coerce and force your queen to obey your will."

She leveled a straight arm and finger at them in a slow arc. The northern earls Northumberland and Derby, both covert Catholics who could raise a rebellion, stood next to her dear Robin, Earl of Leicester. All visibly braced themselves and flared their nostrils as if they were stags scenting a wolf on the wind. A frown furrowing his brow, Hosea Cantwell from the Commons glared back at her.

"How have I governed?" she plunged on, clasping a fist of dangling pearls in her free hand. "I need not say much, for my deeds speak for me. And do not use the words *fatal fashion* to me. Fatal fashions are treasons, greed and lust, adultery and murder—and rebellions—in my kingdom. England must take a stand for justice. You must see to the proper punishment of law breakers and even to your own sins. Best tend to the safety of your country and your queen and not by trying to force her to wed and bed, but by helping, not hindering her."

More than one man shifted his weight or shuffled his feet. Several turned their caps about in their hands. This utter refusal was obviously not what they had expected. 'S blood, did they not know her yet?

"Some of you have whispered that I fear death in childbirth. Oh, yes, I know your thoughts, that and others," she added, looking directly at the northern earls whose shires bordered Scotland. "I do not fear death, for all men are mortal, and though I be a woman, yet I have as good a courage as ever my father had. I am your anointed queen. I will never be by violence constrained to do anything. I thank God I am endowed with such qualities that if I were turned out of the realm in my petticoat, I would be able to live in any place in Christendom."

Robin looked amused by the petticoat point, yet her stare wiped the smile from that handsome face. Cecil seemed almost smug while the others stood stunned by her defiance. No doubt those who'd had to settle for the back of the crowd now blessed their good fortune.

Elizabeth of England said no more but stood several moments, as if daring them to gainsay her. She only prayed no one guessed that her pulse pounded and the velvet neckband of her cartwheel ruff was soaked with sweat.

She glanced at the massive portrait of her father, hanging behind her audience. They probably thought she nodded to them before she turned and strode from the chamber. She thanked God they could not see that, beneath her skirts, her silk-stockinged legs shook like a child's.

ALSO BY KAREN HARPER

THE LAST

Boleyn

In the bestselling tradition of *The Other Boleyn Girl*, this is the story of Mary Boleyn, whose beauty captured the hearts of two kings, and whose star rose and fell before that of her tragic sister, Anne.

0-307-23790-7
$14.95 paper (Canada: $21.00)

Available in February 2006 from
Three Rivers Press wherever books are sold.

www.crownpublishing.com

New York Times bestselling author

KAREN HARPER

Julie Minton thought nothing of her fourteen-year-old daughter, Randi, leaving home earlier that morning to go Jet Ski riding with Thad Brockman. But now Randi and Thad are missing—and the hurricane that hours ago was just another routine warning has turned toward shore.

With the help of Zack Brockman, Thad's father, Julie begins a race against time to find their children—but first, they must battle not only Mother Nature, but an enemy willing to use the danger and devastation of the storm for their own evil end.

HURRICANE

"Harper has a fantastic flair for creating and sustaining suspense."
—*Publishers Weekly* on *The Falls*

Available the first week of June 2006 wherever paperbacks are sold!

MIRA®

www.MIRABooks.com